CONFLUX

SEVENTH Story From
space fleet sagas

DON FOXE

The Appendix at the end of the book has a list of characters and planets.

Written by Don Foxe. donfoxe.com

Produced by Caballus Press, USA Division
www.caballuspress.comm

Stock images are used for illustrative purposes only.
Some stock imagery from Pixabay.com, Pexels.com and Stock-adobe.com

ISBN: 9781393114727

Library of Congress Control Number: TBD

Acknowledgments

Thanks to Nancy Thurmond for expertly editing my manuscript. She makes me appear a much better writer than I truly am.

Author's back cover photograph courtesy of Abri Kruger Photography, South Africa.

Cover graphics are mine, for better or worse. I do listen to others with more experience and talent, but I have a vision, so I go with it.

Dedicated to my wife Sarah. Without her I would have no reason to write. She makes it possible for me to spend the time required to create, edit, and publish. During the months this story developed it was an especially stressful time. Her continued love and support, as always, kept me positive and on track. Everyone should have a Sarah in their life.

Introduction

The Space Fleet Sagas began before the creation of Space Fleet. The story started when a United States mission to Mars discovered a mountain on the red planet had been hollowed out. A huge hangar existed within. Inside the hangar sat a saucer-shaped space ship. The facility contained pieces and parts of advanced technology and a cache of cut crystals of various size.

Over the years scientists reverse engineered some items, but it was not until a young linguist decoded the Martian language did the secrets of interstellar space flight come to light.

During this time Earth was overwhelmed by a highly contagious and deadly weaponized virus. A worldwide pandemic resulted in the loss of fifty-percent of the planet's population. By the time a cure was discovered, few bastions of civilization remained. Much of the world became a dystopian landscape. Criminals, renegades, and power-hungry militia terrorized people as economies failed and countries dissolved.

The movement to recover the planet and protect humanity from mobs began when the United States of America and Canada merged. Their united military forces issued forth to stop the carnage and bring rule to the entire planet. There would be no more borders.

The loss of borders did not prevent long-held feelings of national pride. To stem potential revolutions, the United Earth Council was established. Regions and former sovereign nations would send representatives to form a centralized government. A single body in command and control that recognized the importance of cultural pride.

While the Earth experienced years of despair and turmoil, the scientists on Mars continued their work. Among the discoveries was the ability to travel at faster than light speeds, the largest impediment to viable interstellar voyages. Space-fold: lasers striking a faceted crystal could create a "bubble" in time. This bubble developed in front of a ship and dissipated as it flew forward. In essence, by accessing space-time vast distances were folded, making star systems accessible in days instead of centuries.

Another discovery had to do with biology. The Martians had a method of reengineering humanoids. The process enhanced metabolisms. An enhanced individual would be stronger, faster, with a much improved immune systems and the ability to self-heal from non-lethal injuries. Characteristics necessary for extended treks through deep space.

The newly-formed UEC needed a public relations program designed to create pride in the united population and replace nationalism. A way to unite diverse cultures with shared gratification. With the discoveries on Mars exciting the war-weary world, the creation of Space Fleet filled the need. Earth would use its united strength to create a force dedicated to discovering the galaxy.

To further the concept of cross-cultural buy-in, spaceships sent into potential peril would be protected by an elite military unit: Space Rangers. The best volunteers from military, law enforcement and recognized aligned militia from around the planet would undergo the Martian biological reengineering process. This multi-cultural unit would lead the way across space.

During the work to prepare the Martian bio-reengineering process, another potential benefit was discovered. The process could reactivate the Methuselah gene. The dormant genetic code human's retained from the time of Methuselah. A time when humans lived for centuries, not just decades.

The culmination of the Space Ranger Project arrived when two-hundred-twenty volunteers entered bio-vats. Only twelve survived. No one could determine why these twelve survived and two-hundred-eight equally qualified men and women died. The process was shelved, but Space Fleet was born.

Over the next three decades the UEC continued to coalesce its power while funding the construction of the Earth Moon Space Station (EMS2). The orbital site would be used to build an interstellar vessel.

The surviving Space Rangers gravitated to careers on Earth. Enhanced beings with extended lives existed. The planet had, in essence, meta-humans.

Among them Daniel Cooper and Elena Casalobos. These two joined the Can-Am navy, became fighter pilots and advanced to exo-atmospheric flight test pilots. Smaller ships with space-fold capability were tested by these two. The Angel series became the first vehicles built from a combination of human engineering and Martian technology. The first space ships capable of FTL flight.

Fifty years after the discovery of the Martian saucer, Daniel Marcel Cooper, "Coop," commanded Space Fleet's first interstellar capable ship. It was designed to perform missions of discovery and built as a battle-ready military vessel. The SFPT-109, the *John F. Kennedy* disembarked from EMS2 and began the SPACE FLEET SAGAS.

Note from Don Foxe:

I hope the introduction helps make the saga you are about to read more understandable. If you are new to Space Fleet Sagas, especially if this is your first adventure, it can be daunting. The series was named BEST IN GENRE, SPACE OPERA by Books Gone Viral. Space Operas can be difficult because they are, by nature, large in scope.

The basics for the Sagas is actually simple. First, I wanted to explore how a planet of diverse cultures and borders could unite to back galactic travel. It would require a united world to accomplish such a mission. Part of each novel is used to examine the trials of establishing a viable centralized planetary government.

Second, accepting the ability to travel to star systems lightyears distant, what would we discover? What dangers existed. When we met aliens, what would result?

There are billions of stars and millions of possibilities. I am presenting a relative few, but a few among millions adds up quickly. A lot of characters, human and not, pass across the pages. This is universe-building in space thrillers.

To make it a bit easier a simple synapsis of each preceding novel follows. I have tried to give you a foundation without spoiling those stories because my hope is this saga entices you to explore the future with me. Read, enjoy, and don't get too caught up in details. The books are fun to write and should   be   fun   to   read.

THE SPACE FLEET SAGAS

CONTACT AND CONFLICT / Bk 1

Aliens and Humans.

The Launch of the PT-109, *John F. Kennedy*. Daniel Cooper makes First Contact with aliens trying to escape capture by an invasion force that attacked their planet. At the edge of the solar system contact turns to conflict when an armada of vicious aliens arrive in pursuit of the refugees. A maiden voyage becomes a test of survival.

CONFRONTATION / Bk 2

Aliens and Humans. Allies and Enemies

Earth begins to develop alliances with other worlds. It turns out the Martian technology has leapfrogged Space Fleet beyond the capabilities of aliens involved in deep space flight for thousands of years.

Peaceful systems are being invaded and threatened with genocide. The military experience of humans is needed to confront and repel these attacks. Space Rangers move to the forefront in the fight for freedom.

On Earth a dangerous cabal of powerful people are determined to dissolve the central government and return the planet to chaos. The fight for survival heats up on and off world.

CONFLUENCE / Bk 3

Humanity stands at the confluence of space and history. Earth must decide between isolation or intervention.

Daniel Cooper is replaced as Captain of the 109 by Elie Casalobos. He leads a new mission with a new team. They need to stop the Camarilla Dissolvere from destroying the UEC and the unity necessary for the planet to succeed.

In deep space a flotilla of Space Fleet ships are outnumbered by a powerful foe. Making it worse, they are forced into a wild part of space capable of destroying them if the enemy did not do it first.

CONNEXIONS / Bk 4

Daniel Cooper is shanghaied and transported to the far side of the galaxy. His expertise as a military operator is needed to save a Princess and prevent the fall of a confederation of peaceful planets.

His new allies are pirates and his new team is a female three-dimensional holograph.

The reward for services rendered? The secrets of the Martians and the origins of humanity.

CONTRAVENE / Bk 5

Elie Casalobos is stranded on the planet of Phisor. While she and Storm fight for their lives, the 109 is under attack above and unable to help. Genna, the ship's avatar, must decide between saving the Captain or saving the crew.

The Camarilla Dissolvere is planning a major attack on the central government. The only thing in their way is an unexpected and unusual team of operators led by a dead Space Ranger.

When Daniel Cooper returns from the far side of the galaxy, will he find his universe destroyed while he was busy saving another one?

CONDUITS / Bk 6

Daniel Cooper joins new UEC Marshal and fellow Space Ranger Tab Barnwell on Earth. They pursue a dangerous militant determined to destroy the concept of a united planet.

Elie Casalobos is tasked with the PT-109 to explore new space. The mission is part discovery, part diplomacy, and totally dangerous. It is her job to find out if the planet Devisator is a misunderstood ally or the most dangerous enemy Earth has faced.

Fragments from the past help explain current events and shape   the   future.

Part One

Before a conflux can occur, there must be two forces, natural or societal, moving toward identical points. That these forces will meet is inevitable, *but the result is not.*

Chapter One

Deep space

The ship shook like a rag doll in the grip of an excited child. The gravitronic systems were overpowered, allowing anything not secured to end up on the deck. This included more than one crew member.

"Battle harnesses," Coop ordered. "Find a seat and strap in. Cassandra, what's happening?"

"Extreme turbulence," the ship's Artificial Intelligence (AI) responded.

"I already know that," he replied. "What is causing it?"

"Forward wave of a massive stellar event," she answered. "This system's supergiant orange star has a 2,430 solar radii. It is large enough for its photosphere to engulf the orbit of Saturn if placed at the center of Earth's solar system. The star experiences temperature changes. A drastic change resulted in a particle-dense flare."

"Flares aren't particularly dangerous," he said. "The ship's hull should protect us from radiation."

"In a normal solar flare it would," Cassandra returned. "This is not normal. A super-heated stellar wind is driving a wave of charged densely packed particles toward us. The turbulence was a harbinger."

"If that was a precursor, will shields protect us when the flare gets here?"

"Doubtful," she replied.

"Should have led with that," he murmured. "How far do we need to go to minimize the effect?"

"3,670,050,000 miles."

Coop had been incapacitated when the left side of his skull was hit by laser fire. In the year required to recover, that portion of his brain revivified to function more efficiently. It was the part that handled reasoning skills such as math.

"A flare travels at the speed of light." He murmured aloud as his brain worked.

In the time he spoke those eight words he determined at the ship's in-system max space-fold speed of .7ls, or 469,431,640.3, it would take seven-hours-forty-eight-minutes to reach a safe distance.

The stellar flare, moving at 670,616,629mph, would overtake them in five-hours-twenty-eight-minutes. He engaged space-fold and pushed the laser array to full power.

"Listen up," he called ship-wide. "A stellar event will make impact in five-and-one-half-hours. I have no idea how strong it will be when it connects or how much the sonic forcefield will deflect its power. You have four hours to secure anything and everything. We don't need a coffee mug turning into a missile. In four hours you will don type three excursion suits for maximum radiation protection. No later than five hours and one minute from now I want you at battle stations and strapped in. Cooper, out."

"Cassandra, can you estimate the effects of the flare making contact in five-point-five hours while we are under space-fold drive and within a time warp bubble?" he asked.

"I have no idea," she answered. "Calculating speeds and estimating the flare's radiation and force at eighty-nine-percent is simple. I cannot factor our traveling in space-time while the flare is in natural space, nor any variable from the sonic shield or crystal force field. There is no data to extract from."

"We'll be the first ship to experience this. Hopefully we'll be around to share the data."

"I have opened a channel to the science station on EMS2.[1] They have been informed of the situation. I will stream data real time. If the ship is destroyed they will have the information," the AI informed him.

"That's not a comfort."

Five hours later Coop began his final pre-event checks. His crew would be wearing IEVA (intra/extravehicular activity) suits. The type three protective wear was designed on the METS (Multi-Environmental Tactical Suit) worn by special operators when deployed in hostile situations. Instead of being projectile and laser resistant, IEVAs were radiation resistant. Form fitting, they allowed for easier movement than the older systems, which were bulky and required the user to plug into shipboard oxygen and power sources. With the hood up and plexi-flex face shield in place, they were closed off from external variations in atmosphere, pressure, and temperature.

From the pilot's chair he reviewed the long-range scans. The flare was still expected to overtake them in less than thirty minutes.

"I'm going back," he told the young woman seated to his right. "Call me if anything changes."

"Aye," Chaspi replied. She was the co-pilot and a Bosine from the planet Osperantue. Chaspi was one of the first aliens Coop met during First Contact. She and her family were refugees aboard a cruise ship running from the Zenge invaders who attacked her world. Luck brought them to the solar system and the attention of Coop during the final shakedown voyage for Earth's first interstellar battle-ready space ship, the SFPT-109, *John F. Kennedy*.

The doe-eyed, small eared brunette was a graduate of the Space Fleet Academy and certified space ship pilot. This voyage was her first assignment behind a yoke of an actual vessel operating in the voids of outer space.

The area behind the cockpit of the Corsair class ship opened up into a large operations center with twelve-foot-high ceilings. The first station on his left was Systems Control. ASkīlamentrae, nicknamed Sky, from the planet Fell, sat in front of a wall of monitors surveying major and minor operating system within the ship. From her desk she could call for a holo-representation of any framework she wanted to more closely exam.

Her blue skin was hidden by the IEVA, but golden cat-like eyes shined behind her face shield.

"Ready," she assured him. "If Cassandra gets caught up in repairs I can handle anything else."

The IEVA covered her skin color, but the form-fitting material revealed everything else. Even seated she was obviously tall, strongly built with slender hips and large, full breasts. They had met aboard the Osperantue refugee ship, the *Star Gazer*, where she acted as his security. They had sex the first day.

To her right was her cousin, AStermalanlan, known as Storm. She was in charge of the Communications console, including the solid state tachyon module that embedded messages onto sub-atomic particles to be broadcast at faster than light speeds or decode messages arriving the same way. Fellens were considered the galaxy's premier computer and communication systems experts. Not as tall as her cousin, Storm had more curves and even fuller breasts. She and Coop ended up in bed the second day he was aboard the *Star Glazer*.

"Data to EMS2 is on automatic feed," she told him. "Dr. Trent is on stand by, but he has no more ideas about what to expect than we do," she reported.

To her right sat Billy Elkman. He watched over the Engineering station. He would normally oversee operations from the Engineering level, but Coop felt better having him work from the command center.

"I can monitor and work with Cassandra if we have internal maintenance issues," he told his commanding officer. "I won't be much help up here if an external problem occurs."

"I want everyone where I can see them," he told the young Space Fleet Academy graduate and engineering phenom. "Use robots if you can. If something has to have you hands-on, you can get there quick enough."

"I hope," he replied. Billy was the grandson of Elliott Fairchild, the scientist and explorer who discovered the hidden alien hangar and technology on Mars. This included a flying saucer and files left by the ultra-advanced Nakki civilization who seeded the galaxy with sentient lifeforms. Information used to build Space Fleet and provide Earth major advantages when introduced to the galaxy.

He was also Chaspi's boyfriend.

Behind Billy's position and across the wide deck sat a short, shaggy-haired being with eyes nearly hidden by thick red brows and face obscured by a wild beard. Petra was a mining expert from the planet Rys and a Dward. Coop often believed the name of his race had been translated by his communication and universal translation device to something similar to dwarf because of their appearance.

"You'll have to put on the hood and shield," he told him.

"Uncomfortable," the taciturn miner responded. He seldom spoke and when he did used few words.

"Your suit was designed especially for you," Coop said. "The hood and faceplate will cover you, allow you to breath, use your HU^2 displays, and keep you alive if we're bombarded with radiation. If you want comfort, shave and get a haircut."

Petra grumbled, but he pulled the hood up and affixed the shield.

"Your monitors cover the exterior. If you notice anything, let me know."

Petra grunted.

Beside the Dward sat his Japanese friend and fellow Space Ranger, Hiroshi 'Hiro' Kamura. Following the Space Ranger Project, he returned to Japan, but not to his former position with the Emperor's Personal Guard. Hiro decided to make a hobby an avocation by getting his Doctorate in planetology. When he joined Coop's new crew he was living on Fell and teaching martial arts classes.

"This is extremely exciting for a planetologist," he told Coop. "Not the die by radiation poisoning, but the effects of a stellar flare from a supergiant star."

"Sorry I had to pull you out of the observatory, but I needed someone to monitor medical telemetry."

"No problem. Everything is being recorded. It won't kill me to watch everyone's vitals," he replied.

"If it does, you'll be the first to know," Coop quipped.

To Hiro's right was his significant other, Cynthia Shah. Former Space Fleet Security Forces Colonel and the ship's Weapons and Tactical officer.

"Everything set, Cindy?" he asked.

"Cannons are secured," she confirmed. A holo-image of the Corsair hung in the air above her desktop.

The ship was dove grey with navy blue stripes running along either side from bow to stern. The upper deck was flat from a chisel-shaped bow back until the hull widened. It continued the same width to a slightly rounded stern. A low conning-style tower sat two-thirds of the way behind the ship's nose. A half-dozen antennas of various heights rose from the deck and around the tower. A STORM-HATCH[3] catch and sender array was attached to the deck, ten yards behind the tower. The effect was similar to a submarine.

"Wings and stabilizers for endo-atmospheric flight are retracted to reduce pressure within the airframe," she said. When deployed, delta-style wings and a tail fin enabled enhanced endo-atmospheric flight.

On the bow a railgun sat on a track. A twin was stationed on the keel, connected by the revolving track.

"The conveyer belt is locked," she assured him.

Cindy spun the image to a view of the ship's bow.

"Built it to look like a classic Bugatti Chiron's grill," Coop said. "Nathan Trent is an avid classic gas-powered car enthusiast. The Wraith-class ship Cassandra came from had a nose that mimicked a Shelby Cobra."

"If you say so. I have no idea what a Bugatti Chiron or a Shelby Cobra looks like," Cindy responded. "Tachyon cannon on the port side hull and photon cannon on the starboard side are retracted and secured. Same cannons are also stowed away at the stern."

"A lot of firepower," Coop commented.

"Too bad we can't shoot a flare."

"Let's see the keel," Coop requested.

She waved her fingers and the view dropped beneath the ship.

Venting for environmental and mechanical overburden appeared, set flush to the bottom. An anomaly appeared half way between the nose and stern.

"Spirit Two fighter," Cindy said. "Docked to the corsair. Mag-clamps will keep it secure."

Coop recalled the *Renarde's* stats. She had a 1,600ft length, 180ft beam, 320 feet tall with a fifty-two-foot con tower. Longer than a PT, but only thirty-six-percent the width and one-third the height, not counting the available tail fin. The Delta-style wings added two-hundred-twelve feet to the overall width when deployed.

The holo-image spun and they faced the rear of the sleek ship. Painted across the wide transom was CC-01. Under the numeric designation: Renarde.

"The Fox," he translated from the French.

"She is that," Cindy agreed.

Chapter Two

"Thirty minutes, give or take," Nathan Trent said..

The Space Fleet Director of Sciences was too anxious to sit so he stood before a wall-sized display. A dozen boxes framed within the screen provided streaming data from the *Renarde*.

"Anyone have any theories on what to expect?" Pam Patterson asked. Space Fleet's commanding Admiral was as anxious, but remained seated.

"Theories? No," he answered. "Guesses. Everything from nothing to being tossed into another dimension, but nothing useful."

The two shared the room with a half-dozen uniformed engineers and four civilian scientist-consultants. They were aboard EMS2, the five-miles wide, three-miles long orbital station primarily used as a construction and repair facility three-hundred-twelve-miles above the planet.

"How far away are they?" she asked.

"Thirty-two-point-three parsecs," he replied after reading the intel from a box she had equal access to. "Furthest exploration for an Earth ship to date. Eighth system they dropped out of space-fold to search for crystals."

A special type of crystal was used by the majority of known planets capable of interstellar travel. The majority of these came from mines on Rys and a reclaimed planet owned by Rys. Another type, a black crystal, had been discovered by Dward miners on another uninhabited world controlled by Rys . The planet was Neuvarusry. Black crystals, also dubbed black diamonds, produced significantly more energy when activated by a light source directed onto facets cut for purpose. Because of their density, smaller black crystals could replace larger clear ones and still provide more power and a longer lifespan. The mines on Neuvarusry dried up. The *Renarde* was tasked with locating a new source.

"Rys ships looking for black diamonds are limited to using wormholes to travel between systems," Patterson said. "The *Renarde's* space-fold drive allows us to go further faster and cover a lot more space. While Coop hasn't discovered a black diamond source, the information sent back has been invaluable. We're learning new things about our galaxy each day that ship is out there."

"Let's hope it's still out there in," he paused to look at the top right box, "twenty-one minutes."

"Any luck with recovering the files on the Wraith?" she asked, changing the subject. "The ones Coop erased."

The Wraith-class ship, Cassandra, had been a personal project of Trent's, who also owned the private advanced engineering company, Trent Industries. He had given the small ship to Daniel Cooper as a means of escaping Earth during a time he was out of favor with Space Fleet. Following a horrific battle with a psychotic messianic figure known as The Prophet, Cooper, the ship, and its avatar had been wrenched from space-time into natural space by a band of pirates. Shanghaied to help rescue a princess on the far side of the galaxy. Payment for his help was secrets of the Nakki, the galaxy's first civilization. The ones responsible for the technology found on Mars, and, according to Coop, for the creation of humanity and many other beings in the galaxy.[4]

"He doesn't believe we're ready to know what was on those files. He didn't just erase them. He bleached them," Trent told her.

"So no luck."

"Not with the files. Not so far. We think we may have more luck with the avatar."

"I thought the avatar was compromised."

"One of my techs erased a sub-routine that affected the AI's personality profile." While he talked, he watch the screens on the wall. "It caused a loss of memory. We're attempting to reboot the sub-routine to see if the Nakki information was copied to it."

"Does Coop know you're trying to restore Cassie?" she asked, using the name Cooper gave the AI.

"He knows, he just doesn't know the real reason. He won't be happy if he ever finds out."

"I'm not planning on telling him," Patterson assured him. She scanned the wall, her eyes coming to rest on the list of locations watching the same data stream she was.

EMS2. MSD, the Mars Shipyard and Docks. SFPT-89 in orbit around Mars. SFPT-99 in the Aster System. SFPT-109 on assignment near the Galvari border. The Destroyer *Pegasus* and Carrier *Elliott S. Fairchild*, also in the Aster system. Finally, Space Fleet headquarters in Toronto and the office of the Chairman of the United Earth Council's Board of Governors.

"A lot of people are watching," she commented.

"A lot of people are worried," Trent replied. "Five minutes."

Deep Space

"Five minutes," Sky called.

"Everyone make sure your harnesses are secure," Coop ordered from the cockpit.

A battle harness was built into each seat. It deployed and fit over the user, covering shoulders and torso. Besides keeping the wearer in their seat during violent shakes, it protect them from dangerous G-forces resulting from high speed maneuvers.

The ship began to shake. A slight tremor progressed to a violent quake.

"It's early," Coop said.

"The forward edge of the event has not reached us yet," Cassandra reported. "The oscillations are being caused by . . ."

"By what?" Coop demanded. "Cassandra, report."

"AI off line," Sky called. "Multiple systems are fluctuating."

"Space-fold drive just shut down," Billy told them. "Our speed hasn't changed," he said, disbelief obvious in his tone.

"External pressure has doubled. Interior pressure rising," Sky reported."

"Brain functions becoming impaired," Hiro said.

He and Coop remained conscious a few seconds longer than the others because of their enhanced biology, but both passed out before the hot, dense stellar-driven particles reached the ship.

Around the galaxy, monitors streaming data from the *Renarde* went blank. On EMS2 one box in the top right remained on. It read TIME TO IMPACT 0:00.

Chapter Three
Deep Space

"Should I set a course for their last known co-ordinates?"

The question came from Ensign Fallenitsch at the navigation console on the command deck of the SFPT-109, *John F. Kennedy*. Called Folly since her arrival at Space Fleet Academy, she was a Bosine from the planet Osperantue. She was also a member of the *Star Gazer* crew when they made first contact with Captain Daniel Cooper and the 109. When other refugees returned to their home world following the defeat of the Zenge invaders, she had been one of those electing to remain on Earth. With her experience in deep space travel she was welcomed by Space Fleet. Folly was one of fourteen aliens among the 109's sixty-eight person crew.

"No," Captain Elena Casalobos responded. "Until we hear otherwise we assume the *Renarde*'s communications were affected by the stellar event."

Everyone on the ship's command deck had gone silent when telemetry from the *Renarde* ceased streaming. Following thirty-minutes of hope the flare caused a temporary disruption, fear for the crew began to set in.

"We're the nearest Space Fleet ship to them," Folly said.

"We are also fifty-one-days-eight-hours away," First Officer Genna Bouvier responded. She stood beside the Captain, who was seated in her command chair.

The strawberry blonde with blue eyes and freckles looked fresh out of college and too young to be second in command of an interstellar battle ship. What could not be seen was her unique connection to the ship's AI operating system. Genna's name was derived from **G**enetic **E**ngineered **N**euro-**N**etwork **A**vatar. She had been electronically connect to the Artificial Intelligence during her embryonic stage in a bio-laboratory. She had been grown to provide the AI access to real-world sensations. This was in response to the fear an AI could go insane as it evolved into sentience and found itself trapped within a two-dimensional existence.

"Unless we receive other orders from Space Fleet Command, we resume our mission," Casalobos told her bridge crew. "Mags, put us back on course for Aranthine."

"Aye, Captain," the pilot replied. Mags was Lt. Mary Margaret Moore, assigned as a pilot for one of two Spirit Two endo-exoatmospheric fighters kept ready in the ship's hangar. She was equally qualified as a pilot for the larger Patrol and Torpedo (PT) class. Mags had crewed with Casalobos the longest, beginning as her co-pilot on Demon 1, a precursor to the current Space Fleet vessels. She was with Casalobos on Demon 1 when they joined Cooper and Angel 7 to defend the *Star Gazer* against a Zenge battle group at the edge of the solar system.[5]

Mags was friends with Daniel Cooper and several of the people aboard the *Renarde*. She knew not to question Elie's decision.

"Izzy, has Tascarvinavox Oison responded to our call?"

Lt. Izabella Dominczyk, Izzy, was Polish. A slender blonde and member of the 109's original crew.

"Nothing yet, Captain," she reported. "His contact method is space normal communication (SYNC) channels. With the time lapse between our location and Aranthine, it could take days. That's not factoring in SYNC does not operate when the ship is under space-fold drive."

"We'll connect after we arrive in the system," Casalobos replied. "Genna, take command and go to minimum bridge crew. I'm not expecting anything of interest to happen until we reach Aranthine."

"Aye, Captain." The avatar watched Casalobos rise and exit the command center. She made no move to take the Captain's chair.

Elie contacted Admiral Patterson from her office adjacent the bridge. The miniature hologram of the Admiral manifested atop her work desk.

"We're alone, Pam," she told the Admiral's holo-image standing on her desk.

"We don't have any more information regarding the *Renarde.*" The blonde commanding officer answered the unasked question.

"OK. I've returned to mission. I assume you'll let me know about Coop and the others as soon as you get anything."

"Promise. What do you expect to discover on Aranthine?"

"We've been tracing the Parrian cargo ships the raiders used on Vista. They've been on an Aranthine moon for a week. Rachelle said the leader of the raiders was purple skinned. While on Devisator I met a trader from Aranthine. Tas Oison. He was purple. I thought we should learn more about the planet and its people."

"What do you already know?"

"Only what we got from our Devee contacts. It's a more or less independent world on the edge of Galvari space. They are aligned with the Galvari Confederation but have traded with Confederation worlds for three centuries. There is minimal Galvari influence now, but the general belief is they expect the Galvari to assert more control over them sooner or later. I got the impression from Oison he was not a fan of the Galvari."

"What do they trade in?" The Admiral's image leaned precariously as the real Patterson sat against the edge of her desk at Space Fleet HQ.

"The Aranthine civilization sounds advanced, but the planet has nothing of significance to trade," Elie said. "They are apparently excellent dog robbers."

"A naval officer who acquired scarce goods, from military equipment to liquor, often staying barely within the letter of the law. Where did a Spanish legionnaire learn about the old dog robbers?"

"Coop. He loves military history, especially the unusual things."

"Makes sense. You think Aranthinians procure hard to get merchandise for a fee?"

"At least some do. It explains the raid on Vista by purple aliens and the cargo ships showing up on Aranthine. I'd like to find out how much of a slave trade exists out here and who's financing it."

Elie went about preparing a cup of espresso as they talked. Her image would be going on and off the screen in Patterson's office, but caffeine trumped focus.

"The Devee have admitted to abducting people from other systems. Maybe this is another of their operations," Pam mused.

"Ginea Tabilis⁶ admitted to slavery, but told me it was no longer practiced," Elie responded.

"You believe her?"

"I'm not prepared to believe anything a Devee says," the Spaniard replied. "Another reason to check things out for myself."

"Elie, you and the 109 seriously humiliated a Galvari admiral. With a ship one-twentieth the size of their battlewagon, you kicked their ass and sent them running. Flying into Confederation space may not be a wise decision," the Admiral warned.

"We'll be sneaky, Pam. I promise."

"Promise me you'll get out at the first sign of a military reaction to your presence. I don't need two lost sheep."

"Spend your time locating Coop and the *Renarde*," Elie told her friend and superior officer. "I won't cause you another problem."

"I wish that came with a guarantee. Be careful, Elie. Patterson, out."

The image disappeared. The DO NOT DISTURB order ended at the same time. She received a call within seconds.

"Elie, it's Mags. Okay for Rachelle and me to come by?"

"Come to my cabin, Mags. I'll leave the door unlocked. As soon as I update my log I'll be there."

"Roger that," the reply.

The Captain's quarters were accessed through the Captain's Office or the hallway. It consisted of a living space with a comfortable sofa and chairs around a square coffee table. One corner held a work desk and chair. The kitchenette included a replicator, cabinets for dishes and tableware, sonic cleaner, small fridge and a personal espresso machine. A door separated the bedroom and ensuite from the rest of the cabin.

Elie entered to find Mags in sweats curled on the sofa with a glass of wine and Rachelle Paré seated in a chair. She wore a blue polo and Space Fleet grey slacks. She also had a glass of wine.

A steaming cup of espresso sat on the cocktail table. Elie's first act was to sip the brew. Mags was one of the few people allowed to mess with the Captain's espresso machine.

"Perfect," she said. "I'll change and be right back," exiting through the bedroom door, cup in hand.

She returned in five minutes wearing a black tank top and baggy black shorts. No shoes. After a trip to the espresso maker and she joined Mags on the sofa, feet curled under her butt.

"You're the only person in the galaxy who drinks coffee to relax," Mags said. "Two of those and I'd be awake for days."

"Did Patterson tell you what happened to the *Renarde*?" Rachelle asked.

Rachelle Paré was American and French Canadian. Oddly the same mix as Daniel Cooper. She was also a survivor of the Space Ranger Project. Unlike Coop and Elie, Rachelle had been a Can-Am Naval pilot her entire adult life, until transferring to Space Fleet. The most taciturn of the Space Rangers, she was also the least public. It was known her mother had been an Ace Can-Am fighter pilot who went MIA during the Pandemic. She was also considered unbelievably accurate with air-to-target weapons, earning her the call sign 'Rain.' When you were under fire and needed help, you called for 'Rain.'

"She doesn't know," Elie answered. "She promised a contact when they found out."

"Last time he went awol with a ship he landed on the other side of the galaxy working with a bunch of pirates," Mags said. "I'm still waiting on the entire story."

"Me, too," Elie admitted. "He hasn't offered a lot about what happened and I haven't pushed."

"What do you plan on doing?" Rachelle asked. Her brown eyes held Elie's black ones.

"Going back on mission. Nothing I can do about Coop and the others until we know where they are and if they even need help. It could be something as simple as the STORM-HATCH is offline. Storm designed much of the system, and Sky is almost as good with communication engineering. They're both on the *Renarde*."

"If it's more?" Rachelle pushed.

"We'll do whatever necessary, Rachelle. Until we know, we return to exploring this region."

"What will we be exploring on Aranthine?" Mags asked, changing the subject to get the other two to set Coop's situation aside.

"Whatever we look for, we have to do it under cover. It's a Galvari Confederation world and we're not going to be welcomed."

"You're trying to contact the Aranthinian we met on Devisator," Rachelle said. "Is that smart? Letting him know we're on the way."

"You were there, Rachelle. Tas has no love for the Galvari. I think he can help us get on-world and collect more intel on what's happening in this region," Elie answered.

"He was also operating a trade ship for the Galvari," Rachelle reminded her.

"It's a gamble," she admitted. "Everything this far out is."

"Hey, Rach, I heard you met Coop before anyone else. True?" Mags asked.

"Trying to get us to not talk work?" Rachelle inquired.

"You betcha. I'd hate to waste Elie's wine listening to crap I hear all day every day," the green-eyed brunette admitted.

"We met soon after the cure for the virus was discovered, only we didn't know until the Space Ranger Project."
"Finally, a good story. More wine for you. No more caffeine for you, Elie. I'm bringing you a glass of wine," Mags announced as she unwinded. "And more for me."

Chapter Four

Earth - Past

NIGHT EAGLE[7]

(This short story excerpt occurs concurrent and following
the events in *PANDEMIC*.)

Facts:

• The US Navy's Sixth Fleet is stationed in Naples, Italy.

• Sardinia is an Italian-owned island east of Naples.

• Constantine, Algeria, known as the City of Bridges, is
one of the most beautiful sites in North Africa.

• All characters and events are fictitious. Any similarities
to real people or events are coincidental.

Sardinia

"Toni, you have to stay here. If your father calls or gets
through, you need to be here for him and your brother."

The cargo hover-copter awoke with a hum from the
power plant. The sound low, warm, and reassuring. Michele
Paré, wearing a grey flight suit with no insignias, not even
her Captain's bars, sat behind the left yoke. Her eighteen-
year-old daughter stood beside and behind her, between the
pilot and co-pilot seats.

"Mom, you can't go alone. You can't leave me here
alone," she said.

She pleaded once more to accompany her mother. An
appeal repeated regularly since learning of the desperate
plan to locate Toni's father and younger brother.

The two remained somewhere on the Italian mainland.
Vice Admiral Murphy's emergency order to redeploy the
entire Sixth Fleet to Sardinia included setting the exact time
for the last ship to sail. Anthony and Michael never made it

to the fleet-assigned docks in Naples. When the last ship sailed, anyone not aboard would need to find another way to escape the Italian mainland.

"Your father and Michael will be at the farmhouse north of Naples," Michele told her daughter. "That was the plan. If we ever got separated, we would head for the Ricci's farm. I can fly there, get them and return in a couple of hours."

"And get courtmartialed for stealing a Navy hover-copter," the younger Paré added.

The Naval ships, over-filled with personnel, support staff, and families, disembarked the District of Capodichino base on orders issued out of fear. Fear the spreading pandemic, having arrived on the European continent, would be too difficult to defend against with the city of Naples surrounding fleet activity headquarters.

Vice Admiral Murphy, without express consent from the Navy, ordered the emergency relocation to southern Sardinia. The twenty-four hours required for the relocation created chaos, but no panic. Military people and dependents drilled for emergency removals. Forced evacuation was a potential fact of life for anyone stationed overseas.

"Maybe," Captain Paré said. "But if it means Anthony, Michael, and you are safe, I'll happily pay the price. Now get off the copter. Stay by the sat-link comm unit. I'll stay in touch. You need to listen for your father. If he contacts you, let me know where they are."

The tall, slender teenager gave her mother a quick kiss on the cheek, backed out of the cockpit, and jumped down from the side door to the tarmac. She ran a couple of steps and turned. Brilliant brown eyes, damp with tears, watched the shuttle lift on compressed air. Her mom smiled and waved.

She returned the wave, continuing the gesture as the hover-copter flew across the asphalt and concrete, the shoreline, and out to disappear over the blue Tyrrhenian Sea.

Sardinia

(Two Years Later)

"Paré! Just what-the-fuck do you think you're doing?"

Naval Flight Officer (NFO) Turner Irving stood with hands on hips, feet spread, and face twisted into a countenance guaranteed to bend wills, if not steel.

"I am not a fucking aircrew trainer. I train pilots, Paré. You ain't a pilot."

"I'm not aircrew either, Ty," the twenty-year-old countered. "I guess I'm just a mutt."

When her mother never returned, and her father and brother never made contact, Antoinette Rachelle Paré became a ward of the US Navy's Sixth Fleet. It was not an official designation. She simply became one of hundreds of armed services dependents caught alone in the aftermath of the deadly contagion coursing across the planet.

Vice Admiral Murphy basically invaded Sardinia and annexed the port of Cagliari on the southern tip of the island. Marines maintained control of a large triangle encompassing the docks through the south-central section of the town.

Armed Marines allowed no one into the restricted area without extreme caution.

First, they had to be US citizens, and second, they would spend a required two weeks, minimum, in a special quarantine facility.

When the virus jumped from the mainland to the island, restricting access became deadly. Panicked islanders trying to escape the disease forced military personnel to fire. In the beginning they fired water hoses or rubber bullets. This escalated to gas. Finally, deadly force. People tried sneaking in from the water and by air. Every attempt turned back, sunk, or shot down.

During the two years following her mother's unauthorized departure, Toni Paré underwent a transformation. The giddy, light-hearted teenage girl became a stern, no-nonsense young woman.

She dealt with loss by filling her time working for the Navy. No job needing done seemed unimportant. If the cooks needed a dishwasher, her hands drowned pots and pans until her skin burned red. If garbage needed incineration, she was there. She acted as a clerk in administration and cleaned weapons for the armory.

She also learned. She learned close quarter combat from the Marines. She practiced with personal weapons stored in the base's arsenal. She was good at both.

Very good.

The Warrant Officer in command of small arms training called her 'the most natural shooter' he had ever seen. She simply did not miss.

No one needed to teach her how to fly. Her mother, a decorated Naval pilot who flew everything from hover-ships to the latest super-sonic exotropospheric fighters, taught her daughter to fly before she could ride a hover-bike. She continued to hone those skills with a flight simulation program stored on her computer. The 3-D sims helped her escape the pain which threatened to tear her down any time she allowed herself a quiet moment. It kept her near her mother's spirit.

The NFO's face untwisted. This young woman had become family. Her insistence on helping around flight operations and her ability to fix anything capable of flight made her an indispensable member of his staff. The loss of so many people from the virus, to the hurried relocation and the desertions following setting up shop on Sardinia, left most sections short-handed. Paré filled a lot of needs for a lot of commanders, but no one received more of her time than NFO Irving.

"Toni, you can't go 'round calling yourself a mutt," he said. "It ain't fair to dogs."

"Rachelle," she said.

"What?"

"I prefer people call me Rachelle." Toni was the name of the girl who lost her family. Toni laughed, danced, and wanted to become a teacher. Toni hurt all the time. Rachelle was none of that.

"Okay, *Rachelle.* Changing your name don't suddenly make you a pilot," the NFO said.

"Lt. Simmons is the pilot," Paré said. "You're sending her on a support mission to Malta. Malta is one of the few places on Earth completely free of disease. It is also under attack by renegade Italian sailors trying to fight their way ashore. Every possible copilot is already on a mission or too exhausted to stay awake. Ty, you know I can handle the second seat. Simmons can't fly, shoot, and watch her own six, even with the advanced computer systems. I'm here. I'm qualified. You decide."

Irving boasted thirty-plus years in the Navy. The thin, ramrod straight black man from Kansas intimidated everyone who came into his sphere of influence, including those of higher rank. Except one skinny, brown-haired determined twenty-year-old.

"Go, but Toni . . . sorry, *Rachelle* . . . if you get killed out there, don't you dare come back here."

Rachelle Paré strapped into the right seat of the fighter. Lt. Simmons, herself only a couple of years older, welcomed the help. It was not the first time Paré sat next to the pilot.

She begged ride-alongs whenever she could. She knew the routines, and she knew the systems.

Dahlonega, Georgia

At the same time Rachelle strapped into her seat for the flight to Malta, on a secure US Army Ranger training facility near Dahlonega, Georgia, USA, an eighteen-year-old Daniel Marcel Cooper stood before his father, Colonel Robert Cooper.

"You sure?" the elder Cooper asked.

"I am. I want to enlist," Daniel replied. "Going to college now makes no sense. With the new Can-Am-Mexico alliance, the military is going to be important if the world is going to survive. When they find a cure, someone will have to deliver it. After the pandemic is stopped, the whole world will become a war zone. I'll do a lot more good as a soldier than a student."

"Can-Am Alliance," the elder Cooper corrected. "Mexico can't control the cartels trying to slip refugees into North America. They've been cut out of the alliance. Your Mother would have wanted you in school," the career Army man added.

"She would want me to make a difference."

"You can enlist here, but I have no idea where the army will send you for training."

"Doesn't matter. As long as they train me and put me where I can help."

Constantine, Algeria
(Two Years Later)

"Thirty of our guys northwest of the airport are backed against a ravine," Ivanov told Coop.

Serg monitored comms while Coop used the night vision on his scope to track the action around the Boudiaf Sky and Space Port.

The two formed a crew-served sniper team. Specialist (SPC) Daniel Cooper did the shooting, and PFC Serg Ivanov acted as spotter, support, and protection.

Their current assignment to a Can-Am Force Recon company of one-hundred-twenty Rangers started the same way their previous dozen missions began. Hurry up. Wait. Drop into unknown territory and fast-foot to a hot zone. Wait. Shoot or don't shoot. Get out.

Except all hell broke loose.

"That would be the western fire teams," Coop replied. "Eastern units have reassembled with the northern teams." He set the rifle down. The weapon wrapped in gunny sack cloth to keep it safe from the dirt and sand. "I can't see the South from here. Anything on sat-rad?"

"Just the guys northwest. Even their radio signals are sporadic," Serg responded.

The Russian sat with his back against an artificial dirt-bank created decades before when the Algerians built the N79 highway. He faced abandoned buildings. The airport-spaceport facility lay east of their position, on the other side of the roadway.

Coop lay atop the rise. The position provided line-of-sight over the entire airport, as well as most of the flat farmland around the tarmac.

Sat-rad, short for satellite-fed radio system, allowed the units and individuals on the ground to remain in touch at all times. It also allowed the company to stay in communication with home base in Tunis, Tunisia.

"Makes no sense," Coop said. "We should be able to talk with and hear everyone."

"Jammers," Serg answered. "Not the latest or the best, but good enough to cause the sporadic results."

The Can-Am Rangers were on site at the request of the Algerians. Constantine, a beautiful city, and once the home to 750,000 people, needed help. Former army soldiers from France arrived after the cure for the pandemic had been distributed. They laid siege to the city's 125,000 survivors. Using military hardware and tactics, the French mercenaries killed the few remaining police and militia. They set up command and control at the former air and space port and began demanding taxes from the population. Intimidation, rape, and murder followed.

The City of Bridges became a city of fear. The reforming government in Algiers agreed to join the United Earth movement if Can-Am agreed to remove the French infidels choking Constantine. They estimated between two-hundred and three-hundred heavily armed former armée de terre. These military-trained opportunists used the port facilities and adjacent hotels for headquarters and garrisons. From these fortified locations, they ventured in and around the city framed by ravines. Constantine was accessible primarily by bridges.

The bridges, for vehicle and train traffic, and the river remained guarded twenty-four-seven by members of the self-titled Brigade Nouveau. Armed patrols kept residents in, visitors out, and maintained a close watch on all activity around Constantine. With mobile antiaircraft guns stationed at the spaceport, the New Brigade maintained control of their fiefdom.

"Algerian Intel reported two or three-hundred former French army grunts," Coop said. "We get dropped five miles east, trek across a desert valley, in summer heat, divide into four fire and depression units, and surround the port. We're outnumbered, but we're trained, and coming in before dawn to surprise them. Sneak in, hit 'em before they know they have company. Clean up the outliers next."

"They actually number closer to one-thousand than two-hundred. Our guys walked into a beehive," Ivanov finished. "Hold on, Coop. Getting something through from another unit." The former Russian commando closed his eyes, which did not help him hear better. He cupped his hands over his ears, which did.

"The combined northern and eastern groups are under the A1-N79 junction. Using the concrete for cover." Ivanov opened his eyes. "Forty total. That means twenty KIA or MIA. They are surrounded. Incoming fire heaviest south of their location, north of the airport."

"Thirty northwest, caught between a ravine and bad guys, and forty north, surrounded and taking heavy fire," Coop repeated. "South?"

"Nothing."

"Home base?"

"I keep trying, but nothing is getting out or coming in," the PFC replied.

Coop started to reply when a buzz in his earbuds stopped him. He cupped his hands over both ears.

"This is Shooter One. Do you copy?" he asked the buzz, hoping it represented someone live on the other end.

He gave his spotter a questioning look and received a head shake in reply.

Whoever reached Cooper, had not been heard by Ivanov. That should not have been possible, but Jammers were never perfect. They often created anomalies for communications tech.

This anomaly became a scratchy male voice.

"This is Sixth Fleet communications control, Sardinia. We are receiving broken transmissions, over."

"Sixth Fleet, I am with Can-Am Force Recon. Location, Boudiaf air and spaceport facilities in Constantine, Algeria. I have soldiers pinned down in multiple locations by unexpected superior numbers. I need air support as quick as it can get here."

Static and reverb almost made Coop remove the earpiece. He resisted, fearful of doing anything resulting in loss of the shaky connection.

"Sixth, please repeat."

"Sorry, Shooter one," came the response. More of a gargle than garbled. "All air assets are currently engaged. We have nothing available. Can you retreat? Over."

"Negative. One group is backed against a ravine. One group is caught beneath a highway overpass, taking heavy fire. I have another group unaccounted. Can you pass intel to Can-Am HQ Tunis? We have bad comms."

No reply. No static. Dead air.

"Sixth Fleet? They're gone," he told Ivanov. "Even if they reach Tunis, our guys will be toast before anyone arrives to help."

"What's the plan, Coop? I'm sure as hell not bugging out."

"Do you realize how difficult life is going to be when you get your third stripe?" Coop asked. "You'll be Sarge Serg."

The spotter dropped his optics and let his forehead sink to the sand.

"Only you think of things like that at times like this," he said. "Do you ever get rattled?"

"Whatever is jamming the signals has to be damn powerful," Coop said. "It's capable of squelching point-to-point and sat-rad communications. It isn't perfect, but affective. We need to find it and take it out. If we can improve comms, we can work out a strategy with the teams and find the South group."

"Any clue what to look for?"

"It will be up high. It will either be flat and round, or on a swivel to affect an area this large," Coop answered. "A swivel would explain why we have intermittent access."

"It could be up on a mountain or on top of a building somewhere is the city," Ivanov complained.

"Anything important will be close to the commander, and the commander is at the spaceport. The eastern sky is getting lighter, Serg. Use your optics to check the tops of structures around the port facilities."

Ivanov adjusted his optical scanners and began a grid search of the airport. Coop recovered his gunny sack. He extracted a tool and used it to remove the barrel of his rifle. He pulled a longer, wider bore barrel from the sack, and set to work attaching it to the stock. By the time he completed all the adjustments, Ivanov had located the suspected jammer.

"When did we get a cannon?" the former Russian soldier asked.

"The original piece belonged to my great grandfather. My Dad had the parts re-milled so it could be mounted on a standard frame. What did you find?" Coop asked back.

"A dish on top of an old-fashion control tower, making three hundred-sixty rotations slowly. Location is fifty-yards east and center to the main runway."

"Distance?"

"Two thousand-six-hundred-forty-three meters," came the response. "We need to get closer for you to have a chance of taking out any operators."

"Closer means the potential of being seen before we can make a shot," Coop said. "It also means moving to a lower elevation. From the top of this hill to the top of the tower, how much elevation change?"

Ivanov consulted his optics and replied, "Twenty-one feet."

Coop extended the carbon tripods and settled the weapon on the crest of the hill.

He opened the chamber after extracting a projectile from the gunny sack's side pouch.

"Mother Mary of God, Coop," the private exclaimed. "That's a fucking artillery shell."

"2,400 grains of lead and 240 grains of smokeless powder," Coop replied, placing the mammoth round into the slide chamber. "A .905 caliber capable of twenty-one-hundred feet per second."

"Your normal load is two-hundred grains of lead. What kind of kick is that thing got?"

"Two-hundred-seventy-seven foot-pounds. I've modified the frame with additional absorption and added extra venting to allow more gas to escape. It's still going to kick like a mule, but a smaller mule."

"So a jackass," Ivanov quipped.

"Call the target, Spotter."

"You have distance and elevation. Forty-eight percent humidity and zero wind. No mirage effects on the board. I have no idea what a .905 does over distance, so the shot is yours. Hit or miss. I still don't see anyone to target."

What the shot did was contact the base of the jammer disc. The force of impact shattered the steel and carbon into shards. Eight French mercenaries operating and protecting the equipment died from shrapnel. Ivanov watched in amazement as the entire thirty-foot circumference dish tilted. Gravity took control and the jammer fell from the top of the ancient control tower.

"Holy Mother, Coop. Coop?"

The recoil dislocated Cooper's shoulder. The rifle lay to his right side. He held his right arm across his chest. Ivanov had to put it back in the socket.

"Didn't expect that," Coop said a few minutes later, needing the time to bring the pain under control. "I don't think I set the barrel properly." He loosened the utility belt at his waist, gingerly lay his hand across the front of his hip, and tightened the belt over the wrist, securing his arm to his side.

"Coop, you just took down a massive electronic jamming station, from over one-and-a-half-miles, with a bullet. If I didn't have the optics system video, no one would believe me."

"Can-Am Recon, this is Sixth Fleet pilot nearing Constantine. Can anyone hear me?"

The discernibly female voice spoke in Coop's ear, but Ivanov's reaction indicated he received the same request.

"Pilot, this is Shooter One. Jammer has been destroyed. We have comms. I'll be your eyes on the ground. What do I call you?"

The hesitation lasted long enough Coop and Ivanov were starting to worry the French renegades had more than one Jammer.

"Call sign *Orphan*, Shooter One. Where do you need me first?"

Sardinia
(Sixth Fleet Communication Center)

"Sorry, Shooter one," responded SPC Hadley. "All air assets are currently engaged. We have nothing available. Can you retreat? Over."

"Negative. One group is backed against . . ." and the reply ended. Communications once more interrupted.

"Is there anything we can do?" Rachelle asked the comms operator. Tentative light gave color to the eastern horizon when Rachelle requested Hadley's attention. She had no official qualifications, certainly no Fleet certifications in communications systems, but knew her way around the sophisticated equipment. During busy times, the communications commander used her to listen for random signals. When aviation assets were engaged with multiple missions, the trained, limited availability specialists, like SPC Hadley, needed to concentrate on those messages.

The erratic chatter from North Africa caught her attention. Once she grasped the situation, she asked Hadley for help.

"I'm forwarding copies to Can-Am, Tunis," Specialist Hadley replied. "I don't think they have air capability to reach those guys in time, but maybe."

"He sounded calm," Paré commented.

"Sniper," Hadley responded. "Call sign Shooter One; has to be a sniper. Those guys have no nerves."

The Specialist rolled his chair three-feet to a second monitor station, swiped a couple of requests on a built-in trackpad and read aloud the result.

"One hundred-twenty Can-Am Ranger special operators sent to Constantine, Algeria to eliminate an estimated two to three-hundred French ex-military. Sounds like their intel sucked. Unexpected numbers probably means more than a thousand."

"Will they get out?"

"Some might. Rangers are tough. If they can make it to open land, they'll disappear into the deserts and mountains. If they are caught without an exit, most are dead or captured."

"The sniper?"

"Crew is probably in a safe place, high enough and far enough away to cover the killing field. They could bug out. But they won't."

"Why not?"

"Rachelle, there is something not quite sane about snipers and the crew who work with them. They'll lay down cover fire until someone pinpoints their location and lobs a mortar on top of them. Hey, where you going?"

The door closed behind her without a reply.

Constantine

"Hold, Orphan." Coop turned comms over to Ivanov, pulled the extended rifle up and opened his scope. While Cooper took visuals, Ivanov made contact with the two groups under fire.

"The guys at the ravine have cover," he told Coop. "They're pinned, but they can keep their heads down. They have enough firepower to keep the Frenchies back.

"The two groups under the bridge are getting hammered. Coop, my portable laser-designator isn't going to be able to pinpoint targets at either location accurately from this distance."

"Let me have your laser rifle," Coop said, placing the gunpowder weapon down.

"Tell both groups to release green smoke."

He turned his attention back to the flyer.

"Orphan, do you copy?"

"Copy. I'm two-minutes out and hot."

Any girl with a jet and missiles is most definitely hot, he thought to himself. Aloud, he said, "Green smoke will be good guys. Two groups. One north of the space port under a highway overpass. Second group northwest caught in a ravine. Highway bridge is priority. We're too far away to lase the bad guys. I'm going to use a shoulder-fire laser rifle to light the spots you need to hit. Can you target on my shots?"

"Don't know until we try, Shooter One. Beginning my run; fire away."

Ivanov's laser rifle did not come with a scope. It was a defensive weapon designed to protect the sniper crew in case of detection. Coop relied on remembering what he saw with the sniper-scope earlier.

The laser rifle stock set against his left shoulder, weapon supported across his freed damaged right arm. He fired four times, left to right, aiming center of where he recalled mercenary groups positioned and firing on the encircled Can-Am Rangers.

The sniper crew neither heard nor saw the fighter, but hell rained down on the four marks Coop hit.

"Holy shit and my Mother is a whore," the Russian said. He said it twice. The first time in English, followed by Russian for emphasis. "I don't know which is more unbelievable. You hitting targets from this distance, with a fucking unreliable laser rifle, left handed, or a pilot dropping missiles on the exact spots without a guidance system."

Laser fire from near the airfield erupted into the dim sky of night-morning. Two mobile anti-aircraft units attempting to hit the fast-moving fighter.

Coop did not hesitate. He trained the laser rifle on the two enemy sites, and triggered bursts back and forth, trying to disrupt the gun crews.

One of the mobile units turned to face his position, attempting to use the surface-to-air weapon to target and eliminate the threat he posed.

Two missiles streaked in from the West. One for each gun. The incoming missiles eradicated the weapon systems and everything around them.

"Orphan, are you ready for the ravine?"

"Waiting on you Shooter One, but I did get a look when I flew over. Your guys are close to the bogies. I'll have to use my mini-gun. Can you set a pattern from north to south?"

"Say when."

"When."

Coop fired seven times into the smaller team positions established by the renegades along a highland east of the ravine.

With the sun rising over the horizon, rays of light cleared the mountains east of Constantine. Coop and Ivanov could see the Can-Am fighter as it flew from the North, above the city skyline. The belly of the aircraft skimmed feet above the tallest rooftops.

Twenty-caliber death and destruction tore into the ground, beginning from the spot furtherest the sniper crew's location, moving south, through all seven enemy positions. To get to the ground, they had to pass through a lot of bodies.

"North team commander says they are wiping up the leftovers from Orphan's missiles," Ivanov reported. "They have a few mercenaries north of the overpass, but nothing they can't handle. Team West has exited the ravine. The few bad guys left are surrendering."

"South?" Coop asked. "Have we heard anything from the group there?"

"Negative. Jammer is gone, but still no contact. Comm systems must all be off-line. Dead or damaged during the firefight," the spotter surmised. "Individual comms may not have enough power to reach beyond their immediate field."

"Orphan, this is Shooter One. Can you recon south of the airport? We're missing a group of thirty Rangers. No contact in hours. I have no set location other than south of the airfield."

"On it, Shooter One."

The fighter, an older US Navy stealth in-atmosphere superjet called a Night Eagle, crossed from the West, low to the deck, and headed south. The black and dark gray plane, flying now below mach, created little sound as it passed.

"Shooter One?"

"Copy, Orphan."

"Your people are in a wadi surrounded by a couple of hundred bad guys. They're taking heavy fire, including lasers. I see a transport-mounted jammer that's causing the interference with comms. More importantly, light artillery is being positioned. If they range in, no way anyone gets out of that ditch."

"Anything you can do, Orphan?"

"I used all six missiles. I'm almost empty on the last gun-pull. Lasers aren't accurate for air-to-surface, but I don't seem to have another choice. How fast can your other groups get three-miles south of the airport?"

"Spotter is on the horn. Reports both groups headed your way, but forty-minutes minimum," Coop relayed. He and Ivanov were already setting a quick pace headed southeast. Slowed by his damaged arm, they could still get within firing range in a third the time needed by the other groups.

"I'll do what I can. Orphan out."

The sniper crew heard the battle long before getting to a high spot where they could see. Topping a hill, both came to a jarring, jaw-dropping stop.

"I got nothing," Ivanov said. An amazing admission from a man prideful in his ability to find a curse for any occasion.

The Night Eagle employed hover thrusters to remain steady above a desert wadi.

They could barely make out Rangers huddled under rocks and overhangs, heads down as the wash from the thrusters churned sand, dirt, and rocks into the air. The cloud of debris helped hide them from enemy guns.

At the same time, the ship rotated in a slow circle, the pilot firing laser bursts to keep French ex-army soldiers from advancing on the Rangers caught in the wadi.

Projectiles pinged off the armored ship, with an occasional laser burst singeing the Navy paint job, but not penetrating the reinforced airframe.

The Russian tapped Coop on the left shoulder. He pointed to the Northeast. A half-mile from the Rangers and Night Eagle, the mercenaries were setting up a heavy mortar.

Neither soldier needed to say it out loud. With the fighter stationary, a mortar round would cause a lot of damage. It might not destroy the ship, but it would bring it down. A shell impacting near the cockpit would take out the pilot.

Coop handed the laser rifle back to Ivanov. He pulled the sniper rifle out of the long gunny sack the Russian carried on cross-country run.

"You can't switch the barrel with your arm screwed up, and you ain't got the time anyway," the PFC said, watching his younger superior lift the weapon out left handed.

"For a descendant of the great Russian poet Vyacheslav Ivanovich Ivanov, you use the word '*ai'nt*' a lot. Lie down," Coop ordered.

Serg did not bother to argue. He dropped belly down on the hilltop. Coop placed the now-folded gunny sack across the prone man's back. The weight of the barrel soon rested atop the cloth.

"Damn. That thing's heavier than it looks, and it looks like it weighs a ton."

"Shut up. When I tell you, take a deep five-second breath, then let half out using a three-count, and don't move. They're getting ready to fire the mortar."

Less than five-seconds later: "Take your breath."

Recalling how loud the first shot used to destroy the big jammer rumbled, the Russian cupped his ears as he took a breath. The boom, followed by the weight removed from his back, brought agony and relief.

Too interested in observing the result of the .905, he ignored the ringing in his ears.

"Damn, Coop. You hit the fucking shell at the same time they fired it."

The blast, muted due to his hearing temporarily disrupted by the rifle's retort, must have been loud. The result of the explosion left total devastation. Nothing within one-hundred yards of the artillery piece stood. The blast crater and surrounding damage could only have occurred due to the detonation of the mortar shell.

He turned to congratulate his partner and experienced his next heart-stopping moment.

The .905's recoil knocked the young NCO backward. Judging from the angle of his arm, the kick-back dislocate the left shoulder. Luckily SPC Cooper lay unconscious, so the pain was under control.

Tunis, Tunisia
(Two Days Later)

Daniel Cooper sat upright in his hospital bed.

Reinforcements arrived from Tunis, but they arrived to find Constantine under control of the surviving Can-Am Rangers.

The two other groups converged on the wadi. The withering laser fire from the Night Eagle, the aftermath of the mortar explosion, and the loss of many other assets resulted in a short skirmish, followed by the French laying down weapons and raising hands.

Ivanov informed the pilot Sniper was down, but okay. He watched the outdated Navy fighter disappear into the morning sun, headed home to Sardinia.

"You look like shit, Coop," Ivanov said. He procured Coop's lunch, sat on the nurse's stool he wheeled in from the hallway, and began eating.

"At least my looks are temporary," he quipped. "You, on the other hand, are stuck with ugly for life."

The Russian would have replied, but decided eating provided a better use for his smart mouth.

"How many did we lose?" Coop asked.

The question made his visitor place the tray back on the stand.

"One third," he replied. "Would have been a total cluster fuck if Orphan hadn't shown up. Speaking of, you don't know the rest of the story."

"Nurse told me reinforcements from Tunis teamed up with the special operators still standing and finished the mission," Coop replied. "Took the space port, swept the bridges, and collected the remaining ex-armée de terre deserters."

"Not the most interesting thing," Ivanov said. "Not even close. Turns out Orphan is a civilian. She stole a Navy Night Eagle to save our asses."

Coop sat up, grimaced, and leaned back quickly. The pain meds failing to keep pace with the double dislocated shoulders. "Give me the whole story, Serg. Don't make me ask."

Ivanov recounted the rumor he heard from an SPCl assigned to the Tunis Command Center.

"A civilian, a woman, the daughter of an MIA Navy pilot, donated her time to help around the Sixth Fleet since the relocation to Sardinia. She was helping out in the comm center and overheard our request for air cover. When Sixth responded with a '*no-can-do*,' she commandeered the Night Eagle. The old fighter was kept armed, fueled, and ready in case of an emergency. They stashed it in a make-shift hangar at the end of a city street. Scuttlebutt says Sixth maintains a couple of hold-out fighters, hidden around the docks in case they ever run out of carrier-based assets."

Ivanov, his recitation proving his lineage to the twentieth-century playwright, wheeled the nurse's stool closer to the bed. Though no one else was near enough to hear him had he shouted, he delivered the next information quietly.

"Orphan, real name Rachelle Paré, opened the hangar doors, drove the fucking Eagle down the street, and took off. She radioed control her plan after she cleared the island."

"Paré?" Coop asked.

Serg scooted back a foot, and resumed at a normal volume.

"Father was a French-Canadian businessman working in Naples while her mother, US citizen and Navy pilot, was assigned Sixth Fleet," Ivanov replied, understanding the one-word question. Time together under the conditions the sniper crew operated led to a great deal of simpatico.

"Your contact seems to have heard a lot. What will they do to her?"

"Good news. She can't be courtmartialed," Serg said. He retrieved the food tray, his appetite returning.

"If General Durand [Commander of the Can-Am North African Army] has his way, she'll get a medal. He already told Admiral Murphy she's welcome to come fly Army fighters."

"Anything else I should know about?"

"I'm getting promoted to SPC, and can expect a Bronze Star. For valorous action in the face of the enemy," he answered. "Ain't much of an honor. They said I had to stay on crew with you."

"Congratulations anyway, Serg," Coop said. A smile helped ease a tiny bit of the pain.

The Russian finished a mouthful of warm jell-o before saying, "You get a Silver Star and a stripe, Sergeant."

"Okay, Serg. Why so glum about the medals and promotions?"

"Fucking classified mission. We can't tell anyone." He looked at his friend, closer than a brother, and added, "Who the fuck wants a medal if you can't use it to get laid?"

Sardinia
  (One Week Later)

"Well, well, it's the felon who fell into a load of shit, and came out smellin' like a hero." NFO Turner Irving stood with hands on hips, feet spread, and face twisted in a smile.

"That was the most convoluted thing I have ever heard, Sir," Paré said. She stood in front of the training officer, dressed in an official Sixth Fleet Can-Am Naval-Air flight suit, complete with ensign rank and name patch.

"Yea, well now hear this, Ensign Paré. The state of the Navy must be one of extreme disrepair if the Admiral of the Sixth Fleet is willing to ask the Prime Minister of the Can-Am alliance for a special dispensation to give a civilian, nonmilitary cadet, wet-behind-the-ears, skinny, twenty-something a commission and assignment to Flight Training School." All said without pause or breath.

"She's a bit more than that, NFO."

Irving snapped to attention a wink quicker than Rachelle.

Admiral Murphy appeared from around the corner of the hangar wherein the borrowed Night Eagle again resided.

"She's the only service member, hell, the only person I have ever heard of to receive a military medal for bravery in battle before officially being a member of the military."

Rachelle broke protocol, dropping out of attention with wide, questioning eyes, and a "Sir?"

"Both of you, at ease," The Admiral ordered. "The PM received video from over a dozen cameras attached to the SO company sent to Constantine. She watched your actions from a lot of viewpoints. Every angle proved you saved a lot of lives, Toni."

She did not correct his use of her 'former' name.

"We can't have an official ceremony, because it was a classified mission," he said. He continued in a hushed voice. "We do not need the world to know you stole a government aircraft."

He returned to his normal, slightly gruff tone.

"I don't have an actual medal yet, anyhow. But for the record, Antoinette Rachelle Paré, you are hereby awarded the Can-Am Navy's Flying Cross, earned for demonstrating extreme bravery during battle."

The new ENS Paré excused herself to attend her first official squadron meeting.

Lifted spirits evident in the way she glided across the pavement.

"Has anyone told her how close she came to not coming home?" NFO Irving asked the Admiral.

"Not that I'm aware," Murphy replied. "We'll leave it that way, Ty. Sooner or later she'll find out a grunt on the ground saved her ass with a one-in-a-million shot. By then it will be another footnote. Let her have her day. She earned it."

"Wow," Mags said. "When did you find out the sniper was Coop?"

"During the Space Ranger Project," she answered. "We were comparing notes on the campaign in North Africa. Especially when he mentioned 'Orphan.' I had that call sign less than a year before changing it to 'Rain'."

"Wow," Mags said a second time. "I need more wine." She stood, stopped, and turned back to Rachelle. "Can I see your medal?"

Chapter Five

"Where are we?" Elie asked.

"Fixed position above the system's first planet," Genna answered her Captain. "We're between the planet and the system star. Detection dampeners are on. The ship should be invisible to general scans from Aranthine or ships in the area."

"Izzy?" the Captain addressed her comms officer.

"Still no response from Tascarvinavox Oison," her Comms officer reported. "We currently have a three-minute lapse with space-standard radio. Are you sure we have his receiver code?"

"It's the code he gave me on Devisator," Elie responded. "Keep it on auto. If we don't hear anything in twenty-four hours we'll go in for a visit and see what happens. Genna, a quick rundown on the system."

The avatar answered, "Orange dwarf star and five planets in orbit. According to the Devee files, the Aranthinians call the star Ortoka. Aranthine is the second planet, sixty-eight-point-twenty-two-million miles distant at its current position. No other inhabited planets or moons. Two wormhole gates. The nearest at 28,800,000 miles from the planet. Well within visiting distance for ships.

"Aranthine is eighty-five-percent Earth's size at 6729.875 miles in diameter. Ninety-two-percent gravity. Three moons, each roughly one-half the size of Earth's moon. Class M, Goldilocks environment.

"One of the moons is designed for interstellar ships to land or dock at one of two orbital stations. The Aranthinians do not allow alien ships inside the troposphere. Cargo shuttles transfer goods and people between the planet and moon bases."

"The inhabitants?" Elie asked.

"Once again I'm relying on the Devee," she qualified her answer. "Approximately three billion. Humanoid. Purple skin pigmentation due to a combination of star light and diet over millennia. Considered extremely intelligent. Information on the history of the civilization is sparse. Apparently catastrophic environmental failure destroyed most of the crops used for trade as well as decimating the population. They currently import the majority of the world's food. They perform service work in trade. It was after the environmental disaster they joined the Galvari Confederation."

"Izzy, are you still receiving pings from the Parrian cargo ships we tagged on Vista?" Elie asked.

"Affirmative," the reply. "Both are on the surface of the moon used for visitors."

"Captain," Genna addressed Elie formally. "The Devee report a Galvari presence on the planet. A small, permanent base. It would be unwise to simply drop in for a visit. Our scans indicate four surface-to-space laser cannons. After the confrontation with the Galvari battlewagon in the Devisator system, I doubt we would be welcomed."

"Let's hope Tas answers our call." Elie replied.

"As a matter of excellent timing, Oison just responded," Izzy announced.

"Put him through to my office," Elie ordered. "Genna, join me. Kennedy, have Captain Paré report to my office. Lt. Nassar, you have the bridge."

Anwar Nassar at the Systems console answered, "Aye," as Elie and Genna departed.

Inside her attached office, Elie said, "Kennedy, pipe Oison here."

"Yes, Captain," the AI responded. "Captain Paré is in route."

"Tas, this is Captain Casalobos."

There was a six-minute delay. Three for her message to reach the planet and another three for the response.

"Hello, Captain. I must say I was surprised to hear your call," the Aranthinian's voice issued from a speaker embedded in Elie's desk. "This is Galvari space, Captain. You are taking a dangerous risk."

"What about you? How risky is it for you to take this call?"

"I'm safe," he assured her. "The Galvari do not monitor this bandwidth. It is not on the approved list for space normal transmissions. I assume from the lapse you are near the planet En. Is there a reason worth incurring the Galvari's wrath that brings you here?"

Rachelle Paré entered as Oison finished his question.

"Two reasons," Elie replied. "Our mission is discovery. I want to know more about the Galvari Confederation, as well as more about Aranthine. I am also interested in two Parrian cargo ships currently moored on your moon. We tracked them from a planet called Vista. Do you have any ideas as to where it would be best for my fighters to land without creating an uproar?"

"There are areas around the planet we know the Galvari do not watch. Flying from space into our atmosphere and moving from the troposphere to the surface will be more difficult. I believe I can arrange a short glitch in the planet's scanners. No more than fifteen to twenty minutes," he answered.

"Send the coordinates for the surface location. Let me know the time you will begin your glitch. The fighters will be on the ground in under fifteen minutes," Elie assured him.

"Very well, Captain. When I know I can arrange a break in the scanner operations I will contact you with when and where. It may take a day or two."

"We'll be here, Tas," she replied. "Your channel is monitored at all times. Contact us when you are ready. Casalobos, out."

"Do you trust him?" Genna asked.

"I don't know him well enough to know," Elie admitted. "But the value of the potential intelligence is worth the risk. Rachelle, your opinion?"

"I don't know him any better," she said. "But the most valuable asset you have against a potential enemy is intelligence. The more we can learn about the Galvari Confederation, the better for Space Fleet if it ever does come down to a confrontation."

"It would take the fighters six days at max speed to get from here to Aranthine," Genna said. "That presents a lot of opportunities for detection, even at their size."

"Too risky and too long," Elie agreed. "I have an idea how to reduce both."

Chapter Six

"Rain. Magpie. Report," Elie ordered.

Tension on the bridge rose as the 109 neared the planet's horizon. When they crossed the ship would be exposed and in a position where they could be seen on scanners. Lt.JG Lesego Ndaba piloted the ship, timing their emergence with the exact time Tas Oison told them a *glitch* would temporarily suspend scanner operations on Aranthine. If she was off or he was wrong, the mission would be a bust.

"This is Rain," Rachelle responded using her callsign. "Ready to launch on your signal."

"Magpie mounted for pony express," Mags replied. It was her unique way of telling the Captain she was in the fighter and ready for a fast departure.

"Lesego, time to drop zone preset?" Elie asked her pilot.

"Aye, Ma'am. Three-point-six-seconds at in-system max space-fold," she replied.

"Anwar, force fields?" she inquired.

From the Systems console, Lt. Anwar Nassar responded. "The crystal shield is on. The sonic force field kicked in with ion-fusion drive. The combination should be sufficient to protect us from the planet's gravity well. I can add the electro-magnetic generator shields if you want. "

"Save the EM," she replied. "Am I crazy, Genna?" Elie asked her First Officer.

"Adventurous," the strawberry blonde responded. She stood to Elie's left. "Space-fold to the planet. Launch the two fighters. Space-fold back into hiding. The Spirit Two's have fourteen minutes, give or take a few seconds, to enter the atmosphere, reach the coordinates provided by Oison, land and cover the ships. Right out of Daniel Cooper's playbook."

"Basically the same gambit he, Hiro, and Mags used when they attacked the Prophet's ship in the Aster system," she explained.

"It works if the shields hold and Oison isn't a Galvari agent setting us up," Genna said.

"Horizon in twenty," Lesego called.

"Get in a seat," Elie told Genna. "Battle harnesses," she ordered, in case the return to natural space was rough.

"Ten," the pilot called.

Ten seconds later, "Space-fold drive engaged." The mission to place Space Fleet personnel on the surface of Aranthine began.

At .7ls, or 7,823,844 miles per minute, the 109 traveled 29,339,415 miles in three-point-seven-five seconds arriving one-thousand-ninety-eight miles above the surface of the planet.

"Launch fighters," Elie commanded when the ship did not dip due to the gravity well and no one took a shot at them.

The original Spirit fighters, like the Angel and Demon series before them, were built to operate in the unique conditions of outer space. They could fly in atmosphere, but they did not perform nearly as well. The Wraith ship Nathan Trent built for his personal use and gifted to Daniel Cooper proved to be capable in multiple environments. Many of its design elements were used in the construction of the Spirit Two.

This smaller new Spirit Two retained the sleek boomerang shape of the Spirit, but a variety of retractable vertical and horizontal stabilizer fins and wings could be arranged to compensate for atmospheric conditions. Alien worlds came with a variety of atmospheres; different air densities and elemental compositions. Weather variables and gravitational fields ranging from zero to crushing required adjustments. Adjustments would need to be made on the fly - literally.

Rain exited the hangar first. Magpie followed.

As they turned toward the surface, the 109 disappeared as it reengaged space-fold drive.

The first thousand miles were covered in fifty-five seconds. Next they hit the entry point of the planet's atmosphere. Flames surrounded the two ships as the heat soared.

Spirit Twos were capable of indo-atmospheric speeds up to Mach 7. Not wanting to cause a sonic boom and alert people on the ground, they maintained a modest four-hundred-miles-per-hour. Because the 109 delivered them directly above the coordinates Oison provided, they reached the LZ in less than three minutes. Ship to surface taking an incredible four minutes total.

They landed in an experimental hydroponics garden. By radio, Oison directed them into a massive barn-like structure where both ships fit with plenty of space left available.

"Five minutes to spare," Tas said as Rachelle and Mags appeared from beneath their ships. "I am Tas Oison," he introduced himself to Mags.

"Mags Moore," the pilot replied leaving off her rank.

"Captain Paré, welcome to Aranthine," he said.

"Where are we and what is this?" Rachelle asked.

"We are one-thousand-miles from the city of Avendal. Avendal is the planet's technology center. It is the hub for high tech research and enterprises. This is an experimental hydroponics farm. More specifically, this building was used to house the vehicles used for crop management," he explained.

"Was used?" Mags asked.

"The experiment failed," he said. "My civilization embraced the concept of expansion and growth regardless of potential consequences. As a result pollution fouled the atmosphere. A mixture of chemicals resulted in a miasma that destroyed much of our flora. The loss of plant life meant a reduction in oxygen and food. The fight to live led to global conflicts. We almost exterminated ourselves."

"What changed?" Rachelle asked.

"Two things. The same technology driving us to overburden the environment also created artificial food sources. Second, and more incredible, a huge silver space ship arrived. No one knows who they were or where they came from. The aliens provided machinery capable of reducing the deadly chemicals in our air. In the centuries that followed, we maintained and reproduced them. There are large sections of the planet which remain unlivable. Plants have recovered a little, but there remains a toxicity in our air that hampers growth. Farms like this one periodically attempt new procedures. Thus far only botanical gardens within bio-domes produce positive results. We cannot grow enough food to support the population without artificial replication and imports from other worlds."

"What happened to the alien ship?" Mags asked.

"It left," he answered. "No fanfare and no contact. All we have are the original converters. No idea who they were or where they came from. I have a house nearby. It will be more comfortable to talk there."

"Your home?" Rachelle asked.

"Family home," he said. "For centuries my family has experimented with farming. Between attempts we survive by running errands for other worlds."

"Like the Galvari?" Rachelle asked.

"Among others," he said. "Here comes my sister. We'll take you to our home and continue there."

Crossing the expanse walked a slender female. Her purple-hued skin and interesting veining criss-crossing her features marking her Aranthinian heritage. Attractive, as her brother was handsome, with short dark hair in a shaggy style that showed small ears. She wore cargo-style pants and a dark grey t-shirt that displayed muscled arms, a flat stomach, and firm chest. Her grey eyes indicated a mix of curiosity and concern.

"This is my sister, Tamina," Tas said. He stopped talking when he saw his sibling freeze in place. He turned and found Rachelle holding her side-arm, pointed at the newcomer. "We've met," she said.

Chapter Seven

Toronto

Guy Arcand, Chairman of the UEC Board of Governors, stood contemplating a holographic representation of the African continent hovered in the air. The dapperly dressed French Canadian's black hair was shot with grey above his ears, a sign the job of leading the planet to a place of unity came with stress.

The man in charge of the United Earth Council's security services, Paris Cassel, sat nearby with his left leg crossed over his right. As slender as Arcand, the top spy had a full head of white hair earned in his forty-plus years in espionage. Unlike the fashion-forward suit the Chairman wore, his blue suit was nondescript. If you passed on the street, nothing would draw your attention toward him. If asked later, most people would not remember anything about him.

"I'm trying to decide about title changes," Arcand said.

His statement had no relationship to the map or to Cassel's position. Over the years he had gotten used to Arcand's tangent thoughts spoken aloud. The Chairman used the security director as a soundboard because he knew nothing he said would ever be repeated.

"When I hear *Chairman* Arcand I remember my world history class and how communist party leaders had the same title."

"Once you sanction a global election you can go by *President* Arcand," Cassel said.

"We may all be dead before that happens," Arcand responded. He turned from the hologram to look directly at the other man. "We finally agreed to a universal monetary system, and writing a constitution is a bag of snakes. That has to be done before elections can occur."

"At least the World Judicial Courts are up and operating," the older man said.

"United Earth Council is dated," Arcand said, returning to his concern for titles. "It was fine before we became involved in galactic politics. It makes it sound like Earth is governed by paid board members. We can't continue to introduce ourselves to extraterrestrials this way. Space Fleet should represent Earth, not a council."

"The UEC is the planet's central government," Cassel said. "There is no reason we cannot simply say we represent Earth when meeting aliens."

"Perhaps. Instead of UEC we could be the World Assembly," Arcand said. "Say it like we are united, not trying to convince people we're combining our differences under one roof."

"Sounds like a church group," Cassel said, earning a frown by his boss.

"What's the latest intel on Col. Katherine Chanda?" the Chairman asked, returning to the actual reason for Cassel's presence.

"She took your offer seriously," he replied. "She's overseeing four construction projects, three schools and a hospital. Her militia has put down one wannabe warlord and absorbed another group. Her combination of humanitarian work and no nonsense handling of criminals and insurgents is making her a hero to the Africans."

"That's good. They love her and she represents us."

"Maybe. Her forces still don't wear UEC uniforms. You could be financing the next major threat to unity," the security expert said.

"It is a risk," Arcand agreed. "Do you have anyone inside her organization to keep us apprised?"

"Of course," the answer.

The holograph changed from Africa to the western hemisphere.

"Which leaves us with Lorenza Aragon."

"I have Tab Barnwell keeping an eye on her operations," Cassel said.

"Watching, not arresting? What's the point of having a Marshal Service if they aren't bringing in criminals?" Arcand wanted to know.

"We aren't going to eliminate crime, Guy," the older man replied. "Aragon is a known quantity. Her cartel runs the major illegal businesses from Argentina to Can-Am. More importantly, she is no longer interested in overthrowing the UEC."

"Deal with the devil you know," the politician said.

"Exactly. If her people step too far out of line, the Marshals will act. Otherwise, we keep an eye on her operations and concentrate on continuing to fully unite the planet."

"After we ratify the constitution and hold elections we can work to eliminate crime," Arcand reasoned.

"Good luck with that," Cassel rejoined. "As long as people populate the planet, I have a feeling criminals will break the laws."

"We can hope, Paris," the Chairman replied.

Arcand's personal assistant interrupted over the intercom.

"Chairman, Director Ishihara is here for your next appointment."

"Thank you, Henry. Make her comfortable for five minutes," he replied. To Cassel he said, "Keep me informed on Chandra and Aragon."

The Director of the United Earth Security Establishment (UESE) greeted the Director of Exo-Legal Affairs on his way out. Arcand waved Aya Ishihara into his office.

The attractive Japanese woman took the same chair Cassel's had used. Ishihara had been a brilliant student of the law, and developed a reputation as an attorney and legal counselor in Japan. The Japanese representative on the UEC brought her to Toronto as a member of her staff. Her talents were quickly recognized by the other members. With the arrival of extraterrestrials, it was decided an agency would be needed to provide Earth with legal advice when dealing with other worlds. Aya, despite her youth, was asked to create and direct that agency.

She was the daughter of Kai Ishihara, the close quarters combat instructor at Space Fleet Academy and part-time Deputy Marshal when needed.

"Chairman Arcand, I appreciate your time," she said.

"You've been the Director long enough to call me Guy, Aya," he told her.

"Arigato, Guy," she replied. "I need clarity on a couple of possible issues. The relationship between the Trade Alliance Worlds and the new Orion Spiral Alliance and the potential problem with the Galvari Confederation."

"We could all use some clarity on those relationships," he said. "I'm not sure I have a handle on Earth politics, much less galactic intrigue. How can I help?"

"My department's responsibility is to provide guidance for our representatives dealing with aliens. We've spent a great deal of time and effort learning the regulations and procedures our galactic partners use when trading. Judge Tasha Korr has been invaluable in helping to flatten our learning curve."

"Is the Judge still in the Aster system?"

"She is," the lawyer answered. "She is assisting Admiral Kebede restore order and formalize interplanetary rules of engagement. There remains a lot of resentment toward the Mischene. Fortunately Ventierrans like Tasha have been settling disputes between Trade Alliance worlds for centuries. We communicate regularly thanks to the STORM-HATCH system."

"Your issue?"

"OSA is primarily a joint defense pact," she said. "The Trade Alliance is for economic exchange. Thus far the OSA members are also Trade Alliance participants. Do I treat these as separate entities or should our laws be written to cover both groups equally?"

"Excellent question," he said. "The OSA is new and is an Earth initiative. I believe you should allow the legal staff at Space Fleet to handle the regulations and codes of operation between the member planets. Exo-legal will act as a consultant. If there is a dispute over any particular precept for OAS participation, action or interplanetary interpretation we'll convene a council to review the issue and make a final decision. Your department will concentrate on the more civilian rules of engagement between Earth and aliens relative to commercial and diplomatic interactions."

"It helps," she responded. "Do we consider the Galvari a diplomatic or military relationship?"

"Since we're in a wait-and-see situation until they make the next move, leave the Galvari to Admiral Patterson. If they initiate conversation over confrontation, we'll get you involved," he said.

"That makes my current workload simpler," she said. "Exo-legal will make sure we're on the proper footing when dealing with Trade Alliance partners. Tista Korr, the Judge's daughter, was helpful before her assignment to PT-109."

"Captain Casalobos is in a fluid situation on the border with the Galvari Confederation," Arcand reminded her. "Tasha Korr is there to help her negotiate dangerous waters."

"Of course. I was simply bemoaning her loss."

"I would suggest hiring a replacement," he said. "There must be other aliens who would be willing to join your department and help provide context from an extraterrestrial view."

"I'll begin a search," she said. "Again, thank you for the time and the clarity, Guy."

Chapter Eight
Aranthine

Mags placed her hand on top of the laser pistol strapped to her right thigh.

Tas, confused, alternated between looking at his sister and back to the human holding a deadly weapon.

Tamina Oison kept a nonchalance stance, left hand on her hip and neutral expression. Her grey eyes may have squinted a hair as she scanned the woman in front of her.

"I don't think so," she said. "I'd remember you."

Rachelle Paré stood five-ten. Her deep brown eyes, inherited from her French-Canadian mother, level with the Aranthinian's light grey ones.

"You led the raid on Vista," she said.

"I never saw you on Vista," the purple-hued alien countered.

"But I saw you," Rachelle responded. "You were there kidnapping civilians, even children. You killed people who resisted."

"Tamina?" Tas queried.

"Fish-heads," she said. "Damn Piscium mercenaries were kill-crazy. First and last time I work with them."

"I warned you about Piscium," he said.

"Excuse me," Mags interrupted. "There's still the whole kidnapping children issue."

Tas turned to Rachelle and said, "I told you on Devisator what happens to the family of people who defy the Galvari. They call it culling. Once a year they demand an Aranthine ship must collect slaves from this region. Our people detest the entire thing, but resistance is handled by more than placing the insurgent's family into bondage. They execute a number of others. When we were initially ordered to raid worlds it was for goods. Precious minerals, specialty items and tech. The first time they required sentient lives, our people resisted. After a couple more times it became too costly to fight. Each year a different crew is selected for the culling raid. It was Tamina's turn."

"You were the reason they were able to escape," Tamina surmised. "It was so damn obvious they didn't have the ability to overpower my crew, sabotage my ships, and figure out how to use advanced weapons. I want those back. Laser rifles are expensive."

"Why haven't the Galvari punished you for failing?" the woman with the gun asked.

"Because they don't know," the Aranthinian answered. "Communications are slow between us and the Confederation home world. I still have time to make a delivery."

"You plan on making another raid?" Rachelle asked.

"As soon as I find replacements for the Piscium crap," she responded. "Have you not been listening? I deliver a sufficient number of slaves or my family takes their place and people die."

"Don't you know what will happen to the people you deliver?"

Ignoring the laser pistol, Tamina Oison walked to within inches of the human questioning her. The pistol on Mags' thigh slowly cleared its holster. Tamina's pupils darkened. The veins on her face and forehead grew thicker.

"Yes, I damn well know what happens to them. Women are used for galley work and sex. Men labor under unbearable conditions, become sex objects, or, if lucky, use their skills for Confederation projects. Intelligent children are taught to be good little Confederation workers. Those not as smart are used as trade. The Galvari do not care what they are used for afterward. We don't have a choice. You helped a bunch of stick-litters beat mercenaries with modern weapons. Can you imagine how we would make out against the Galvari military?"

"Stick-litters?" Mags whispered to Tas.

"Hicks," he whispered back.

Rachelle holstered her pistol. Tamina took a step backward. Tas and Mags released pent up breaths.

"There must be an answer," Rachelle said. "You cannot continue to supply the Galvari with slaves."

"When you find the answer, please share it with me," the Aranthinian woman said. "Meanwhile, you are my brother's guest and it's time for dinner."

She walked past Rachelle headed for a door.

Mags holstered her sidearm and said, "Yeah. Food."

Tas and Tamina's mother was an older version of her daughter. An attractive woman, but with a different musculature. While her daughter was a warrior, Resula Oison was a farmer.

If she was surprised by the arrival of two alien pilots, or having her barn used as a hangar for spaceships, it did not show in her welcoming demeanor when introduced.

"You can hang your weapons on the wall," she told them. "I prefer they not come to the table."

Rachelle and Mags obeyed, hanging their laser pistols on wall pegs before sitting at a medium size wooden table placed beside a spacious kitchen.

"Tas did not tell me you were coming until the last minute," she complained as she placed serving dishes on the center of the table. "I didn't prepare any meat. I hope pasta and plants will do."

"It looks and smells wonderful," Mags said as Tamina and Tas sat.

"Is your husband joining us?" Rachelle asked.

"He and our brother, Torvan, are hauling minerals," Tas said. "Besides the farm we own two old cargo carriers and a fast transport ship. We keep them moored on one of the space stations."

"Thank Hena," Resula said. "The farm is hit and miss. The ships keep us going. The family is apart much too much, but we survive. The pasta sauce is a mix of fresh masto and herbs."

"I love it," Mags said. "It's like a zesty spaghetti sauce."

"If you say so," the mother said. "The plants are grown in a small hydroponic barn."

"Excellent," Rachelle said. "Human and Aranthine tastebuds must be similar."

"Why are you ladies here?" Resula asked, apparently the matriarch of the Oison family was used to controlling the conversation at her dining table.

"We're new to this region of the galaxy," Rachelle said. "Our mission is to learn about new cultures and discover what we can about the Galvari Confederation."

"Tas told us you have a ship that kicked a Galvari battlewagon out of the Devisator system," Resula said. "He said you use space-fold drive instead of wormholes. Why should we trust you? Our experience is the powerful take advantage of those who can't stand against them."

"Power corrupts," Rachelle said.

"Absolute power corrupts absolutely," Mags added.

"We understand your concerns," Rachelle said. "Our world has experienced several periods in our history when people with power abused their position to cause harm. Good people have always risen up to stop them. I would like to think Space Fleet represents the best of human nature."

"It would be nice if true," Tamina interjected.

"We should assume the best," Tas said. "While on Devisator I heard stories of humans helping other worlds fight invaders. I saw Captain Paré and Captain Casalobos come to the aid of the Devee when the Galvari threatened to annex Devisator."

"Would Space Fleet come to our defense, Captain Paré?" the farmer asked.

"I cannot speak for Space Fleet," Rachelle answered. "Devisator is a member of the Trade Alliance Worlds, which Earth recently joined. Aranthine is a member of the Galvari Confederation. It makes involving ourselves more difficult."

"Even if we do not wish to be a member of the Confederation?" Tamina asked.

"We can take information back to our superiors," Rachelle said. "I'm sorry, but that's all I can promise."

"How many people feel like you do?" Mags asked.

"The vast majority," Tas answered. "There are a few the Galvari have placed in positions of power who are happy to bow to our oppressors."

"The more intel we can return with, the more likely we can convince our superiors to consider assisting Aranthine. What can you tell us about the Galvari's military capabilities?" Rachelle asked.

"They believe bigger is better," Tamina said. "Nuclear power is used for space flight. It's inefficient, but provides a lot of straight-line speed. Because they use oversized vessels, they aren't nimble and turning ratios are huge. Ionic drives powers their drones. Otherwise the Galvari Confederation uses magno-driven electricity generators to power weapons and shields."

"My daughter is the warrior in the family," Resula interjected. "She has studied military methods since she was a child. She hopes to learn enough to build a ship able to rival those used by the Confederation."

"They use laser cannons powered by electricity," Tamina continued. "Their force fields use the same generators.

Similar systems are employed on their ships and drones. The deadliest weapon in their arsenal is the centrifugal cannon. It spins at a high rate and ejects a large metal projectile with enough kinetic force to shatter an asteroid. Because it uses rotation to fire there is no significant sympathetic vibration. It is capable of firing projectiles as soon as they are loaded and brought to speed."

"We saw them up close and personal," Mags said.

"They use similar dense metal projectiles with external thrusters to attack planets," Rachelle added. "Kinetic bombardment capable of mass destruction."

"I didn't know they could do that," Tamina admitted.

"What about their army?" Mags asked.

"Same commitment to numbers," she answered. "The Confederation puts as many boots on the ground as they deem necessary to eliminate threats. They have mobile laser cannons as well as a combination of long-barrel cannon, short-barrel high-angle cannon, and smaller tri-mount mortars using explosive charges for propulsion and different types of shells. The individual soldiers carry kinetic sidearms and battery-charged short range laser rifles."

"Sounds like military units on Earth two centuries ago," Mags said. "I'm surprised a civilization committed to military culture isn't using more advanced weaponry."

"Sounds like there hasn't been a reason to evolve," Rachelle said. "Their tactics have been successful for centuries. There has been no motivation for change."

"They did invent an ion disruption weapon," Tamina said. "When it is released a region of millions of square miles are affected. Any machinery using ion-powered systems will be inaffective until the disruption fades, which takes twelve to fourteen hours."

"We saw it," Rachelle said.

"Elie shot it down before it went hot," Mags added.

"Elie?" Resula queried.

"Captain Casalobos," Tas answered. "She's the commander of the ship that defeated the battlewagon."

"Strange they have a method to disrupt ion-driven systems, but don't use particle-beam weapons," Rachelle said.

"They use it to prevent space ships from escaping," Tas responded. "Many, if not most, of the interstellar ships in this region use ion-drive systems. A Confederation ship with an ion-disruptor can leave an enemy adrift in space. Even if the dead ship has electro-magnetic shields, being bombarded for hours on end will kill everyone on board."

"Are foot-soldiers mainly Galvari?" Mags asked.

"Just the opposite," Tamina answered. "They conscript men and women from Confederation planets. The officers are predominately Galvari."

"This has been an incredible wealth of intelligence," Rachelle said.

"Pay us back by telling Earth we need your help," Tas said. "And Aranthine is not the only planet that would secede if given the opportunity."

Rachelle agreed to the request. Mags added, "What do I have to pay for the recipe for your masto sauce and a to-go plate?"

Resula chuckled and said, "No charge, Lieutenant."

"Please, after this wonderful meal, call me Mags."

"Okay, Mags," the lady farmer replied. "I'll get you the recipe and a basket of fresh plants and herbs to take with you."

"I have something for you as well, Captain Paré" Tas said. He handed Rachelle a tip-drive. "System charts for Confederation controlled space between here and Galvari. I don't have access for the regions beyond their home world."

"Thank you, Tas. Please call me Rachelle."

"This is all warm and touchy, but if it doesn't help us escape the Confederation it's been a huge waste of time and effort," Tamina interjected.

"Tamina," Resula spoke harshly. "There is no reason to be rude. If Rachelle and Mags can help, they will. I know a good heart, and they are both honest people."

"It's alright," Rachelle said. "I'd feel the same way if my planet was under the control of another world. I'll head back to my ship and contact the 109. Tas, how much time will you need to arrange another glitch?"

"I expected you to stay longer," he said. "Give me an hour to reach my friend and I'll have an answer for you."

"I'll walk to the barn with you," Tamina said.

"I'll help Resula collect goodies," Mags chipped in.

The walk to the barn was taken in silence.

"Would you like to see inside the Spirit Two?" Rachelle asked.

"You don't mind an alien looking around your fighter?"

"I don't," the answer.

The Aranthinian followed the human beneath the ship. They rode the personnel lift up and inside.

Rachelle left Tamina to look around while she went to the cockpit to contact the 109. Tamina joined her as she completed her short conversation with the Comms officer.

"They're waiting to hear back with time and details," she told the purple hued young woman in the co-pilot's seat.

"I've never seen a more beautiful ship. Inside or out," Tamina said.

"Endo and exo-atmospheric flight capable," the pilot told her, aware of the woman's unvocalized curiosity. "She has retractable wings, tail, and stabilizers to make her maneuverable within an atmosphere. Ion-drive."

"How? Ionic engines can't function inside an ionized atmosphere."

"Earth scientists created a gridded electrostatic thruster that uses xenon gas to direct the positive charged ions and shield them from the effects of naturally occurring ions in the atmosphere. By using grids, or layers of laser-produced plasma, we are able to super-heat the ions and create instant acceleration and high-end speed," Rachelle replied. "All Space Fleet ion drive engines use this method."

"I don't know what xenon gas is."

"It's a trace gas found in Earth's atmosphere. It may be in yours. I'll have Kennedy provide an analysis when I return to the 109."

"Kennedy?"

"The name of the ship's Artificial Intelligence operating system. It's also the name of the ship. The *John F. Kennedy.* 109 is its Space Fleet designation number," Rachelle explained.

"And it has a space-fold drive?"

"It does. We travel between systems at one parsec every twenty-four hours."

"Great Hena!" Tamina exclaimed. "Your fighter?"

"Is not equipped for space-fold."

"Weapons? Unless it's a secret."

"Mini laser cannons embedded in the wings. A railgun with EMP and kinetic capability. A plasma cannon. Both retractable," Rachelle answered. "Powered by crystal-laser array. Special crystals act like power generators when activated by light."

"This small ship is more advanced, more powerful than anything I have ever seen or imagined. Earth must have been involved with interstellar travel for millennia."

"Less than a decade," Rachelle said. "How we got involved is a story for another time," she told the slack-jawed woman.

"I have to collect slaves for the Galvari," Tamina said in a sudden twist of subjects. "I know what you think of culling, but I don't have a choice. It isn't only my family who suffers if I refuse. Every member of my crew and their families would be punished for failing."

"I don't like it, but I understand better now," Rachelle admitted. "Tas is outside."

"There is one more thing," Tamina said. She handed Rachelle a data coin. "When I work for Galvari interests they equip my ship with a Quantum Key communications system. During three jobs where I had access I took the system apart. The data coin has diagrams and instructions on how to build my own transmitter and retriever. It's three-quarters of the way complete. I planned on building systems for the family ships and farm, to use in case of an emergency."

She handed the human a piece of paper.

"If your engineers build a QKD receiver, assign the bottom code as the activator. The top code will activate the one here, as soon as I finish building it. If there is a serious reason, use it. The transmissions can't be hacked, but quantum streams can be detected and traced."

"Thank you, Tamina. I will make sure we're careful," Rachelle promised.

Aboard the 109, following a reversal of the tactics used to get the two pilots onto the planet, Rachelle and Mags briefed Elie on what they learned.

"I'd say this adventure into Galvari Confederation space has paid off," the 109's Captain said.
"Like you would not believe," Mags said. "Wait until you taste masto and noddles."

Chapter Nine

Deep Space

Coop woke first. It required a couple of deep breaths before his head cleared. He checked on Chaspi beside him before he swiveled the pilot's seat to find the rest of his crew harnessed in their seats, somnolent.

He unstrapped and went to each station to check. Everyone was alive. Hiro awoke while Coop was making sure no one appeared injured by whatever anomaly they experienced. It was no surprise the two Space Rangers recovered first.

"Sit and breathe," he told the Japanese. "It takes a few seconds to clear the dust. Everyone appears okay, just out."

"What did we hit?" Hiro asked. "Or what hit us? The stellar flare?"

"Not sure. Cassandra. Report."

There was no response from the AI.

Coop went to the Systems console where Sky sat with her head tilted forward.

"Only system operating is environmental," he told Hiro, who had released his harness to check on Cindy.

"What possible phenomenon could shut down every system except the one keeping us alive?" Hiro asked.

"I'm having a deja vous moment." Coop looked around the cabin. "Clyde?"

"Welcome back, Captain Cooper," a voice replied. Distinctly male, it came from the air around them. "I apologize for not warning you before the abrupt tether from space-fold. The flare was about to reach your ship. You would not have survived the Orange star's radiation."

"Who is Clyde?" Hiro asked.

"Complex Linear Inter-Dimensional Drive, or CLIDD," Coop answered. "Not who, but what. Clyde is a trans-dimensional drive vessel that belongs to the Nakki. Is D'Sey aboard?"

"I am without a crew. I was patrolling this side of the galaxy and picked up your communications. I am sorry Cassie cannot be with us."

"You have already scanned my ship's files."

"Of course, Captain. Collecting data is my first priority. The rest of your crew will recover in two-minutes-twenty-one-seconds. It may be more comfortable for everyone in my lounge. Environmental systems are adapted and there is cold cola, if you wish."

"Are there any damages to my ship?"

"None," Clyde assured him. "I shut everything down as a safety precaution."

"Cassandra?"

"The ship's AI is now available and has been updated."

"Cassandra. Report," he ordered.

"All systems except communications are available. There are no external or internal damages to the the *Renarde*," she responded.

"Clyde, why are you stopping communications?" Coop demanded.

"They will be restored shortly, Captain. We can continue this in the lounge."

Before he could mount an argument, the crew began to revive. Concerned they would be disoriented and panicked, he and Hiro went to each person as they roused.

Petra was the last one to awaken. He was not as disoriented as he was grouchy.

"Listen up," Coop called after everyone appeared recovered. "I won't get into the details yet, but here is a quick synopsis. We are docked aboard a Nakki ship named Clyde. The ship is sentient. It used a teether ray to pull us out of space-fold and away from the stellar flare. This is the same ship that shanghaied me and the Wraith ship Cassandra was originally assigned. I know you are aware I was asked to help a group of Nakki agents on the far side of the galaxy. I recognize I have not been forthcoming with many details regarding that mission. What you need to know is I trust we are safe.

"We are going to exit the *Renarde* and go to the crew's lounge on Clyde. I intend to find out why we are not allowed to communicate with Space Fleet. Once that is settled, we will depart. I know you all have questions. Hold them."

They used a cargo ramp to depart the *Renarde*. The hangar the ship rested in was lit around their vessel, as well as an area between the ship and a door. Otherwise the hangar was bathed in black. It did not prevent the perception the area was massive.

Exiting the hangar through the door, they entered a lounge. The view caught everyone's attention first. A wall to the right displayed a black hole in the distance. Space around the hole vibrated with yellow light. Colored gases of solid and mixed hues fluttered throughout the void between their perspective and the black hole. Thousands of twinkling stars scattered around the edges of space. It was impossible to determine if the view was from a window or a projection.

The room contained three large sectional sofas, a dozen club chairs, and a stocked bar along one wall. It rivaled the bar in the Officer's Club on EMS2, the space station between Earth and its moon.

"You'll find a fridge and ice maker behind the bar," Coop told the others. "Stay away from the bottles on the shelves. I need everyone sober. Anything in the fridge will be safe."

Hesitant at first, when soda, juices, and crushed ice, real ice, were found, people began to relax. With glasses in hand, they found seats.

"We're here and we're ready, Clyde," Coop said aloud. "Get on with it."

"We thought it might be easier if I spoke to you, Captain Cooper."

The man speaking stood at the bar. He had not been there earlier and no doors had opened.

"Who are you?" Coop asked. He held a hand out to calm Hiro and Sky. Both jumped to their feet when the man first spoke.

"I'm surprised you do not recognize my voice. I am KSS-delta-one-nine-one-six, the verbal guide you named Arty."

"You never had a body," Coop said. "You were only a voice on the saucer left by the Nakki on Emperatus. You were inactive for two-hundred-thousand years."

"I was. When you reactivated the ship I was reintroduced to the Nakki mainframe. I can access any Nakki vessel or system within the galaxy. Because this ship has a hologram matrix integration ability, I created a body. I thought it would be more comfortable conversing with a solid form and not a disembodied voice."

Arty appeared to be a man of average height; fifty to fifty-five. He had short grey hair, light blue eyes, and laugh lines around his mouth. He wore a maroon shirt tucked into navy blue pants and black loafers.

"Okay. You're here. If you want me on some mission on the far side of the black hole, no dice," Coop said.

"Nothing of the kind, Captain. The Nakki offered you the opportunity to work as their agent on this side of the black hole."

"I turned the offer down."

"Yes, you did. As it turns out, it did not matter. It appears you and your comrades from Earth are determined to keep the Orion Arm of the galaxy secure without Nakki assistance. You were in trouble, a ship capable of rescuing yours was available, therefore we intervened." The solid holo-being appeared comfortable among the humans.

"Thank you," Coop said.

"Most welcome. The Nakki have no intention of interrupting your trek. They would like to offer you an invitation to visit someday in the future, when you are not quite as busy."

"Orion's Belt?"

"Alnilam, Alnitak, and Mintaka are the stars which form a constellation humans call Orion's Belt," Arty said. "The Nakki home world orbits Alnilam, seven-hundred-thirty-six lightyears from Earth."

"The trip would take over two-hundred days," Chaspi interjected. Aware she spoke aloud, she quickly added, "Sorry. I didn't mean to interrupt."

"The Captain is aware we can arrange for a faster means of transport than space-fold," Arty said.

"I'll consider it. I need to contact Space Fleet to let them know we are okay."

"Of course. Just one more thing."

The holo-being placed his hand out. A data tip-chip rested on his palm.

"Coordinates for planets with a high potential for power crystal deposits. The ones once used by the Nakki are much too distant to be of use to your alliance. These planets were never mined, but they have markers consistent with crystal deposits."

Coop took the chip.

"Some are within thirty lightyears of Earth. The furtherest is ninety-two lightyears distant. All are located within systems with at least one wormhole gate. There are charts. If you find a suitable planet, the charts will map out which wormhole combinations are needed."

"Why? Truth. Why all of this help?"

"I told you," the Nakki avatar replied. "But there is a little more. D'Sey considered the Devee the most dangerous civilization in this sector. He thought they were destined to cause a disruption in the evolution of cultures over dozens of systems. Captain Casalobos changed that. Her actions delayed, perhaps halted the destructive path the Devee were taking. Unfortunately her good deed is going to lead to a more consequential confrontation."

"The Galvari Confederation," Coop said. "They're a bunch of bullies. Elie sent them packing. They don't have the tech to compete with Space Fleet."

"They had grown complacent. Without a reason to improve, they simply relied on blunt force to control the planets in their confederation. Captain Casalobos poked them in the eye. Trust me, Captain Cooper, they have access to the knowledge to advance their technology quickly. They have the assets needed to improve their ships and weapons. Now they have a reason to do so. Your Alliance is going to need crystals. We believe a conflict is inevitable. It will not be as one-sided as you think."

"This is the Nakki interfering without interfering. You have a strange way of protecting the galaxy."

"Perhaps. I appreciate your time. Your communications systems will operate when you are ready."

The holo-image disintegrated.

"Holy crap on a corn dog, Coop," Cindy Shah said. "You have some strange friends. There has to be more you know about the Nakki."

"We'll talk aboard the *Renarde*. Everyone back to the ship and prep for departure. Storm, plan on contacting Space Fleet after we clear the hangar. Go. I'll follow in a few minutes."

After the door closed behind the last of his crew, Coop called out to Arty.

"It took being back here to remember, but Doc's home world of Kanistar is part of the Galvari Confederation. They were the ones who forced her to be a sex slave before D'Sey freed her." He spoke aloud to the empty room.

"Actually it was the Setites, but with Galvari approval," Arty responded. "Some things have changed since she departed this side of the galaxy, but much is the same."

"What's happening on the far side? What is D'Sey and his crew involved in?"

"With your help, the Kashōn were dealt a significant defeat, losing their most powerful battlecruisers. But the Kashōn Empire is vast. They were dangerous before they built their super ships. It is a war of survival for the Helacene Alliance. The Menace is a major obstacle for the Kashōn forces, but she is one ship. You have your own wars to prepare for, Captain Cooper. Veresk D'Sey will fight his battles."

"How do I contact you, if I should decide to visit the Nakki?"

"The information is with Cassandra," the body-less voice answered.

"If you can access my ship remotely, why did you hand me a data chip with systems and wormhole charts? You could have downloaded all of it."

"Do you recall I told you my personality profile was based on the great Nakki philosopher Ninart?"

"I remember. The hunter of truth."

"He was known for his dramatic presentations on philosophical ideals. I thought handing you an actual chip added a nice touch of drama."

The *Renarde* slid easily into space and moved away. Beside the giant kidney-shaped trans-dimensional vessel, the corsair class ship appeared the size of a fly buzzing around a horse.

The silvery Nakki ship shimmered and disappeared.

"Storm, tell Fleet we're back on line and headed their direction. We have a few promising leads to follow and will send regular reports," Coop instructed.

"When they ask where we've been?" the Fellen asked. "Tell them we have been dealing with technical issues. Hiro, you and Petra have the data. Select a good location and let's go prospecting."

Chapter Ten

Deep Space

"You had me worried," Elie said.

"Never my intention," Coop replied.

Elie sat on the sofa in her cabin. The call from Coop transferred to her receiver. Due to increased radiation somewhere between them, their conversation was limited to audio.

"Sounds like everything turned out for the better," she said. "Hiro has a possible planet to check for crystals. That's a win."

"He and Petra have six they're high on. We're going to test them as they fall in line between our current position and Earth. Pam has the list and ships from Rys are going to investigate those nearest to them. Petra believes finding crystal deposits that can be mined is probable. Whether they contain the black diamonds we need is only a hope."

"No desire to fly off to the other side of the galaxy and spend time with your pirate buddies?"

"I'd be lying if I didn't admit I'm worried about them," he told her. "They have their battles and we have ours."

"I'm not sure how to take the Nakki warning about the Galvari. I was not impressed by Admiral Particus. The 109 flew rings around their prize warship. Even the Devee cruisers did well once they had a plan."

"Don't forget you went against the Prophet following Space Fleet Admiral Stephen Hawks. His incompetence nearly cost the loss of the entire battle group. Every military has their idiots who rise too high. You overcame his mistakes and kicked butt," Coop said.

"Particus could be the exception and not the rule. You're probably right. If the Galvari make adjustments based on the data they collected during the skirmish over Devisator, we can't expect them to use similar tactics if we meet again."

"You've collected some valuable intel from your contacts inside the Confederation borders. Add it to what you learned fighting them and you should have a decent concept as to what to expect."

"I'm wondering if we should wait," she said. "I'm going to advocate for Aranthine. Earth should take a stand. If it makes the Galvari uncomfortable so be it."

"If they defend their borders?"

"Holding a planet hostage to fear is not defending anything. If we have to fight to free those people, then we fight."

"You're being pretty generous with Space Fleet assets, Elie. The UEC may disagree. You only have the word of three Aranthinians their world is oppressed. One of those is an admitted raider. Pretty slim evidence to start a galactic war."

"You think we should ignore what's happening out here?"

"I'm giving you a taste of what to expect from the brass and the politicians. The Aranthine situation is too similar to a story I heard of another planet under the thumb of the Galvari not to believe it. That you and I understand these worlds are victims of despots isn't enough to get Earth and the OSA to act."

"The 109 remains tasked with exploring this region. The more I can discover about the Confederation, the more ammunition I will have to present when we return home."

"I'm on your side, Elie," he said. "When you're ready, I'll back your play."

"Stay safe, Coop, and tell everyone hell-o. Hasta luego."

With his call completed, Coop left his cabin to join the rest of the crew in the mess.

"Chaspi, status?" he asked his co-pilot after taking a seat in a comfortable chair.

"Auto-pilot," she answered. "We're in space-fold, eighteen hours from entering natural space. Cassandra will let us know if anything needs our attention."

The formal tables that originally furnished the ship's mess hall had been removed and replaced with a combination of chairs and small sofas. It had become more of a lounge than a place for meals. Coop recognized the similarity to the crew's lounge aboard Clyde and realized it was the inspiration for the changes he requested prior to beginning their mission.

"Are you going to tell us about the Nakki?" Cindy asked.

Coop surveyed the room. These men and women joined his crew voluntarily and deserved his trust. Even Petra who sort-of joined on his own accord.

"I was told that for millions of years Nakki vessels explored the galaxy," he said. "They discovered billions of worlds with the potential for life. For life to occur, to produce the most simplistic forms of living organisms, all the right things necessary for the spark to occur must happen within a relatively short window of opportunity. For those life-forms to evolve into sentient beings is an astronomical crapshoot. The Nakki decided to enhance those odds.

"They seeded orbital bodies with the greatest potential with the biological and chemical agents necessary for the development of living organisms. They assessed the trial planets and moons over time and boosted the evolutionary process along on those indicating promise."

"The Nakki are responsible for the creation of sentient life in the galaxy?" Hiro asked.

"Not all sentient life," Coop answered. "Life developed and evolved naturally on millions of worlds. There are sentient, highly evolved races whose appearance would scare a human to death. Billions of planets remain barren of life, or provide a home to non-sentient lifeforms.

"However, there are hundreds of species which are direct descendants of the Nakki."

"The Nakki were humanoid," Storm said.

"Apparently. The saucer Elliott Fairchild's group discovered on Mars was designed for use by humanoids. The ship, and the tech discovered in the storage hangar, led to the creation of Space Fleet. As I understood it, of all the worlds, in all this time, humans are the only ones to reverse-engineer Nakki technology in order to develop our own interstellar engines and access space-fold."

"Amazing," Hiro said. "Not the time taken, but that it occurred at all."

"Have other species discovered abandoned Nakki technology?" Billy asked.

"There are hundreds of abandoned Nakki outposts in the galaxy. More than a few discarded sites have been discovered by indigenous civilizations. I visited one on a planet called Emperatus. A hangar with a fully functional flying saucer."

"A working saucer," Billy, the engineer and grandson of the man who discovered a saucer-shaped ship on Mars exclaimed. "Did you get it turned on?"

"We can talk about that at another time," Coop responded. "Let's keep this conversation on the Nakki."

The Captain continued by telling them, "The Nakki cleared the majority of their stations before departing. The discovery of ruins has become unexplained mysteries for those finding them. I was told there are at least a dozen depots discovered with abandoned equipment, records, and trash. Of those discoveries, three civilizations, including Earth, were able to reverse engineer portions of the technology left behind. Only humans recreated the space-fold arrays."

"The other two?" Sky asked.

"I wasn't told."

"Nakki seeded potential planets, and then stepped away to see what would happen?" Hiro inquired.

"The Nakki prefer life to evolve as naturally as possible. They believed, left to their own devices, a few of these species would mature into the benevolent guardians the galaxy needs in order to expand and grow until time ends."

"Benevolent guardians. Is that how the Nakki see themselves? Guardians?" Cindy asked.

"Are you familiar with the Sagittarius Dwarf Galaxy?" Coop asked.

"A group of around a billion stars swallowed into the Milky Way Spiral," Hiro, the planetologist, replied. "No black hole in the center known of. It is on a deteriorating elliptic orbit as the Milky Way tears it apart and absorbs the pieces."

"Much of the Orion Arm originated within the Sagittarius Dwarf Galaxy," Coop said. "There are eleven Dwarf Galaxies currently being eaten by the Milky Way. Over the past billion years, stars, and other matter, slipped from the Sagittarius Dwarf Galaxy into the Milky Way."

"Scientists are aware of this," Hiro replied. "The current orbit of Sagittarius is bringing it closer to our star. The dark matter emanating from the dwarf system appears to be reviving the ozone layers of Mars, along with other effects on planets and moons in our system."

"Dark Matter within Sagittarius does have unique, rich properties," Petra unexpectedly commented.

"It is home to a species called the Basfor Flyn," Coop said, taking a sip from an almost forgotten glass. "The Basfor Flyn were not a result of the Nakki seeding program. They evolved and conquered a large part of their galaxy. They were neither benevolent nor restrained. Five-hundred-thousand years ago they dispatched drones into the Milky Way. These drones came to build millions of wormhole channels. The Basfor Flyn created the use of wormholes to travel between star systems. The dark matter from their galaxy provides the glue necessary to keep the channel walls intact."

"The wormhole channels used by the space-capable planets in our galaxy?" Chaspi asked.

"The same. Channels used by all of the interstellar travelers in this galaxy, except Nakki, a small number of Nakki agents, and, now, the planet Earth. Channels once used by Basfor Flyn armadas to invade the Milky Way Galaxy 500,000 years ago."

"Really. And no one knows about this invasion? I've read a lot of alien histories over the past year. None of the races talk about an invasion from the Sagittarius Dwarf Galaxy," Hiro objected.

"Our own history records stories of incredible battles in the skies of our planet, Hiro" Coop said. "Indian mythology gives detailed descriptions of nuclear warheads. There are ancient sites with pictographs of ships, aliens, weapons, and battles. These confrontations occurred throughout the galaxy."

"You said a half-million years ago," Hiro countered. "Civilization on Earth is not that old."

"The current civilization is not," Coop replied. "Civilizations existed on Earth long before scientific records indicate. Do you honestly believe a planet able to sustain life for hundreds-of-millions of years only recently developed a sentient culture? Civilizations have come and gone a half-dozen times. Destroyed by wars, astronomical phenomenon, planetary shifts, pandemics, and new ones rebuilt on the ashes.

"One of the major battles between the Nakki and the Basfor Flyn occurred in our solar system. It resulted in the end of life on Mars. Astrophysicists discovered a large portion of Mars had been ripped away. The destruction occurred when Basfor Flynn ships blasted the planet with nuclear-tipped missiles."

Billy said, "I remember my grandfather talking about the Martian surface. He said it was covered with a thin layer of radioactive substances, including uranium, thorium, and radioactive potassium. There is also elevated readings of the gas Xenon-129 in the Martian atmosphere. Xenon-129 is a rare substance which is typically found in the fallout of nuclear explosions."

"It also explains the disappearance of carbon in the Martian atmosphere," Hiro added. "Carbon had to be reintroduced artificially to allow terraforming."

"Where are the Basfor Flyn now?" Chaspi asked.

"The Nakki pushed the Basfor Flyn out of the Milky Way. Thanks, in great part, to technology like space-fold travel. The Nakki who survived remain in their home system. They keep an eye on the Sagittarius Dwarf Galaxy. They also created a provisional force. Agents dispatched to keep the playing fields safe inside the galaxy."

"Galactic cops?" Billy asked.

"My understanding is their agents act more like referees. The Nakki never stopped wanting worlds to evolve as naturally as possible. They stay out of the way until a species evolves to the point of interstellar travel. Thereafter, they begin to take more of an interest."

"What kind of interest?" Cindy wanted to know.

"When a civilization decides to forcefully disrupt the development of other worlds, they become more concerned. When a disruption turns violent, or worse, genocidal, they dispatch an agent. The agent decides if an intervention is necessary. It was my impression the Nakki might intercede to save an endangered sentient species."

"Is that why Arty invited you to visit the Nakki?" Sky asked. "They want you to become an agent."

"They asked before and I said no," he answered. "I have enough problems looking after the seven of you. And that is all for now. Rest and begin thinking about our immediate mission."

"I do have a question that has bothered me," Petra said.

"By all means, Petra, ask."

"Ms. Shah, what kind of animal is a corn dog?"

Chapter Eleven
Red Dwarf System

"Persistent little bastards," Cindy Shah said.

She leaned around the bolder she took refuge behind and fired her laser pistol.

"Don't hit them, Cindy," Coop warned. He was tall enough to see above the boulder he shared with the ex-Marine. He fired his laser, hitting the ground in front of a half dozen beings.

"I hope this is worth the effort." She regained her breath, resting her back against the large rock.

"Hiro and Petra have to complete the drill tests." Coop kept watch while they remained protected.

"I know. We lure the locals away from them and make sure none of them are harmed. Can't we ask them not to harm us in return?"

"They're primitive, Cindy. Their spears can't penetrate our METS[8]. We simply need to keep them occupied and away from the drill site."

"Gotta love the little devils." She stuck her face around the rock for a look down the hillside. "We're firing laser pistols and all they have are wood spears and stone axes. They have guts."

The first three planet on their list of possible locations for crystal deposits proved unsuccessful. Drill samples at prime sites came up negative. They were now on the fourth option. A small planet orbiting a red dwarf star. It was a Class M world, sustaining wildlife and large forests between two polar ice caps. The atmosphere was breathable and the gravity seventy-percent of Earth. It was twice the strength of Mars, but it still made lugging heavy equipment easier.

"They're getting restless," Coop said. "Let's go."

Cindy pushed off the boulder and sprinted up the hill, juking around rocks of various sizes and shapes as she ascended. Coop kept pace a couple meters behind his security officer. With his enhanced speed he could easily outdistance her and the tribal hunters following them. But the point of the exercise was to keep the residents engaged chasing them, leaving the Japanese planetologist and the Dward miner to chase veins of quartz. While Coop and Cindy played fox to the local hounds, Billy and Sky maintained guard over the mineral test. Storm and Chaspi remained aboard the *Renarde*.

Cindy took cover behind a roughly rectangular stone left from a landslide centuries before. It was ten feet long, six feet thick, and four feet tall. She rested her arms on top and fired three short bursts that landed a few feet in front of their pursuers.

Coop walked backwards the last six yards to the stone. He had his weapon up and watched as the short people scurried to the protection of fallen rocks. A single spear arched up into the air from behind a boulder. The tip stuck into the hard surface six feet in front of him.

"Their aim is improving," he commented, no inflection in his tone. A simple statement. "You have to give them credit. That's actually a pretty decent throw from that distance."

"*Magmatic and volcanic activities, along with the planet's crustal thickness and the porosity of the crust, combined with a liquid core are prime indicators of success,* Hiro said." Cindy mimicked her significant other's slight accent well.

"You remember all of that?" Coop remained in the open. He fired, a laser burst chipped shards and dust from a rock face.

"I live with it," she said. "How much longer before we can stop playing tag?"

"Storm, it's Coop. Any timeline from the drill site?"

He contacted the Fellen using the trans-comm chip subcutaneously embedded in his neck. With a transmission boost from the *Renarde*'s system, it easily reached the ship overhead. Going through Storm instead of directly calling someone at the drill site would not distract the crew members working there.

"Coop, Chaspi has already picked everybody up. The team and samples are safely on board," she responded.

"How long ago?" he asked. Cindy, without access to his private channel with Storm gave a stern frown as she listened to Coop's question.

"Thirty minutes," Storm replied. "We have long-range optics on you and Cindy. It has been quite exciting to watch you tangle with the locals."

"Storm, have Chaspi get her Bosine ass down here," he ordered. "We're less than one-hundred feet from the summit. Tell her to hover and drop the belly cargo ramp."

"Ten minutes, Storm out."

The pair were two-thirds to the LZ when the Spirit Two soared down through the capri blue sky. They fired multiple bursts to deter pursuit and sprinted forward. They jumped onto the extended ramp and scurried into the antechamber as Chaspi lifted away, closing the plug door as the fighter ascended.

After docking, they took turns exiting the fighter. Chaspi followed Cindy and Coop onto the command center where Sky, Storm, and Billy welcomed them with applause.

"Fuck all of you," Cindy said, but could not contain a smile. "Where are our miners?"

"The lab," Storm answered. "That was the last of eight samples. They're checking them for content."

Coop, Chaspi, Billy and Cindy sat amid a comfortable quiet in the lounge. Sky was alone in the cockpit making herself better versed in the the *Renarde*'s flight controls. Storm was asleep in her cabin. Petra and Hiro examined the geological samples recovered from the planet.

"I think we should name the fighter," Chaspi said, breaking the silence.

"Why?" Billy asked.

"Ships have names," she replied. "Spirit Two is a classification. It's generic."

"What would you name it?" Cindy asked.

"Well, this ship is the *Renarde*, the fox," the young woman from Osperantue said. "If a fox has a baby the French call it kit de Renarde. I think the Spirit Two should be called *Kit*."

"You've been thinking about this for a while, haven't you?" Billy asked.

"I like it, Chaspi," Coop said. "Cassandra please add to Space Fleet vessel SF Spirit Two dash zero-three the appellation *Kit*."

"Aye, Captain," the AI responded.

Hiro and Petra entered the lounge. The contrary Dward went directly to the food replication unit. Hiro handed Coop a flex data sheet before joining Cindy on one of the sofas.

"What am I looking at?" he asked.

"Results," Hiro replied. "Three of the eight sites are extremely promising for the type of crystal used as a power source. All three are moderate to good for black crystals."

"That's great," Billy said.

"It's good," the planetologist rejoined. "Now we have to mine the location and see what's down there."

Petra joined them with a bowl of food with steam rising from it.

"What do you need?" Coop asked.

"We need to put the Remote Autonomous Mining tech on the sites and begin the tunneling process. We will not know for sure until we look," Hiro answered.

"Billy, give the RAM a pre-operation check. Chaspi, get the location from Hiro where we need to set down. Cindy, we'll need to keep a presence on the mining site at all times. Pull together what will be needed for a secure camp. We'll rotate two teams of three. Chaspi is our shuttle, so she's off surface duty. Hiro, Cindy and Billy are Team One. Petra, Sky and I will be Team Two. Storm has the *Renarde.* Questions?" Cindy said, "Hiro, please tell me the location isn't near a tribal settlement."

Chapter Twelve

Deep Space

Izzy sat in the chair at the Comms station. She read messages from home on her personal tablet. Elie, who sat in the Captain's chair with her legs extended and crossed at the ankles, noted the blonde's short hair was in need of a trim.

The 109, as all Space Fleet vessels and orbital platforms, operated on Universal Time (UTC), which is equivalent to GMT. On board it was 3:11am. Which meant it was 3:11am in London and breakfast, 8:11am, at Space Fleet HQ, Toronto.

The ship employed a twelve-hour day-night internal lighting schedule. From 8:00am to 8:00pm UTC the common areas were well lit. From 8:00pm to 8:00am UTC those areas would be dimmed. At the moment it was night aboard the *John F. Kennedy*.

Nothing in Fleet regs required a Captain to take one of three eight-hour shifts, especially not the dead shift from midnight to 8:00am. Elie had always added her name to the rotations. Coop had done the same before her. It was a small consideration appreciated by the crew.

"Elie?"

Formality during the dead shift did not exist. As long as there was calm, the two officers in charge of the bridge interacted as friends and co-workers.

"Yes, Izzy."

"The pings from the Parrian cargo ships we tagged on Vista left the orbital station on Aranthine two weeks ago. We got another hit indicating they exited a wormhole into a star system four lightyears inside Galvari Confederation space. Is there a reason we're not following? What if they're on another raid?"

"First, they are in Confederation space and we need to be careful out here. Second, we're not interfering with alien ships unless they are bad actors against Alliance assets or non-aligned worlds who request our assistance."

"Those are the rules of engagement now?"

"They are," the Captain answered.

"What if aliens attack a planet like Vista where the people are unable to call for help?" the junior officer asked.

"Grey area. We're on site, we decide."

"Meaning you decide. That's a lot of responsibility."

"Any interesting updates from Fleet?" Elie asked.

"The Carrier *Fairchild* is ready for assignment. Ten Spirit One fighters have been berthed and the crews have all been certified by Colonel Tal. We have a lot of friends flying those fighters."

Elie recalled former teammates, "Noa Tal, Jim Huard, Jason Wren, Ryan Fox, Harper Leigh, Wild Bill Story, and Sky's sister, Stacey."

"I thought there were more than ten fighters built."

"Lack of crews," Elie replied. "The Fairchild has less than half the number of crew it is designed to carry. Space Fleet Academy can't certify people fast enough to provide most of our ships with full compliments. The PT-class ships are doing best, mainly because of the number of extra-terrestrials added to our rosters."

"Why aren't we recruiting more talent from the Trade Alliance worlds?"

"There hasn't been a dedicated effort. Plus most of our alien friends aren't military minded. The best potential are the Mischene and no one is ready to trust them yet."

"Elie, are we out here taking on more than we're ready for?"

"I hope not, Izzy. I hope not.

Chapter Thirteen
Galvari

The planet orbited a red dwarf star twenty-percent the size of Earth's Sol. It received half as much light from its parent star as Earth received from the sun. The planet was one-point-four times the diameter of Earth and six-point-six times its mass.

The dense atmosphere was composed mainly of nitrogen and oxygen. A slow rotation, eight continents, and oceans with dynamic up flows created the perfect place for an abundance of life.

The Galvari system was one-hundred-thirteen lightyears from Earth. From this point the Galvari Confederation spread forty lightyears in every direction, eighty lightyears from border to border. Galvari was the only orbital body in a system with six wormhole gates providing easy access to their empire.

"Sayuss and Particus are the two most inept officers in the military," Admiral Scendunt said. "If not for their families they would have been dismissed long before being handed their own ships."

"General Sayuss is an ass and a poor tactician, but he isn't stupid," Admiral Magnum said.

"He's worse, he's greedy and corrupt," Scendunt countered. "Qualities making him the perfect envoy to the Devee witches. We knew he would steal a percentage of each trade, but he was adept at getting items we needed. Why did the Council of Elders send Particus to pressure the Devee into joining the Confederation?"

"Because his father is one of the five council members," Magnum reminded his fellow officer. "The old man refuses to admit Particus is incompetent. We did have one of our best Captains at the helm of the battlewagon. Otherwise they may not have returned at all."

"Did we learn anything from that fiasco?"

"Quite a lot. We know the humans from Earth have advanced technology and are shrewd strategists. We haven't had a foe with their abilities since the disappearance of the pirate who plundered our ships and depots."

"We need to be better prepared for when we face the humans again." Scendunt rubbed the embroidered rings circling the cuff of his tailored coat. The rings identified him as co-commander of the entire Galvari military machine. "I guarantee it will happen."

"The positive result of Particus' failure was to get the Elders' attention," Magnum said. "We have the finances and their permission to update our systems."

"We've been asking to integrate new tech and improve our current capabilities for decades. Particus' screw up has handed us the opportunity we need. Has your analysis unit made recommendations?"

"They are still reviewing all the data, but some items are obvious. We must reinforce the drones to prevent the loss of their shields when they incur a sudden impact. Find a method to protect the ion-disruption cube after deployment throughout the process until activation. Increase the number of deck guns to make up for a battle wagon's lack of maneuverability. Protect our larger, more cumbersome vessels with our nimble cruisers. We can begin work on these issues while we decide what new tech can and should be added or used to replace outdated weapons and systems."

"We reenforce the dominance of our military," Scendunt said. "We press forward into a brilliant new future. At the same time we reinvigorate pride in the Galvari Confederation armada by recalling the first expansion of power and we were known as the Crush."

"You work on the psyche and I'll work on the tech," Magnum said. "There is one more thing you need to accomplish."

"What?"

"Eliminate my cousin Particus without pissing his father off. We cannot afford his level of ineptness any longer."

While the Admirals made plans to advance the military to the next step, the Council of Elders, the five Galvari who controlled the Confederation, discussed concerns created by the skirmish in the Devisator system.

"My son would have bested them if the Captain had followed his strategy," Vulpus said.

The Council of Elders convened in a chamber located in an ancient castle built on the summit of the highest hill in the capital city. While the structure was centuries old, the chamber was furnished with modern, comfortable chairs for the members. Five slaves stood rigid against a tapestry-covered wall awaiting any order their owner required.

A secretary sat at a desk with a computer. He was there to recover any data an Elder requested and keep notes.

"We're sure you're right," Colythi said. She was the lone female on the council. "The military will analyze the event. We need to discuss our options going forward."

"Options?" Vulpus responded. "We have one. The galaxy must respect the Confederation. The Admiralty has our approval to upgrade the armada. We must return to Devisator and teach them what happens when you attack one of our vessels."

"Actually, we attacked them. They responded," Turea said. The well-dressed elder sat with his legs crossed and a glass of off-world wine in hand.

"Then we respond to their response," Vulpus countered. The older male outweighed the younger Turea by one-hundred pounds. He moved toward the smaller Elder to intimidate him. Vulpus was comfortable using his size and position to threaten others.

Turea sipped his wine, unaffected by the larger man's presence.

"Are we prepared for a war?" Arrium asked. He was the newest Elder, and had held the position for a decade. "It was one thing to pressure the Devee into joining the Confederation. It's quite different to annex them by force. They are a member of an Alliance. There would be repercussions."

"Member of a trade alliance," Vulpus responded. "The Galvari will never bow to merchants."

"Those merchants had friends who kicked your son's ass," Turea reminded his fellow Elder.

"I told you, his officers did not follow orders," the other Elder said. "Valens, what is your opinion?"

"Humans present a threat if we decide to advance our borders in their direction," the being considered the most influential Elder said. "For the moment it is in our interests to make improvements to our military assets. The military needs to remedy the weaknesses shown to us by the humans. Until those improvements are completed, we will continue to live our lives as we always have."

"We have been slapped," Vulpus argued. "The Confederation cannot pull its head into its shell. We will lose the respect of the populace."

"Since when have we ever cared about their respect?" Valens asked him. "When the improvements are complete, then we decide whether to revisit expansion and the annexation of Devisator. If we do, we will be prepared to face and defeat any threat. Until then, discussing options is a waste of energy. There are planets within the Confederation showing signs of insurgency. We need to address those first."

"Agreed," Colythi said, as did Arrium and Turea.

Vulpus did not agree verbally but did sit down, relenting to the majority.

"Secretary, load the report on Aranthine to our data pads," Valens ordered.

Part Two

"The idea of a *pole*, a centre on which lines of force converge, all having their like ends upon it, is as purely abstract an idea as that of the lines of force themselves. We may give precision to our ideas by calling a solid on which lines of force converge a *centroid*. A *pole-centroid* is, then, the *conflux* of two forces. **The question becomes what magnetism draws two lines of force to a single *pole-centroid*?**"

The Magazine, <u>Science</u>, 1907

Chapter Fourteen

SS-13 / The Abyss

The space station designated SS-13 on Galvari Confederation charts orbited the planet Callustrade 2 in the Parnack system. The system was twenty lightyears from Aranthine and twenty lightyears from Galvari. Two of the system's planets, Callustrade 1 and Callustrade 2 rested in the star's habitable zone. The Confederation maintained a massive garrison on Callustrade 1 and a military-only space station, GMSS-8, where Galvari war ships could dock and receive repairs and upgrades.

SS-13 above Callustrade 2 provided a place where Confederation merchants could arrange or conclude trades, as well as enjoy the many bars and entertainment businesses that provided respite for the rough types who captained and crewed trade vessels. The planet below did a brisk business offering similar distractions geared toward the sailors and soldiers conscripted into military service. Species from every corner of the Confederation with tastes as varied as they.

Keeping the civilian merchants and the military personnel separated prevented clashes that resulted in losses of business assets and lives.

SS-13 was unofficially known as the Abyss. The small bar Tas and Tamina met with the merchant from Settasor, who commissioned the culling, was called the Hole.

"You delivered some scrawny specimens," the fat Setite said. "It will take me weeks to feed them enough to get any work out of them. That costs me extra."

"Suck on it, Staver," Tamina said. "You gave me a number and I delivered. I expect my cargo ships to be loaded with the agreed upon merchandise or I will kick your ass off the Abyss."

"Relax, Oison," he replied. "Your vessels are being loaded as we speak. Where did you pick up this group of malnourished trash?"

"A dying planet. Massive planet-wide drought. Another year and all life there will be extinct."

"So they gave you no trouble?"

"None." She downed the cup of ale ordered when she and Tas sat down. "Didn't have the will to fight."

"So, Tamina, would a simple Setite trader and a few crew members be able to cull this planet without worrying about getting hurt in the process?" Staver inquired.

"You could lower a ramp and they would walk into your cargo hold for the promise of a drink of water." Her grey eyes peered across the table in the same manner as if aiming at a target. "*If* a simple Setite trader had the coordinates of the planet. There's a lot of space out there."

"I'll double the amount of merchandise you're getting for the cull," he offered. "I can have it here by the time you return from dropping off this load on Aranthine."

Tamina caught the attention of the buxom green-hued waitress and ordered another ale for herself and Tas. She said nothing more to Staver. She had presented the potential for collecting slaves without the expense of hiring raiders.

"Okay, fine. Triple, but no more. It's going to cost me to feed the lot. Plus housing. Not to mention the probable medical expenses."

"You have a deal, if . . ."

"If what?"

"If you deliver the merchandise to Aranthine directly," she answered.

"Thievery, but I'll do it." The trader produced an electronic chip. He quickly had the agreement embedded and certified before the taciturn Aranthinian changed her mind and demanded more. Tamina exchanged it for one with the six points needed for the coordinates a navigator would use to locate the planet in the vast void of outer space.

"And pay for our drinks," she said.

Staver stood, pulled a credit from his vest pocket, and tossed it on the table.

"Next time, Oison. Watch out for your sister, Tas. It seems she plans on taking over the family business."

"I hope to Hena I never have to share air with that shunt again," she said as he waddled out the saloon.

"You did good, Tamina," Tas said. "Those people had no chance of survival. You may have prevented their extinction and made us a huge profit."

"I sold a world into slavery, Tas. I don't think I did them a favor."

"It may not be the best solution, but it was the best option you had. Slaves have a chance. Dead is dead."

"I'm not sure which is worse."

"Dead," he replied. "Every time. I asked Creo to join us here. Do you want to eat before he arrives."

"One, I can't eat after dealing with Staver. He turns my stomach. Two, I wouldn't eat anything served here. No way to know what you're really getting."

"True," he agreed. "Doesn't matter anyway. Creo just walked in."

At the entrance a tall - eye catching tall - alien as thin as Staver was obese, scanned the dimly lit bar. He was a minimum six-six and wore a garnet colored velvet suit with gold cuffs on the sleeves. A bright green shirt, opened and unbuttoned to the pant's belt, enhanced the depth of his burnt orange skin. Long braids of brown hair laced with golden threads cascaded around his slender face and down his back. Spotting the two Aranthinians, he appeared to glide across the floor to join them.

"Peace to you, friends," he said as he took the seat the Setite vacated. "What a filthy place to meet. There are much better establishments on the Abyss than the Hole. In fact, any other bar on the station is better."

"It's private," Tas said.

"True the fact," Creo said. "No one would ever admit to coming here."

"I like the ambiance," Tamina said, which elicited a chuckle from the Jastican. This close, it was obvious his golden eyes matched the threads in his braids.

"What I do for the Oisons?"

"You know a lot about a lot," Tas said. "I thought you might know a merchant looking for haulers."

"Information is a valuable thing. As you can tell by my fine attire. I love the two of you like kin, but I must make a living. The Abyss is a shit hole, but it is also expensive to reside here."

"Especially with your sense of style," Tamina said.

"I am so very glad you notice, Tamina Oison. It can be costly when you possess the fine tastes I have," he told her.

Tamina retrieved a duffle bag from beneath her chair. She removed a smaller cloth sack before returning the bag. She slid the sack across the table.

Creo lifted it, opened the draw string, and let out a breathe of excitement.

"No, no, no. My heart will burst."

He pulled out a pair of dark brown loafers.

"Mastadile leather," she said. "Single hide from a bull. Killed, skinned, tanned and sewn on Aranthine. Your size, I'm sure."

With no regard to his location, Creo removed the half-boots he wore and slid the loafers on. He walked to the far end of the bar and back, a wide grin of bright white teeth affixed as he returned to his seat.

"Beautiful craftsmanship and they feel like clouds," he said.

"Fair trade?" Tas asked.

"I have the contact information on a merchant in need of a hauler undeterred by potential danger," he said. "I suspect it will be lucrative as he has been searching without luck for some time."

"Deal," Tamina said.

"We don't know what the goods are," Tas objected.

"Doesn't matter," his sister replied.

"Here is her chip," the Jastican said. "There is more news you might be interested in. No extra. The engineers on GMSS-8 are working crews around the clock to retrofit armada ships."

Creo placed his boots into the cloth sack before continuing.

"New weapons. Refitting old ones. Adding secret new systems of the most advanced nature," he said.

"The Galvari are normally tight-lipped," Tas said.

"The powers that be have the crews so busy, income on Callustrade 2 has dropped considerably. Equally, those doing all the work are going without essentials like good ale and harsh liquor. An enterprising Jastican with the right contacts might do well trading for information if he could smuggle the proper stuff to the proper people."

"I suppose you have more specific details," Tas said. "What would they cost and why should we care?"

"No cost, my friend, because I do consider you friends. Here is a chip with what details I have learned." He handed the coin-like electronic data chip to Tas.

"You already had this ready for us," the hauler surmised.

"Aranthine has come up in conversations between high ranking officers and overheard by low ranking labor. It could be nothing and have no relationship to the work being done on their ships. But your species has been acting a bit independently in the region for over a generation. It would be unlike our Galvari overlords to let such activity go for long. It sends the wrong message to others who are not fond of our Confederate association."

"You think they will attack Aranthine?" Tamina asked.

"I think it more likely a show of force," he answered. "But with new weapons to play with, should you rub them the wrong way at the wrong time, bad things could happen."

"Thanks, Creo," Tas said. "For the lead and the information."

"Peace with you, brother and sis. I need to strut about the Abyss and show off my new custom made mastadile leather shoes. Good travels."

"Good travels," the Oisons responded and watched the tall alien as he danced out of the Hole.

"Now what?" Tamina asked.

"Contact the merchant and find out what the haul is and what they're willing to pay. Whatever it is will have to wait until we deliver our current cargo home. That's if we accept a deal."

"The Galvari?"

"We'll talk to Dad. We may need to get the word out for everyone to play by Confederation rules for a while. Try to defuse any animosity while we have some time. Make nice with the Confederation delegates on Aranthine."

"Gag me," she said.

"If we have to swallow our pride to save the planet, it's what we do, Tamina. Let's go back to the ships. As soon as the Parrians sober up I want to depart."

Chapter Fifteen
Red Dwarf System

"You needed to see me," Coop said as he entered the geo-lab set up for Petra and Hiro's research.

Hiro tossed him a rock.

The Captain rolled the stone in his hand.

"It looks like black crystal."

"It is," Hiro confirmed. "Thirty-four meters deep in Shaft One."

"This is great." He moved the rough stone from hand to hand, watching light play across the surface. "It's easy to see why they're called black diamonds."

"We're not ready to celebrate yet," the planetologist said. "The next step is to determine if there's enough present to make a serious mining operation viable. I asked Billy to build a mobile surface penetrating sonic resonance machine. We take the sample's resonance signature and chart the area around Shaft One."

"When?"

"Billy estimates twenty to twenty-five hours to construct the SRM. After completion, we make a quick trip to the surface and run scans for results."

"What else do we need to do?"

"Move drill testing to the next site. Whatever the SRM shows, we need more crystals than one mine will produce."

"Get the next location up while Billy completes his build. Regardless, this is good work."

Following the meeting with Hiro, Coop contacted Admiral Patterson.

"We'll know if we have a large enough deposit to warrant a full mining operation within two days," Coop told her.

"Fingers crossed," she replied. "You and your team have done a great job, Coop. How are you holding up?"

"No problems. The *Renarde* is built well and comfortable. Investigating new systems and visiting unexplored planets has kept everyone involved and entertained. There hasn't been the kind of down time that results in space fever."

"Elie's reports are similar. The 109 crew has been away longer, but she tells me the constant new discoveries keep everyone excited. Trent says the data from the two missions is staggering. Analyst from around the world are busy combing through the information. We've even shared system charts with Fell and Rys."

"Speaking of Rys, have their ships found any deposits?"

"They have only investigated one planet," she answered. "It was a bust. Restricted to wormhole travel limits their explorations. The *Renarde* can survey four systems in the same time they visit one. The King assures me they are prepared to provide a mining operation as soon as a viable location is discovered. Their cutters can shape the crystals to design specs as soon as new black material is delivered. Our cutters on Mars will shape the ones needed for space-fold arrays."

"Still no plan to share space-fold with allies?"

"No. The ability to manipulate space-time remains Earth's biggest advantage. If it ever gets out, it won't be long before it is no longer a secret," she said.

"Not if, Pam, but *when* it gets out," he replied.

"We keep it to ourselves as long as possible," she repeated.

Moving on, she told him, "Rachelle Paré and Mags Moore developed a source who provided insight into Galvari military equipment. They have diagrams of their QKD communications system."

"I spoke with Elie. I knew about the intel, but she didn't mention the QKD.'

"Security," Pam said. "We know the Devee can use QKD, but we got the details from a spy."

"You still don't trust the Devee?"

"Not enough to share secrets or tech with them. When the chips are down we'll see how they respond."

"I suppose we will," he replied. "I'll contact you when I have Hiro and Petra's reports."

The two Space Fleet officers ended the connection.

"Cassandra, show me a star chart with Space Fleet assets highlighted," he ordered the AI.

A holographic display appeared.

The *Renarde* appeared in the red dwarf system. They were eighteen lightyears from Earth. PT-99 under Sam Harrison was on duty in the solar system. PT-109 and Elie were twenty-two lightyears distant, thirty-six from Earth.

The Carrier *Fairchild*, Destroyer *Pegasus,* and PT-89 were located in the Aster System, thirty lightyears from Earth, twenty from the The *Renarde* and thirty-two from the 109.

"Spread out and spread thin," he said to himself.

The star chart reminded him of an aquarium with planets and Fleet ships suspended in the water. Distances depended on more than measuring straight lines. You had to account for how high or deep something was also. Toss in orbits and it was like a pump constantly moved objects so distances would change each time you looked. It was why it required six points of data to determine a location when navigating space.

The expanse was too staggering to fully comprehend. The Trade Alliance Worlds, including Earth, comprised roughly one-hundred lightyears. Earth to the center of the galaxy was 25,000 lightyears. To reach the far edge of the galaxy, on the other side of the black hole, was 75,000 lightyears.

In the swath of the galaxy where the Trade Alliance operated, the relatively tiny one-hundred lightyears contained 13,862 stars. Alliance records going back 5,000 years charted one-hundred-twelve planets within habitable zones, of which fifty-six were inhabited with at least one sentient life form. Of those only twelve were evolved enough to travel beyond their solar systems.

It would take roughly a month for a Space Fleet ship with space-fold drive to travel between the member planets on the edges of the Alliance trade routes.

The same ship would require nineteen years in space-time to reach the center of the galaxy or the nearest edge from Earth.

They were exploring .001% of the galaxy and it was daunting in scope. Unless the Orion Spiral was special, he estimated over five-thousand species in the galaxy were capable of exploring outer space.

With his extended life span, if he remained in space every day he had left, it would be impossible to visit the planets with potential life in the Orion Arm. Yet he had visited the far side of the galaxy and encountered the Helacene Alliance and the Kashōn Empire. Clyde used trans-dimensional drive. If he wanted to expand his ability to discover as many new worlds as possible, should he consider joining and working with the Nakki? Or should he limit his vision to his own neighborhood and protecting his home and friends?

Chapter Sixteen
Aranthine

The back porch of the farmhouse provided an unobstructed view of the acreage they hoped would one day again produce food. Resula's greenhouse, an A-frame structure clad in translucent panels, sat off to the right.

Cerulean sky was turning to butterscotch as Ortoka neared the horizon.

Tas perched on the porch's top rail. He faced his family seated on hand-made chairs.

"I spoke with Consta," he said. "She saw the dispatch from the Galvari admiral."

"Who is Consta?" Urvan Oison asked. The older Aranthinian's deep purple hue and dark veins marked his years of labor.

"She works in the command center at the Galvari garrison," he reminded his sire.

"Why would she risk her life giving away Galvari secrets?"

"She's in love with our son," Resula told him. "If you paid more attention to your family and less time on your business you would know that."

"She isn't in love with me," Tas objected.

"She is," Tamina interjected. "You'd see it if you weren't so thick."

"Whether she is or isn't doesn't matter. What does a Galvari military communication have to do with us?" Torvan, the eldest sibling asked.

"It has to do with me," Tamina said. She and Tas discussed the information from Consta before calling for a family meeting.

"It has to do with all of us," Tas corrected. "The message was about Vista."

"Who in Hena is Vista?" Urvan demanded.

"Not a who," Tamina said. "It's a planet. I went there for the cull."

"You turned in the cull," her father said. "We just unloaded two cargo ships full of payment. The Galvari should be happy."

"Those souls came from a dying planet I discovered after I made a trip to Vista," his daughter explained. "Vista is a vibrant world with semi-technical societies and agricultural systems. I had one ship filled when my raiders were attacked. We lost the cull. They used laser rifles taken from my crew to repel us. I left empty."

"You let locals take your lasers," Urvan exclaimed. "Do you know how hard it is to procure laser rifles. How many did you lose?"

"It doesn't matter," Ursula interrupted. "Go on, Tamina."

"Besides taking six rifles, they sabotaged the cannons on both Parrian ships. That's why I bugged out."

"Semi-tech farmers outfought mercenaries, took their weapons, freed your pick, sabotage your ships, and scared you off the planet," Torvan recounted the points in disbelief. "Really?"

"We have since learned they had help," Tas said. "Off worlders with military assets and training."

"Learned how?" Urvan asked.

"I'll explain it to you later," Resula said. "What is in the message Tas?"

"Tamina hired Piscium for the raid," he said. "They told Galvari officials about Vista and what happened. In return, the Galvari have agreed to help the Piscium return for a super-culling. The Confederation is gearing up for a possible confrontation. They need additional labor as well as conscripts for the army. The population on Vista must have sounded like perfect candidates."

"It's bad for the Vistans, but why should it affect my family?" Urvan asked.

"Because I failed and never reported it," Tamina said. "I didn't tell the Galvari about Vista. They will send someone to talk with me."

"Minor infraction," Urvan said. "You delivered an acceptable cull within the agreed upon time."

"There's more," Tas said. "We're going to try and contact the off-worlders who helped the Vistans and ask them to intercede again."

"Why?" Torvan asked.

"Because soon it will be Aranthine the Confederation decides to cull," Resula answered. "Tas and Tamina did not tell me their plan, but I agree with it. If there is a force in the galaxy able to stand against the Galvari, we will need them on our side one day."

"What do you plan for us?" Torvan asked.

"We take our ships, animals, food and anyone who wants to go with us, and join the off-worlders, if they will have us," Tas replied.

"Leave? Everything? Because of a minor infraction?" Torvan demanded.

"The Galvari are wound up," Tas said. "The aliens we're talking about defeated a battle wagon over Devisator. The Galvari will not be satisfied slapping Tam's hand. They will make an example of her and probably the family for good measure. You know how they are."

"That's enough," Urvan said. "Tas is right. There has been a lot of chatter saying the military is ramping up activities. Every time they do, more conscripts are taken. Tamina will be punished and the people of Aranthine will lose many of our young men and women to the Confederation. Do you truly believe you can contact those people?"

"I can try," Tamina said.

"Whether you do or don't, our fate is set," he told them. "We need to make plans to leave. I know of two habitable planets beyond the Confederation border we can relocate to and begin again."

Following Urvan's announcement, Tas joined Tamina in the workshop she kept in the barn.

"Will it work?" he asked as he looked over the QKD system his sister built.

"Most of the parts are second hand and never meant to be used in a communications array," she responded. "Let's find out."

"At least enough ships are licensed by the Galvari Confederation to have QKD systems for commercial use that a signal shouldn't create an alarm."

"I'm sorry I caused all of this."

"You didn't. The tradition of culling for slaves caused it. You might be the catalyst that ends it."

"That will depend on the people of Earth," Tamina responded. She touched *transmit*.

Chapter Seventeen

Toronto

"We do not need to get into another galactic war over internal politics of a Confederation that is not a threat to us," Jeanne Binoche, the French UEC representative said.

"They did try a forceful annexation of Devisator," Arcand reminded the assembled.

"I believe there is a great deal of doubt as to how strong an ally the Devee are in reality," Ewan Tennent, the recently credentialed UK rep, said.

"That action showed how aggressive the Galvari Confederation is, and it brought the Devee in line," Admiral Patterson commented. "It is the opinion of Genae Tabalis that a strong action by the OSA is essential to preventing the Confederation extending their borders."

"Space is huge," Binoche said. "They can expand their borders and never be noticed."

"It isn't only the expansion," Arcand countered, "it's the lives of a planet we are debating. Vista is on the edge of what is considered Confederation space. The population cannot defend against an invasion of superior force."

"Where does it stop, Guy?" Binoche asked. "First we had to defeat the Zenge. Next it was a war against the Mischene. We're rebuilding the Aster system. Our Marines are still on Phisor after taking it away from renegade elements of the Prophet's armada. Elements that remain active in our part of the galaxy, I remind you. When do we stop getting involved?"

"Earth made our entrance into extraterrestrial events at a difficult time," Patterson agreed. "We had no way of knowing what the galaxy beyond our solar system encompassed. What we discovered was that we, though new to interstellar travel, owned superior technology thanks to the discoveries made on Mars. We also displayed strategic and tactical operational abilities that made us the logical species to lead the responses against the Zenge, Michene, and the Prophet.

"Those actions have garnered Earth respect and rewards from members of the Trade Alliance. Because of interacting with our new allies we have FTL communications that can also reach inside space-time bubbles in large part thanks to citizens of Fell. We have advanced crystal power sources provided by Rys . Our weapons have been advanced and improved. The rebuilding of the Aster system includes the construction of a super carrier by ship builders with five-thousand years of experience. Methods and techniques being replicated on EMS2 and MSD."

"What will we gain placing our superior assets at risk over a world sixty lightyears away? A planet that runs on steam power," Binoche asked.

"Evolution," Arcand interjected. "Earth is not where we are due to luck. There must be some providence involved. I do not believe we can, or should involve ourselves in every conflict in the galaxy, but I do believe we have a responsibility to stand against tyranny."

"We have a responsibility to care for our own world first," Binoche argued. "Our planet is united in name only. There remains major areas of concern we must answer before we are truly unified."

"The more people see and hear of our successes in outer space, the greater a sense of shared pride is created," Arcand said. "If we prevent the Galvari from destroying Vista, it has the same effect as stopping a warlord from raiding villages. More so in that Space Fleet represents the entire population."

"What does it do to shared pride if Space Fleet fails?" Binoche asked. "A simpleton like the prophet destroyed the original Elliott S. Fairchild and badly damaged other ships.

My understanding is the Galvari military is more advanced in assets and experience. By your own calculations, failure would damage us in lost ships and irreplaceable personnel, as well as fostering doubt in the capabilities of the United Earth Council. Risk versus reward, Guy. Is the risk of losing worth the cost of losing?"

"There is a more pressing question to be answered," Tennant interjected. "Time. Vista is thirty-five lightyears from the Aster system. It would take days for them to get from Aster 2 and 3 to the system edge and at least another ten days to get assets on site. Estimate two total weeks minimum. What if the Galvari raid occurs sooner? The QKD message reached the 109 three days ago. There was nothing in it about when the attack was planned."

"The 109 is two days away," Patterson said. "The *Renarde* is five days away. The Devee can have ships in the system in ten days via wormhole."

"The Galvari will not repeat the mistakes made in the Devisator system," Tennant, a retired soldier, said. "It would be suicidal for the 109 if forced to face them alone again. The first time they had the assistance of the Devee. If the Confederation moves quickly, it will be entirely alone."

"Captain Casalobos can harass the enemy until help arrives," Patterson responded.

"You hope," Binoche interjected. "You hope the Galvari do not attack Vista early. You hope the PT-109 can perform one more miracle without being crippled or destroyed. You hope other vessels arrive in time. You hope they make a difference, which they may not. You hope our intervention brings unity on Earth. That is a lot of hope, Admiral."

"I believe in my people," Patterson replied. "Hope is the only thing the Vistans have."

"Let's take a break," Arcand told the Board of Governors. "We'll come back, complete our questions of Admiral Patterson, debate the facts and make a decision."

Alone in Arcand's office, Pam asked, "Do you have a feel for which direction the majority is leaning?"

"When we began, I was supportive of intervention," the Chairman replied. "After listening to Jeanne, even I have doubts. It could go either way. I suggest you send the 109 nearer, but not over the border. Move Fleet assets in the Aster system to the edge. If they are called they will not waste days getting there. They can go directly into system-to-system travel."

"Will do," she confirmed.

"Bring your A-game to the Board room this afternoon. Don't try to convince them with words like pride and hope. They are politicians, Pam. Make them see the situation as you do."

The PT-109 / Deep Space

"Appreciate the update, Admiral," Elie said. She closed the communication.

Mags, Rachelle, Genna and Tista Korr were present in her quarters and heard the conversation.

"That sucks," Mags said.

"They didn't say no," Tista said. "Politicians are required to debate. It is an unwritten law of the universe. That Governor Arcand believes he will have a vote in a few hours is optimistic."

"I'm surprised Patterson agreed with helping the Vistans," Rachelle said.

"Pam can read the tea leaves," Elie said. "The Orion Spiral Alliance and the Galvari Confederation is headed for a showdown sooner or later. The longer it's delayed the more time they have to advance their weapons and operating systems. We bested them at Devisator. If they are making improvements they cannot be major changes in so short a time."

"The idea any one species believes it has the right to subjugate another continues to baffle me," Genna said. "I have experienced the Mischene justify their actions under religious grounds. They believed they were the chosen race to rule the galaxy. The Devee admitted to enslaving beings abducted from other planets and say they were improving their lives. Now a group does it because they can. It is insanity."

"Amen, sister," Mags said. "Slavery on Earth was a dark stain on our history. That humans could justify it by considering other humans as animals was sick."

"It hasn't gone away, Mags," Rachelle said. "Human trafficking has been a criminal profit center for centuries. All efforts to stop it have failed."

"We know now it isn't only a human failing," Elie said. "It doesn't make it any less reprehensible to discover other species are involved in slavery."

"What do we do now?" Mags asked.

"Send a message to Tas and have him send us the location they're planning to go to," Elie answered. "We'll move closer to the border. Otherwise, there's nothing to do but wait."

Chapter Eighteen
PT-109

"Kennedy, complete the connection with Coop," Elie told the AI.

The desk in the Captain's office was constructed with an integrated holo-emitter. Following a short flicker, the image of Daniel Cooper, seated in his cabin aboard the *Renarde,* appeared.

"Hello, Elie. Hello, Kennedy," he greeted them.

"It is good to have you aboard, Coop, if only by hologram," the AI said.

"Thanks for taking the time to help, Coop," Elie said.

"I have plenty of it. We're drilling holes and digging tunnels. Waiting for the UEC to decide our next move."

"Tista Korr warned me they wouldn't rush the process," Elie said. "As long as they finish with the right decision, I suppose it's worth a little patience."

"I reviewed the logs on your confrontation with the Galvari ship over Devisator. You handled it perfectly. Went in with a thought out strategy and deployed assets to your advantage."

"Things went well for us. The intel I got from Tas Oison is worrisome. The Galvari brass also reviewed the battle and are making significant improvements to insure a different outcome if they meet a Space Fleet ship again."

"Apprise and adapt. Every good military strategist understands the principal. You want to do the same."

"Sí. For example, there is no way we will be able to get within a few miles of their ship again. It was not a tactic anyone would expect in a confrontation between star ships. It allowed us to destroy their ion-disruptor before it affected my plasma and photon cannons. They will plan against that happening a second time."

"But they don't know their disruptor does not work against our ion-drive flight engines."

"Because we employ gridded electrostatic thrusters that use xenon gas to direct the positive charged ions. The layers of laser-produced plasma shield the engines from the effects of naturally occurring ions in the atmosphere."

"Put a team of engineers on developing a way to grid the ion-energy supply to your weapons. Contact Trent and have him do the same. The knowledge is there, it just has to be adapted."

"Hopefully we have the time and materials."

"Have a plan of attack that does not include your particle weapons in case you don't," he said. "It will limit your offensive options, but it may come to that."

"Roger. Next is their drones. The intel says they are reengineering their shield generator. Bump and shoot isn't going to work again."

"The good news is you aren't going to stop them from deploying the ion-disruptor. Once they do they take their drones off the board."

"True. I may be without cannons and they will be without drones. They are increasing the number of laser cannons on their battle ships."

"What is the most difficult aspect of aiming in space, Elie?"

"Distance," she answered. "By the time your scan locates a target and you fire, if the target is moving, chances of hitting it are pretty low. It's why we fire where we think it's headed."

"It's why we train for three-dimensional battles," he reminded her. "From a defensive position, take advantage of the battle field."

"No straight lines," she said. "There's no up or down. Never give the opponent a flight pattern they can take advantage of."

"And their major disadvantage?"

"Size. They use the massive size of their battle wagon to intimidate, as well as transport thousands of surface troops. It makes maneuvering difficult. They have high-end straight-line speed, but need to slow considerably to turn."

"What happens if they attempt maneuvers at a high speed?"

"G-forces jump. Even with gravitronic dampeners, a ship in space experiences G-forces because of internal environments. With their size, trying to accelerate too quickly could kill the crew."

"It would happen to our crews accept . . ."

"Chairs are designed with harnesses that compensate. Crew members wear IEVA suits if duties require movement during battle conditions," she finished.

"If you need space-fold for an emergency move, the space-time bubble operates without acceleration. It simply is."

"Which leaves missiles and their centrifugal cannon."

"Missile and torpedo defense is what it is," he said. "Shoot them down, avoid them, or hope your shields are strong enough to prevent or reduce damage. The centrifugal cannon is your biggest threat. The size and speed of a projectile launched through centrifugal force will deliver one hell of an impact. An electro-magnetic generated shield or a crystal source shield may not dissipate the force created on impact enough to prevent critical, if not terminal damage."

"Stay out of the way."

"If you know a hit is coming, place the crystal shield at the collision point and rev the fusion drive to produce a stronger sonic force field as well. Maybe multiple layers will work," he added.

"Which leaves me with two fighters, a shuttle, a rail-gun, and an experienced crew."

"The Galvari don't stand a chance," Coop quipped. "You have a good handle on this, Elie. Make a game plan and drill your crew."

"Will do, mi Capitán," she replied with mock seriousness.

Elie and Coop had a more personal conversation before signing off.

"Kennedy, I need you to create a random pattern of maneuvers. Code it Kennedy One," she ordered the AI.

"Aye," the ever-present Kennedy responded.

"Get any data you have on gridded ion-powered systems and send it to Chief Nelson. Send a message to Nathan Trent and include Coop's recommendation on adapting our weapons with plasma grids."

"Aye."

"You've been in more open space fights than I have. Any suggestions."

"Denote areas of the ship based on value," the AI said. "If an impact cannot be avoided, there may be time to place a less crucial area in the path. Reinforce hulls, ceiling, and floor surrounding the space-fold array. If you must retreat, space-fold capability will be essential. There are two planets we charted in the past month with atmospheres containing xenon gas. We need to harvest extra gas for the ion-grids if a design for the cannons is completed."

"Excellent points," she complimented the AI. "Determine the values needed to rate the ship's areas, send a work order to maintenance for the space-fold array cabin, and provide the location of the nearest xenon cache to navigation. Muchos gracias, Kennedy. Good job."

"Will do and thank you, Elie."

Chapter Nineteen
Aranthine

"We're screwed," Tas said.

He and Consta joined his family in the dining room of the farmhouse. It was two hours after sunrise.

"A Galvari cruiser is in the system," the Aranthinian woman who worked at the Confederation garrison headquarters told them. "Shuttle service between the surface and moon has been suspended."

"The next step will be an order to detain Tamina, if not all of us," Tas said.

"Load the coach," Urvan said. "No wasted time and essentials only. Tam, is the QKD you built transportable?"

"The unit and batteries are," she answered. "The antenna is too tall."

"Torvan, cut the antenna into pieces you can lash on top of the coach. Have everything done and everyone loaded within one hour," the family patriarch ordered. "Consta, your family will be in danger."

"Not if I stay," she said. "If I'm back at work they won't suspect me of warning you. Plus I can reach Tas on a private channel with updates."

"You sure you want to take that chance?" Resula asked.

"I'm sure," she answered. "I'll say my good-byes and get back."

She and Tas left.

"Tam, call your friends and tell them what's happening. They will need to avoid this system with a cruiser here. Let them know you'll report anything Consta learns when you can."

His daughter nodded and departed, Torvan close behind.

"What are you planning?" Resula asked.

"We use the bush coach for family camping trips. We load up and head into the hills. I have extra ship materials stored in the barn. I can mask the engine so it doesn't give off a substantial heat signature. If we travel off known routes and stay in the wilderness we should avoid the Galvari."

"For how long?"

"Whatever's necessary," he answered. "There are other places to live on the planet. Keeping the family alive and out of prison are the only goals."

An hour later Tamina informed her father, "I sent the message." She joined Torvan to lash the sections of antenna to the roof of the bush coach.

The bush coach was designed for extended ventures into the Aranthine wilderness. The sixty-foot long, fourteen-foot tall vehicle featured a second story design with a lift up roof design. The upper level had six beds, bathroom, huge galley kitchen and lounge for eight to ten people.

The lower level provided storage, batteries for power rechargeable by stellar panels or off the engine, water storage, and the driver's cab.

The engine powered hover/thrusters that allowed the massive coach to skim over any terrain or across water with a heavy-duty 12-speed transmission, eventually reaching the hovers after passing through a two-speed transfer case.

Urvan commissioned the construction of the coach and had it built from a design he created using a combination of vehicles inspired during visits to other worlds.

The cab was large enough to comfortably hold the five Oisons.

They departed the multi-generational farm, not knowing if they would ever see it again.

"The Captain of the cruiser has ordered the arrest of Tamina Oison," the comms operator told his commander. "Do you want me to dispatch a squad?"

"No. Contact the Piscium scum and offer them a fifty-credit bounty to bring her in," Major Fulzton, command officer for the Galvari Confederation garrison on Aranthine, said. "They started this, let them finish."

"What if she resists?" the comms operator asked.

"Tell them to use their discretion," Fulzton replied.

"Sir, Piscium don't understand the concept of discretion."

"I know," the commander said.

It took the four Piscium fifty-minutes to clear the farmhouse and barn. It required another forty to inspect the smaller buildings before concluding the Oisons had departed.

All four wore liquid-filled rebreather helmets that allowed them to survive the Aranthine atmosphere. The one in a black tunic went to the cross-terrain transport provided by Major Fulzton and rejoined his mates. He carried a handheld particle monitor.

He walked the perimeter of the lot between the house and barn, watching for changes in particulates in the air. He stopped at one corner, called the other three and showed them the read-out. A 294 kilograms increase in CO_2 registered. This indicated battery emissions. The reading would not tell them how long the vehicle had been gone, but it would give a direction. He pointed northwest. The Piscium returned to their borrowed vehicle and headed toward the foothills in the distance. The setting sun reflected off their translucent helmets.

Urvan piloted the big rig over a steep hill and down the other side. Resula sat beside him. A monitor embedded in the console in front of her allowed her to call up views from cameras placed around the bush coach. The windshield provided a panoramic view in front of the coach. She had the rear top-deck camera view on the screen.

Tas, Tamina, and Torvan sat behind their parents in the same manner they had when children.

"The sun will be down soon," Urvan said. "We're an hour from the stream we camped by two years ago. I'll switch to night-sight when it gets dark."

"We can take turns driving and put more distance between us and the farm," Torvan said.

"We need to stop and eat," his father said. "It will give us a chance to discuss what our plan needs to be. No point in driving if we don't know where we're going."

After arriving at the stream, the family moved to the second level. The lounge was a comfortable place to eat and talk.

"We need to stay away from populated areas," Tas said. "The Galvari will put out notices for Tamina when they can't find her."

"The coach is comfortable to stay in for a while, but not forever," Resula said.

"The lower mountains are our best choice," Urvan said. "Fewer people and we can hunt and fish for food."

"Probably enough wild plants, too," Resula added. "Until it gets too cold."

"We can't survive a winter," Tamina said. "What are your plans when the snows come?"

"It won't be that long," Tas said. "When we connect with Captain Paré she'll figure a way to get us off Aranthine."

"Do you believe that?" Torvan asked. "Why would aliens risk pissing off the Confederation for us?"

"I do believe it," Tas responded.

"I liked Mags," Resula said. "If they can help they will."

"I suggest you set up the communicator and antenna to send another message, or receive one if they answered your last call. The external lights will be enough to get the work done," Urvan said.

"We can use circular clamps to put the antenna together and lean it against the coach," Torvan said.

"I'll get the QKD ready," Tamina said.

After the three young people left, Resula asked her husband, "What are we going to do long term?"

"Survive," he answered. "We survive."

Chapter Twenty

PT-109

On the bridge for the dead shift, Captain Rachelle Paré, acting OD, and Ens. "Folly" Fallenitsch. The forward display screen was filled with a colorful mist of purples, greens, and blues. The shape glowed brilliantly against the black space beyond.

"Space clouds are beautiful," Folly said. "I remember the first one I saw aboard the *Star Gazer.* They never get old."

The women watched the cloud move as if blown by the wind. Impossible in airless space. An optical illusion caused by the ship's movement as they travelled through the system with long range scans searching for anything of interest.

Rachelle said, "This one is an emission nebula. A hot, glowing cloud of gas and dust in space. The nebulas absorb the light of nearby stars and reach extremely high temperatures. The high temperature causes them to glow. Knowing what and why doesn't make them any less beautiful."

"Rachelle, do you mind if I ask why you gave up command of the *Pegasus*? I think being a Captain of my own destroyer-class space ship would be a dream come true."

"I thought so too," the French-Canadian replied to the woman from Osperantue. "The battle in the vortex against the Prophet made me realize I wasn't ready for that level of command."

"I read the reports, the *Pegasus* was cited as the main reason the battle group escaped the trap. Your tactics are being taught at the Academy. You brought your ship through with minimal damage while protecting others."

"I remind you, Folly, the *Fairchild* crashed on Aster 3 because of the damage it took in that fight."

"Everyone says Admiral Hawks' mistakes put the carrier in a vulnerable position."

"Sam Harrison saved *Pegasus* by shielding us with the PT-99. By placing his ship and crew in jeopardy he took fire intended for us."

"The report said he did that because the firepower of the Pegasus was greater than a PT boat. You would have a better chance of beating the Prophets battleships. He was right," Folly argued.

"He made a decision that was logical. The act was selfless and brave. Because of his actions, we were able to work with the 109 to escape the ambush. Noa Tal and the original Spirit Squadron had a lot to do with us winning the battle as well. What I realized that day was I did not have the experience to command a ship and crew the size of *Pegasus*."

"It was Space Fleet's first major space battle with our battle group against an enemy armada. No one had real experience."

"I got the same arguments from friends and colleagues. It didn't change the fact that my comfort level is in a cockpit, not a command chair. I will get there someday. It's why I asked for this assignment. Elie Casalobos has a handle on the entire process of captaining a ship. I'm here to watch and learn."

"That makes sense, but I think you did a wonderful job as a ship's commander. I bet your crew did too."

"There's a signal on the comms board," Rachelle told Folly. "You better check it."

Fallenitsch sat before the communications station and listened to the call. She turned to her OD and reported, "It's a QKD from Tamina Oison. Things have gone bad on Aranthine."

Rachelle listened to the message before using her personal trans-comm.

"Loba, it's Rain. We are receiving a call from Tamina Oison. I'm piping it to your cabin. Rain, out."

Five minutes later, she received a reply.

"Rain, it's Loba. Have Izzy replace you and join me in my cabin. Loba, out."

Izzy arrived eight minutes later to take over as OD. When Rachelle entered the Captain's quarters, Elie was in a chair with a cup of espresso and Mags was curled on the sofa in pajamas.

"Don't judge," Mags said. "I didn't want to waste time changing, besides, tiger-stripe pjs are cool."

"The Galvari Confederation cruiser in the Aranthine system doesn't mean it's there for Tamina Oison," Elie said.

"Too much of a coincidence," Rachelle countered. "Her family believes she's the excuse for the timing. They also believe this is the Confederation's first move to tightening controls on all Aranthinians. Tamina and Tas have provided the OSA with valuable intelligence. We can't repay them by ignoring the threat."

"Aranthine is a Confederation planet," Elie responded. "Space Fleet isn't in a position to start a galactic war by sending us to confront the cruiser. Before you say it, I realize they fired the first shot over Devisator. By allowing the battlewagon to retreat we prevented an escalation. It doesn't make sense to throw that away. If future diplomatic negotiations are going to have a chance, lighting a fire now is not the right move."

"Not protecting aliens who are willing to risk their lives for us sends another message," Rachelle said. "Others won't take that chance if they think we don't care about what happens to them if discovered."

"You said it, Rachelle. *Risk their lives*. It's what spies and insurgents do. They know that going in," Elie said.

"We don't have to confront the Galvari," Rachelle said. "We do what we did before. Sneak in, get the Oisons, and get out without anyone knowing."

"There wasn't an enemy ship in orbit last time. Mags, you're being quiet. No opinion?" Elie asked.

"You're wasting time playing the good Space Fleet officer, Elie. I knew we were going to try and rescue the Oison family the minute you told me the situation," her friend said. "You knew it, too."

"Kennedy, determine the coordinates for an arrival in the Aranthine system between the first planet and the sun. Place it in the nav computer," Elie spoke aloud.

"The current orbit of the planet will make it a dangerous location due to gravity wells," the AI responded. "I suggest all force fields be active when we return to normal space."

"Agreed," Elie said. "Time for the trip?"

"One day, two hours, thirty-eight minutes."

"Bridge, this is Captain Casalobos. Izzy, open a channel to the *Renarde*. When I complete that call, open one to Admiral Patterson."

"Aye," she responded.

Twenty minutes later, Elie ordered Folly to lay in the course for the Aranthine system and initiate space-fold.

Chapter Twenty-One

"They're still behind us," Torvan said.

The family first realized they were being tracked at dawn. Resula saw distant movement through the top deck's rear-facing camera. Zoomed to maximum, they could make out an eight-wheeled all-terrain open cab truck.

"Piscium," Tamina said. "I can see their helmets. I must have a bounty."

"The coach's hovers don't leave tracks to follow," Urvan said.

"They must be tracking our emissions," Tas surmised. "As long as we run the engine, they can stick to us. We're faster over rough surfaces, but they won't stop coming."

"If a fight is inevitable, we can pick the place and time," Urvan said. "We'll head up into the mountains and find a good defensive location that gives us the advantage."

"Won't they call for more help?" Resula asked.

"These hills are full of copper and asernium ore," Urvan replied. "Either interferes with radio waves. The combination means you better have a large antenna if you want a signal to get in or out."

"An antenna like the one we have," Tamina added. What she did not say was the Piscium were unlikely to call for back-up even if they could. They would not want to share the thrill of the kill. Even if their orders were to bring her in alive, those orders would not prevent them from murdering her family.

"We're farmers and merchants," Torvan interjected. "They're professional mercenaries. Hiding behind rocks isn't much of an advantage."

"It's all we have, Torvan," Urvan countered. "Unless you want to turn your sister over to them."

"No. Of course not."

"We have six laser rifles," Tas reminded them. "If we get the chance we can disable their truck."

"First, we find a suitable place to fight," the father said. "We disable their ride. Once they can't follow, we load up and run. With a bit of luck we'll be long gone before they can get somewhere they can get a message out."

Two hours later Urvan parked the coach behind a wall of rock. They were two-thirds of the way to the summit of a smaller mountain. The trail they used was once a glacial flow, cutting a path through ground filled with metallic ore.

Tas and Tamina ran to the lower storage bin to pull out laser rifles. Urvan and Torvan made temporary straps to mount the antenna against the vehicle's side. Resula prepped their communicators.

Tamina placed two weapons on the floor beside her mother and said, "The antenna is up. Send a message to Captain Casalobos and leave the channel open as a beacon."

She joined her father and brothers. Weapons in hand, they hurried down the trail to find a safe place to set up their ambush.

From the boulders left of the trail, Torvan and Urvan fired their lasers at the eight-wheel vehicle as it rounded the switchback. Tas and Tamina on the right followed suit. Four laser beams hit the front of the truck, the force pushing backward.

"Damn it!" Tamina shouted. "It's military issue. The hood is reinforced and shielded. Aim for the tires."

Before the Aranthinians could adjust, the Piscium mercenaries returned fire. Two stood in the open cab and raked the rocks with short bursts designed to suppress incoming fire. Two others bolted, one running for cover to the left and the other right. As soon as they were protected they fired lasers up the trail. Under cover of their teammates, the two Piscium left in the truck jumped out, left and right, to join the others.

Tamina moved further to her left, popped up from behind two large rocks, and fired down and across the trail. Her laser blast dug a hole in the hard dirt and scattered chunks. The partially exposed mercenary crouched behind a jagged outcropping retreated.

Taking advantage of a break, Torvan and Urvan fired short bursts down range.

No sooner had they ceased, a Piscium on the right returned fire. He sent short bursts of deadly light.

The personal weapons the Piscium and the Oisons used were smaller versions of the cannons used on spaceships.[9]

Unlike the more compact weapons used by Space Fleet with TSapphire glass mediums and crystal power sources, alien lasers were bulky, heavy, and difficult to aim because of their size and weight.

The blasts from the Piscium's laser missed Urvan and Torvan, but did hit the boulders they used for cover. Rock shards flew, sending the two Aranthinians lower for protection.

The mercenary beside the one firing used the opportunity to slide along the rock wall. He intended to flank the enemy above by finding another path up.

The two Piscium on the opposite side reacted the same way. While one covered and drew attention, the other slinked away to seek another egress.

Above, the Oisons continued to concentrate on suppressive fire, occasionally firing at the all-terrain vehicle in hopes a green beam of concentrated light would penetrate the reinforced hood or blow out a military-grade tire.

"Only two are firing," Tamina said to Tas.

"They could be swapping out," her brother replied. "In those rebreather helmets and enviro-suits, they look alike."

Having spent time with Piscium, the young woman did not believe the mercenaries would be content trading fire.

"I'll be back," she said and moved away before Tas could question her.

She moved adroitly along the crevices and rock falls, slowed by the cumbersome weapon. Twenty yards out the large stones formed a natural crenel where she could rest the laser gun and have a clear view down the slope.

After a few minutes she decided to return when a glint caught her attention. Below, less than one-hundred-feet, the helmet of a Piscium moved between the rocks. She settled the laser rifle on the crenel shelf and waited. The helmet appeared and she fired. The glow of the beam and the resulting blast below obscured her sight. A green flash of deadly light sailing over her head provided the proof her shot missed.

She engaged the mercenary attempting to flank their position. To her right she heard the distinct pst-pst sounds as her father and brothers defended their position.

It was too late to reconsider their decision to ambush the bounty hunters. In the moment she felt they had either over estimated their ability to close the trap or under estimated the capability of the Piscium to fight through it. Either way, they could not afford a stand off.

The Piscium did not believe in a stand off either. The mercenary on the side of the trail covered by Urvan and son was having a difficult ascent, but was making progress.

The two on opposite sides of the pathway began a careful movement upward. While one waved a beam over the area hiding the Oisons, the other rushed forward and up to the next protected position. It was tedious and dangerous, but they did make progress.

"My rifle battery is down to twenty-percent," Torvan said.

"I'm getting low, too," his father said. "Those creeps down there are using the same type of laser. They must be nearing zero. Torvan, run back to the coach. Grab the extra batteries and tell your mother to prep for a quick escape. On your way back give Tam and Tas batteries. Tell them when they hear me yell to lay down a wall of fire and run to the coach. We'll join them and get the hell up the mountain."

Torvan ran toward the coach, careful to keep the rock wall at his back. To help keep him safe, Urvan fired down range. Tas, noting Torvan's departure, added cover fire.

One of the Piscium working up the trail pulled his trigger without result. The gun's power source depleted. Unlike the weapons the Oisons used, the militaristic mercenaries attached holsters with an extra battery to theirs. He adroitly removed the spent battery and inserted the back up. In less than fifteen seconds he rejoined the fight.

Shards of stone flew as a blast shattered the rock above Tamina's position. A jagged fragment cut her left cheek, the gash in her purple skin oozed deep blue blood. She did not return fire. Her battery meter indicated ninety-percent of the power spent. The next few shots had to be affective, and that meant allowing her adversary to get nearer.

Urvan's last shot sent one of the mercenaries cowering behind a low boulder. As his meter hit zero, the Piscium attempting to flank his position reached the far end of the rock wall protecting the Aranthinian.

Tas fell to one knee as a blast from below cut a shallow, painful line across his right shoulder. The superheated beam sliced his skin and cauterized the wound at the same time. Down and injured, he did not see the mercenary beyond his father cross over the natural wall.

Out of sight of the battle, Resula slashed the straps holding the antenna to the coach. There was not time to take it down properly. It would be left behind.

Torvan, inside the storage area in the rear of their vehicle, pushed five batteries into a cloth bag. He used a sixth to replace his nearly empty one before stepping out and closing the hatch.

Tamina could hear rubble shift as the bounty hunter moved closer. She remained still. If he gave her a target she would have one chance. She no longer heard the hissing of lasers being fired or the sound of rocks cracking as beams of solid energy impacted. She was on the far side of a bend, unable to see a Piscium lift his weapon and take aim on her unsuspecting father.

Chapter Twenty-Two

The laser cut through outerwear, skin, organs and bones. Unlike a kinetic projectile that impacts with a small entry hole and exits leaving a large gaping wound, carrying vital body parts with it as it escapes, a laser beam's entry and exit holes are equal in size. The results are the same.

The Piscium preparing to blindside Urvan collapsed.

Rachelle Paré lowered her sidearm.

Tamina Oison was ready to defend herself when several deadly beams of light crossed over her position. The lasers continued raining across the ridge, angled down the far slope. She could hear rubble tossed as blasts tore into the surface. The crack of wood reached her over the multiple pst-pst echos of hard-light weapons. A tree had taken a hit.

Two dark grey shapes stood on either side of her. Humanoids in full body-hugging suits with helmets. They used streamline laser rifles.

In unison they ceased fire. The figure at her feet removed the faceplate and said, "I'm Sergeant Galatti of the UEC Space Fleet Marines. The alien firing on you has retreated."

"My family is in trouble," Tamina said as she stood.

"They're safe," CC assured her. "Captain Paré and Sergeant Vargas are with your father and brother. One alien was killed. Two others retreated back to their vehicle. Lt. Moore is at your vehicle with your mother and other brother. We need to go there now. Corporal Turner will cover watch our backs."

Tamina and CC met up with Rachelle, Urvan, and Tas on the way to the coach. Mags, Resula, and Torvan greeted them.

"Our fighters are parked a quarter-mile north," Rachelle said. "They're not built to transport people. It's going to be tight and uncomfortable getting everybody to the 109.

Collect as few personal items as necessary. We're going to destroy your laser guns and any tech you don't want the Galvari to have."

Recognizing their position, the Oisons made no arguments. Staying alive and free were more important than objects.

Vargas and Turner joined them and added their weapons to the destruction of the laser guns and communications equipment.

They reported the three remaining Piscium had taken their vehicle further down the mountain.

"They're going to put enough distance between them and the minerals blocking communications to call for help," Tas surmised.

"Let's be gone by then," Mags said. She led the group to the Spirits.

With five bodies wedged into the limited space available within each small ship, the fighters rose into the sky. Above interference, a call to the 109 arranged for a quick pick up in space.

Elie greeted the Oisons in a crew mess. The five Aranthinians were with Rachelle and Mags.

"We appreciate your help, Captain Casalobos," Urvan said.

"I'm aware of how much you had to abandon," Elie said. "We will make sure you are comfortable. Do you have a destination in mind?"

"I had a couple of options when I thought we would have our ship and supplies. The only place I know outside the Confederation is Devisator," Tas said.

"I'll contact Genae Tabilis," Elie responded. "I'm positive she'll welcome you."

"What about Vista?" Tamina interrupted. "Are you going to stop the Galvari invasion?"

"Our government leaders are discussing the situation," Elie replied. "I don't believe they will authorize an intervention."

"Why not?" Tamina demanded. "Billions of innocent people are at risk."

"Vista is within the region the Galvari Confederation controls," Elie calmly replied. "Interfering with a military operation would be an act of war. I doubt the UEC or the OSA are willing to do that."

"Captain, Vista is one of a dozen worlds with no idea life exists beyond their planet," Tas said. "They are not members of the Confederation. I can also assure you I know of five planets willing to rebel if they knew a force capable of standing against the Galvari would provide support, starting with Aranthine."

"I'll pass it along, Tas, but I honestly do not believe it will make a difference," Elie said.

"Then tell them their only choice is when, not if, you will be forced to confront the Galvari Confederation," he returned. "When they sent a battlewagon to convince the Devee to join the Confederation it was a move toward your region. That you repelled them will only make them more determined. They are a militaristic society with centuries of forcing their control over less powerful worlds."

"We're attempting to open talks in order to convince them to make no further attempts," Elie countered.

"I would bet you have had no luck getting a reply," Tas said.

"They haven't," Mags said.

"They never will," Tamina added to the conversation. "When you bested the battlewagon, Captain Casalobos, you shamed them. That is one reason they will attack again. The other is even more important to their leaders. Their loss has become the talk of the Confederation. Merchants have known about the Trade Alliance worlds for over three centuries. By opening negotiations with the Devee, the Galvari inadvertently let people know. The news of you forcing them to retreat is spreading. The Galvari cannot allow hope an opportunity. They will respond."

"The Galvari military are not fools," Tas said. "They will learn from their loss and make more changes. If your world waits, if you allow them time, they will attack when it suits them."

"Perhaps," Elie replied. "I still believe the OSA will not make such a provocative move as to go into Confederation space and interfere."

"Saving a planet from slavery is not interfering," Tamina said. "It's mercy."

Chapter Twenty-Three

Toronto

"PT-109 has delivered the Oison family to Devisator," Admiral Patterson told Governor Arcand.

"Captain Casalobos informed me of the Oisons' opinion about the Galvari Confederation planning to make another attack on Devisator," Arcand said. "Genae Tabilis apparently believes the same. She's asking the OSA for protection."

"And our response is?"

"Members are discussing it. I've argued we can't attempt to form a defensive alliance and not offer to defend a potential new member. Having the Devee in the alliance and under a debt is too attractive to ignore."

"What will you suggest?"

"The Aster System is pretty calm. I'm thinking Admiral Kebede takes her new carrier, fighter squadron, and a PT boat to visit Devisator. We leave the *Pegasus* and General Gregory with sufficient ground forces to maintain the peace. I'll also suggest one ship from each OAS planet join her there. That should be a strong deterrent."

"Or a major provocation," the Admiral countered. "We will be parking a battle group on the Confederation's border."

"If what I've heard about the Galvari is true, it might be a smart move to have assets in the area. Unless we can get them to talk, a confrontation sounds inevitable."

"What about the request to help Vista?"

"That is a more difficult question," he admitted. "If we attempt to stop the Galvari from invading, we're asking for a war. Not a confrontation like the Mischene and Zinge fights, but an all-out galactic size war. We have no idea what they are capable of. We could be vastly over matched."

"We defended Phisor after the Mischene rebels invaded," she reminded him. "They were a non-space travel society."

"In neutral space and attacked by an enemy we were already pursuing. The Mischene presence was leftovers from the Prophet's armada, and they held us off for a year. I believe the Galvari military is more organized and more advanced. Do you want to place your people into such a potentially deadly situation?"

"Of course not," Patterson conceded. "But if we had an excuse that allowed us to intervene I know Captain Casalobos and her crew would jump to act."

"Maybe the OSA meeting will find something, but I doubt it. Meanwhile, the other reason for this meeting was to update you on the Camarilla Dissolvere. Space Fleet can take them off your board as a concern."

"Are you sure, Governor? They still have assets that have not been contained."

"Assets, but the leaders are under control," he replied. "Saleh Abd al-Rashin gave up in Saudi Arabia. The last of those holding out beneath the mosque turned themselves over. He was their leader. The two media moguls, Arnold Montack and Alexandra Vasluianu have agreed to testify whenever we go to trials. Benny Claflin, the rogue Space Ranger, is locked away. Wei Zhou Nanke turned out to be a Devee spy. You had her delivered back to Devisator."

"I know Katherine Chandra has agreed to work with the UEC in Africa," Patterson said.

"Not completely. Not yet," he corrected. "We're still on a probationary status. It would help if you call and update her on Space Fleet's current operations. Make her feel more a part of the overall program."

"I'll see to it," she promised. "Lorena Aragon?"

"Tab Barnwell and the UEC Marshals are watching her," Arcand answered. "She runs a criminal cartel. That's his bailiwick."

"Speaking of bailiwick, Sir Daniel Miller?"

"He retired as the UK representative to the UEC. He's basically under house arrest for life," Arcand told her. "Rear Admiral Stephen Hawks died fighting the Prophet in the Aster System. Space Fleet isn't going to be dishonored by having a commanding officer in the middle of an attempt to dissolve the UEC."

Pam Patterson did not mention Captain Sam Harrington of the PT-99. Only a select few knew Sam, also a survivor of the Space Ranger Project, was a Camarilla member. He had a change of heart and no one who did know felt the need to punish him.

"That leaves the computer genius, Hamed Attalan and Dr. Herman Reinhardt," she said.

"Well, I have to admit we've decided to use Attalan and Reinhardt ourselves," Arcand said. "Attalan's skills are helping us streamline the financial services necessary to make the implementation of a global currency viable. In his spare time he's working with Nathan Trent on some project to recover lost data. Reinhardt's research on genetic and bioengineering is too valuable to ignore. We get their expertise and they stay out of prison."

"Must be nice to pick and choose your criminals," Patterson quipped.

"It is actually. A centralized government for the entire planet is a fragile thing, Admiral. My responsibility is to make sure it doesn't shatter. I'll do what I feel necessary."

"I understand, Chairman," she said. "You build with the materials available. If that's all, I have my own responsibilities."

Aya Ishihara, Director of the Exo-Legal Affairs, followed Admiral Patterson on the Chairman's agenda for the day.

"Let's keep this simple, Aya," he said after she sat. "Where are we with the Devee and the Galvari Confederation?"

"Tuito Bailis, the chief exo-diplomat for the Devee, has made a formal inquiry into joining the Orion Spiral Alliance. The other OSA members are reticent. They aren't ready to accept the Devee have seen the light. There is a lot of suspicion."

"Well deserved from what I've read about those women. Plus our own experiences with them. Slow walk the process. Let's make them earn our trust."

"They are making some positive steps. Captain Cooper contacted Genae Tabilis for information regarding Galvari weapons. I understand they are communicating and the results have been positive."

"And the Galvari?"

She exhaled audibly. "Very little. Enough contact to know there is a contact, but difficult. They don't have STORM-HATCH and we don't have QKD. Everything has been relayed through Devisator. They have warned us if we trespass it will cause a war. We asked for details regarding their borders and got back a general map of that entire region of space. Devee traders have done business with them, but they aren't sure what the Confederation deems as their space."

"Do we know anything?" he asked.

"Nothing concrete or positive," she answered. "They are a military society with a five-member leadership council. They are bullies and have no faith in anything but power. I believe the appropriate description is *Galvari Supremacists*."

"Keep working on it. I've been told we have recently obtained plans for QKD communications. Once our engineers build a system it should speed things up. Have you looked over the Vista problem?"

"From a legal point of view, there's no solution," she answered. "We haven't recognized the Confederation's claims on boundaries or ownership of sentient life forms within those borders. On the other hand, within that region of space they make up the laws. You're facing a moral dilemma. Do you intervene and chance war, or do you allow the enslavement of an entire planet to avoid a confrontation?"

"It's more than a moral dilemma, Aya. It's a question of consequences. If we get involved, it affects the galaxy. If we stay out of it, it affects one planet."

"Sounds as if you've already decided."

"The OSA members will decide, but I know my position," he admitted. "If Earth isn't prepared to commit our military resources, I don't think they will vote to intercede. Unless you have anything more, we'll continue at our next meeting."

Aya departed, leaving the de facto leader of Earth alone with his decisions.

Of the eleven members of the Camarilla Dissolvere, only two faced trial. Claflin and al-Rashin. The other living members were being co-opted for the benefit of the UEC.

The Galvari Confederation represented a clear danger, but not one he felt Earth was prepared for at the current time. Which left Vista alone and unaware of the trauma the people faced. Their fate was largely his decision, and he was tasked with the future of this planet, not one trillions of miles distant.

An inscribed plaque sat in a prominent place on the shelves against one office wall. He picked it up and read:

"A true leader has the confidence to stand alone, the courage to make tough decisions, and the compassion to listen to the needs of others. He does not set out to be

a leader, but becomes one by the equality of his actions and the integrity of his intent." --Douglas MacArthur

He turned it over and laid it face down.

Chapter Twenty-Four
Galvari

Admiral Scendunt stood before the Council of Elders. His weekly reports were usually dry, dull, and over quickly. For the last month they had become strained and lasted longer than comfortable. His discomfort began when Particus got his ass whipped over Devisator.

"We're following reports of unrest on several planets," he told the five leaders. "Jastica and Aranthine are the loudest. A cruiser has been dispatched to Aranthine to deal with some citizens who disobeyed orders. It will send the rest a clear message. We're watching Jastica. Things tend to blow over quickly there. The Jasticans find it difficult maintaining a coherent thought for very long."

"Have you found my son?" Vulpus demanded.

"Not yet, Counselor. Admiral Particus has been known to pursue his personal interests and going without communicating. His personal space yacht is gone. I'm sure he will check in eventually."

"We are not overly concerned with Particus' bad habits," Valens said. "How are the upgrades to our battleships progressing?"

"Ahead of schedule," the Admiral assured him. "I have an assignment for GB-3 and a two-cruiser escort. There will be opportunities to test the improvements."

"My son commands GB-3," Vulpus interrupted.

"Captain Lucious is a competent officer."

"Where are you sending them?" Valens asked.

"A neo-industrial planet called Vista. We're going to cull a number for workers to be distributed around the confederation. After that we will begin mining and farming operations, using the locals for labor."

"Doesn't sound like much of a test," Vulpus said.

"The ships will test long-range lasers by firing on the planet from different distances," Scendunt answered. "The GB-3 will fire and drop long rods to measure the force of their respective kinetic impacts. There will be considerable loss of life, but the planet is well populated. It won't affect the culling."

"Resistance?" Valens inquired.

"There are military units. It will be good training for our ground forces. The battlewagon transports 20,000 troops and will use shuttles to place them on the surface."

"Admiral, the Orion Spiral Alliance continues to contact us regarding establishing a non-aggression pact. Do you have an opinion?" Turea asked.

"Most of the OSA members are weak. Earth concerns me. They have access to Nakki technology and are adept at battle strategy and tactics. Engaging them in diplomacy might give us more time to improve our assets."

"Can we steal the Nakki secrets?" Turea asked.

"The Devee tried and failed. They had the advantages of placing a spy on Earth decades ago, and Devisator is a member of the Trade Alliance."

"I did not ask what the Devee could not do," Turea said. The Elder dressed and acted like a dilettante, but he had a core of steel. "Do you have assets capable of stealing the Nakki secrets?"

"No," Scendunt answered and hurried to add, "but I have people who can find a way. We'll need intelligence before we can develop an operation."

"I believe it's worth the effort," Turea said.

The others agreed and Scendunt had the authority to begin building the necessary steps to obtaining the most valuable secrets in the galaxy.

Following the Admiral's departure, Valens said, "We're on the precipice of changes unseen within the Confederation in centuries. It has been a long time since the supremacy of the Galvari has been openly questioned. The Confederation has been content with our current borders longer than the memory of any member of this council. The outreach to Devisator was our first attempt at expansion as the Elders. To have it repulsed is unacceptable. How history views this Council of Elders depends on the response we make."

"We must be careful with any response," Colythi interjected. "History will look on us less favorably if we add more failures."

"Then we must not fail," Valens countered. "We have assembled a huge military and have used that force as a deterrent. Because actions have been limited, the planets under our control are less impressed by our strength. Because our admirals and generals have limited assaults to backward worlds, our officers are overconfident and their troops lazy."

"Are you suggesting massive retaliations against other members of the Confederation, or expansion by invasion?" Arrium asked.

"You call them *members* of the Confederation. You seem to forget, as some of these *members* also do, that Galvari controls the Confederation. It is time to send a reminder who rules and who follows," Valens replied. "It is also time for the planets outside the Galvari Confederation to learn to fear us. The humiliation at Devisator cannot stand unanswered."

"My son's orders were not followed," Vulpus once more rushed to his prodigy's defense.

"Your son is a disgrace," Turea said. "You should distance yourself from him, Vulpus, not make excuses."

"You cannot insult my family like that, Turea," Vulpus angrily responded. He stood, hands clenched.

"Sit back down, Vulpus," Valens ordered. "Or leave. I am also tired of your constant refusal to recognize your son's lack of ability. He would be nothing if not related to you. It is an example of how we have grown apathetic. We can no longer accept disobedience among Confederation members nor incompetence within our ranks."

"I will not stand for this," Vulpus protested. He marched out of the chamber, his secretary rushing to catch up.

"We will need to replace him," Turea said.

"No. He will never give up power over defending his son," Valens countered. "After a little reflection, he will return and act as if nothing has been said. His addiction is stronger than his affection."

"I agree with a show of force to reaffirm Galvari supremacy," Arrium said in an attempt to return the Council to business. "I also agree with Colythi when she warns of the consequences of failure. We are not ready for expansion."

"Then we must get ready," Valens responded.

Scendunt met with Admiral Magnum on his return to headquarters.

"Get General Sayuss. I want access to the witch the Devee placed on Earth. Whatever it takes, I need information she has," he told his fellow officer.

"Do you honestly believe we can obtain the Nakki technology from the Earthers?" Magnum asked.

"I don't know. I don't care," Scendunt admitted. "Turea wants a plan. Since I don't intend to go missing like Particus, I intend to give him one."

Chapter Twenty-five

"A QKD transmission from a Jastican trader was received by Tas Oison on Devisator," Mags told Elie. "I was helping the family settle in at the farm Genae Tabilis gave them when it came through. A Galvari battle group is expected to cull Vista in the next couple of days. They were dispatched over a week ago. The wormhole channels will have them in the system soon. After that it's just the trip from the gate to the planet."

"I'll contact Patterson, but don't expect us to respond, Mags," Elie said.

"I understand. I don't agree, but I understand," her friend replied.

Alone in her office, Elie Casalobos contemplated her options. She wanted badly to call Coop. He would be compassionate, but he could not make decisions for her. She called Space Fleet headquarters. The final decision would come from Earth, not in the heat of emotion rising in the frigid void of space.

"Captain Casalobos, you saved me calling you," Admiral Pam Patterson said. "I'm currently in a meeting of the Joint Chiefs of Staff. The UEC Board of Governors has voted that Space Fleet is to protect the lives and freedom of the people of Vista."

"Admiral, that's great to hear, but I am surprised," Elie responded.

"The Vistans can thank Col. Katherine Chandra," Patterson said. "After I briefed her on Space Fleet operations per Governor Arcand's directive, she contacted him. Slavery is a sore subject for the Colonel. She informed him, quite forcefully I was told, if the UEC would not take a stand against the enslavement of an entire civilization, she could not support the UEC. Either we tried to stop the Galvari or she would not only cut ties, she would personally lead a rebellion to overthrow a central government."

"And he caved?"

"Col. Chandra's positive efforts in Africa have made her a popular figure. News of her work, fully propagated by UEC media contacts, are making her an example of the power of global unity," Patterson said. "Her threat is powerful, Captain."

"What are my orders?"

"That's why the Joint Staff is meeting. The *John F. Kennedy* is the closest ship to Vista. However, sending you is tantamount to a suicide mission. We are not prepared to sacrifice the 109 and her crew to send a message. Especially if the result remains the same and Vista is enslaved.

"The *Fairchild* and PT-99 will be ordered from their current assignment to Devisator and redirected to the Vista System. Our best estimate has them five days away. *The Renarde* is nearby, but fifty-four hours away. If the 109 and the *Renarde* depart at the same time, you will be on site thirty hours earlier.

"No one doubts the capabilities of you or the 109," Patterson assured her. "But no one sees how you could survive thirty hours alone against a superior force. A force better prepared to face you after their recent defeat."

"Admiral, am I going or not?"

"Your orders, Captain Casalobos, is to proceed to Vista and intercept the Galvari battle group. Your primary mission is to engage their commander in talks. Try to convince them not to invade the planet. Failing that, any armed conflict cannot result in the loss of the *John F. Kennedy* and her crew. If it comes down to saving your ship or allowing the Galvari to take the planet, you are expressly ordered to get the hell out of there. Do you understand, Captain?"

"Copy, Admiral. This is not a suicide mission. When do we go?" Elie asked.

"Inform the Devee, prep your people and go," Patterson said. "I'm contacting Admiral Kebede and Captain Cooper immediately. Fair winds and following seas, Elie. Patterson, out."

Elie sat quietly at her desk for a minute to collect her thoughts.

"Kennedy, did you hear?" she asked aloud.

"Of course, Elie," the AI replied.

"Initiate preparations for departure. Inform any crew on the surface or at the space station to return to ship ASAP. Call the command staff on board to the conference room. And open a channel to the Oisons. After I tell them I'll contact Genae Tabilis."

"Aye, Captain. Battle Level Four instigated," Kennedy replied.

Level Four was preparation for imminent conflict. Level One was engagement. Hopefully things ended somewhere in Three or Two. Hopefully.

PART THREE

*"The general pattern downstream of a conflux of increasing stream flow and decreasing slopes drives a corresponding **shift in habitat characteristics**."*

Tim Beechie, John S. Richardson, Angela M. Gurnell, and Junjiro Negishi (2012) "Watershed processes, human impacts, and process-based restoration." In Philip Roni and Tim Beechie (eds.) (2012)

Chapter Twenty-Six

Vista System

"Captain, the Earth ship from Devisator is between us and the planet," the scan operator reported.

"They're hailing us, sir," Communications told him. "They're using QKD and SYNC."

The ship's bridge towered above the top deck, three-quarters the length of the deck from the bow. The Captain's seat was located at the front of the command room. A massive screen on the hull in front of him provided 3D images of his ship and any and all objects within whatever area he requested. Real time displays offered data he felt pertinent. He controlled everything from a heads-up touch hologram he could place anywhere within his reach.

Behind him two-dozen Galvari sailors and officers controlled individual monitors and systems operations. They watched the minutia of war, relaying information requested or reporting on anything they deemed significant. The command crew awaited any order issued by their Captain. He recognized the inefficiencies in the system but changing traditional methods used by the military was difficult.

During his first encounter with the Earth vessel he was hampered by the presence of Admiral Particus. That impairment was no longer present.

"Distance?"

"5,588,460 miles," was called from Scans console.

"Time to reach?"

"At current speed, twelve-hours-five-seconds," Navigation responded.

"Ion-disruptor's affective range?"

"At Eight-million-miles, one-hundred to sixty-six percent," Weapons reminded him. "Sixty-five to zero for another million miles."

"They continue to hail," Communications interrupted.

"Ignore them," he ordered. "Weapons, deploy ion-disruptor when we are four-million-miles apart. I want that ship in the center of the affective range."

"Yes, sir."

"Pilot, begin scrubbing speed at the same time. Bring us down to one-hundred-thousand-miles-per-hour."

High velocity speeds required a controlled, gradual reduction. Even though space was a vacuum, ship's interiors were not. Gravitronic dampeners assisted with mitigating the effects of high-G maneuvers, they could not compensate for sudden accelerations or decelerations done in hundreds-of-thousand-miles-per-hour. Unless a crew was secure within special cocoons, scrubbing speed was the only method to prevent the abrupt change in internal pressures from imploding body organs.

These rules of physics also arose in space ship construction. The idea of a box design being as affective in frictionless space as a more aerodynamic shape was only true for non-crewed or relatively slow vessels. As a ship moved through space internal pressures were created within artificial atmospheres. Squared walls increased these forces, making activity uncomfortable. Curved decks and hulls shucked these forces.

"Yes, sir."

"Where are the escorts?"

"Cruiser GC-10 on our port and eighty-three-thousand-miles off the stern. Cruiser GC-11 is one-hundred-twelve-thousand-miles beneath the keel and thirty-thousand-miles behind us," Scans reported.

"Comms, tell both cruisers to scrub speed when we do, but maintain enough to move ahead. I want them two-hundred-thousand-miles in front of us."

"Yes, sir."

On ship-wide the Captain called, "Battle stations. Two hours to commencement."

"No reply," Izzy told Elie.

"Shut down hails," the Captain ordered. "If they were going to answer they would have."

"Genna, time to impact if they fire lasers?"

The First Officer answered from Tactical, "Thirty-seconds."

"Add the crystal force field to support the EM shield," Elie ordered.

Captain Casalobos looked over her bridge. Lesego Ndaba as pilot. Casey Adams on Navigation. Izzy on Comms and Genna at Tactical. Anwar Nassar sat at the Systems console.

Dr. Bahadur Singh and his medical staff were ready. Chief Nelson patrolled the engineering section, prepared but complaining about wearing an IEVA suit. Rachelle and Mags awaited orders in the hangar's Ready Room. Kennedy was ever ready.

On ship-wide comm she said, "To the officers and crew, we are preparing to go into one more battle. Do your job, watch out for your mates, trust your ship. Watch is over. We are now at battle stations. Captain Casalobos, out."

Two hours later the two cruisers surged ahead of the battlewagon. Much smaller than the enormous main ship, the cruisers were each four-times the size of the PT-109.

The captain of the GC-10 ordered his forward plasma cannons prepared. The electro-magnetic motors hummed as force fields covered the ship in preparation for a response.

The GC-11 followed suit. The nuclear fusion engines shut down but inertia and the lack of friction kept the V-hulled vessel moving forward.

A panel on the keel of the battlewagon opened and a large cube was ejected into space. Five seconds later a directed charge exploded the cube in silence resulting in the release and spread of artificial ionization across a nine-million-mile diameter sphere from the battlewagon forward.

The battlewagon's captain ordered a report from the ship's long-range scanners.

"The enemy ship's engines have shut down," the Scans officer reported. "Electro-magnetic produced force field remains. Cannot confirm the loss of their particle-based weapons, but if they lost propulsion, they probably lost all ion-based systems."

Over his trans-ships system the captain said, "This is Group Command to GC-10 and GC-11. Fire lasers on the enemy. Let's see if they are dead in space or if they attempt to evade."

Laser cannons on the two cruisers used data from scanners and navigation to target the 109's position. Eight multi-megawatt laser cannons with ten-meter mirrors and massive cooling systems rotated on command of targeting computers. The turrets they were mounted on the size of a house. A delay of eight-seconds occurred between the order to aim and the placement of the muzzle. In unison they fired.

"Twenty-one seconds until laser impact," Genna called. "Forward shielding has been reinforced. Crystal force field active and layered."

Elie called across-ship, "Brace for impact in ten seconds."

The wave of lasers impacted the shields and washed over the ship. The impact force lifted the forward keel and pushed the inert vessel 10,000 miles in fifteen seconds. Sympathetic vibrations within the ship resulted in results similar to a magnitude 6 earthquake. A lot of intense shaking.

"Damage?" Elie requested.

"Nothing to report," Anwar answered. "I cut power from the ionic-drive engines when the cube exploded, as ordered. The drives read as ready when required."

"It will appear the disruptor worked," Genna said. "By not attempting to avoid the lasers, it should reinforce the idea we are without maneuvering engines."

"Chief Nelson," Elie called. "Plasma and photon cannons?"

"I cannot honestly tell you, Captain," the engineer reported. "The retro-fits for grids and the xenon gas we collected are in place. We had no way to actually test the new upgrades. Space Fleet engineers said there's an eighty-two-percent positive result expected, but until we try to turn them on we won't know for sure."

"Genna, what have we learned?" Elie asked.

"At four-million-miles our shield success is high. Based on force intensity scaling, their lasers would need to be within two-million miles to cause damage. If they get within 500,000 miles and fire the same number of weapons there is a high probability of breaching the shields."

"Lesego, did you get that?" the Captain asked.

"Aye," the pilot answered. "Keep more than 500,000 distance."

"They have a delay in targeting their cannons due to the size of their housings. The greater the angle of adjustment, the longer the time. According to energy scans, each laser required two-hundred mega watts [200MW]. Each ship used 800MW total. A noticeable reduction in power to their propulsion indicates they use the same nuclear energy source for weapons and drive engines. There was also a large heat reading. They must use massive radiators to rid wasted heat generated by their lasers. This means the weapons require a cool-down period. The longer they fire, the longer they need to radiate heat before firing again."

"Our lasers are crystal-sourced," Elie said aloud. "No wasted heat to shunt and no loss of time or power to other systems. They have size and numbers. We have no recycle rate."

"The cruisers are continuing to move nearer," Anwar reported. "Same line. The battlewagon is following. Same line."

"After seeing our shields hold up they will close and finish us with a barrage of missiles," Elie surmised. "Genna, target the lead cruiser with the plasma cannon. You deployed the rail-gun prior to the laser attack, right?"

"I did. It suffered no damage."

"How long before the first cruiser is at one-million miles?" Elie requested.

"If they maintain their current speed, thirty hours," Anwar answered.

The most dangerous aspect of fighting in the voids of outer space is tedium. The long waits between intense moments of action can create levels of stress that become physically and mentally crippling.

"I want three complete bridge crews rotating every four hours beginning with the current end of shift" she said. "Genna, make the assignments and schedule. Kennedy, if anything, absolutely anything changes you are to alert me immediately."

The shift rotations would place the current bridge crew in place when the Galvari ships reached the critical distance.

Over ship speakers Elie said, "We are at a point of wait-and-watch. For the next twenty-four hours you will handle duties as if we were in orbit over a quiet planet. We will remain on battle watch. If you are mobile, wear IEVA. If you are seated or in your bunk, make sure your battle harness is near. Otherwise, business as usual. Captain, out."

On direct comm to medical she told Dr. Singh, "Keep the people calm who need extra help, but don't lower functionality."

Twenty-seven-and-one-half-hours later, Elie was back in the Captain's chair.

"Anwar, update," she requested.

"Galvari cruisers are one-million-three-hundred-thousand miles out. The battlewagon is three-hundred-fifty-thousand miles behind them," he responded. "We have visual available."

"Put it up," she ordered.

The forward hull operated as a hd screen when needed, turning the wall into a window complete with zoom.

A vessel floated in front of the bridge crew, who all faced the display. The darkness of space, even with a background of stars, was an excellent canvas for visibility.

The cruiser on screen was pointed directly at them. The deep V-shaped keel rose up into a slightly doomed top deck. Four forward-mounted laser cannons were the most obvious structures. Two, port and starboard, placed on the top deck and one on the starboard side and another on the port side. Long barrels connected to disc-shaped turrets setting atop large block housings.

Semi-circular push outs with ominous round openings were located several yards below the side-mount laser cannons. These were for torpedo/missile launching.

A command and control tower loomed in the rear, placed three-quarters back from the ship's nose. A half-dozen round dishes and two tall antenna poles were attached to the tower.

Guns were placed on the deck on both sides of the tower known as a 'fin' among sailors. The view did not display the dorsal surface behind the fin.

"Are those rail-guns, Genna?" Elie asked.

"I don't believe so," the avatar-First Officer replied. "Configuration more consistent with a simple projectile weapon."

"Anwar, the other cruiser," Elie said.

The second ship was pictured at an angle that revealed more dorsal details. Behind the fin sat a second structure half as tall. At the stern, two more laser cannons.

"Any ideas regarding the structure behind the conning tower?" Elie asked.

"Nothing solid, but it does remind me of the generator stations used on Zenge battleships," Genna said.

"Do you have optics on the battle wagon?" the Captain asked.

The largest Galvari vessel appeared.

"Any obvious differences from our first encounter?" she asked.

Genna called out surface assets. "Top side forward is the centrifugal cannon, two-thirds of a mile in diameter. There are thirty laser cannons placed around the hull. That is six additional. Five rail-gun emplacements encircle the command center. Which is the same. Same number of retractible plates on port and starboard hulls for torpedos-to-missiles capability."

"We're going to hope the release of the ion-disruption field will prevent the use of their battle drones," Elie said. "Anwar, give us a wide-view of the two cruisers."

She waited for everyone to see the two ships, one directly in line and the other's aspect from in front and below their position.

"Turn video off," she ordered. The hull returned to a blank wall. The command bridge was located mid-ship, surrounded a protected by bulkheads, ceilings, and floors of extremely strong composites. "Put visuals out of your head. From this moment forward there is no up or down. We act and react regardless of our position or that of the enemy. Are the Spirit fighters ready if needed?"

"Aye," Genna confirmed.

"Casey, navigation will assist all weapons targeting. You need to be prepared for attack and evasion. Chart every object within the system and make sure we do not bump into anything bigger than us."

"Aye, aye," Lt.JG Adams responded.

"Izzy, are we broadcasting to Star Fleet?"

"Yes, ma'am," the blonde at the comms station replied. "HQ, Admiral Kebede, and the *Renarde* are on the board. *Fairchild* currently four-days fourteen-hours away. The *Renarde's* ETA is twenty-seven hours."

"Genna, target the lead cruiser with the rail-gun. I want to bathe it in EMP pulses and disrupt their force field. We will follow with the plasma cannon."

"Do you want the photon cannon to target another ship?"

"Rail-gun and the plasma only. Save the photon for now," Elie ordered.

"On your mark?" the avatar asked.

"No. Anwar, the moment scans indicate either cruiser is moving a laser housing, call it out," she said. "Genna, fire on Anwar's call. Lesego, restart ion-drive at the same time and after the plasma cannon fires, move us to a position where Vista will not be in any line of fire."

The three members affirmed their orders.

On cross-ship the Captain of the PT-109 called, "Battle stations."

The Captain of the Galvari battlewagon watched the enemy ship on the screen in front of his chair. The Earth ship hung in space, slightly tilted nose down. He knew the vessel could space-fold, but no one knew how such a drive worked. The shields surrounding the small ship had withstood laser fire. If the commander had access to space-fold, why did she not use it? Did it also depend on ionic-propulsion?

"Distance?" he called.

"Currently one-million-one-hundred-fifty-three-thousand miles," the response.

"Weapons, centrifuge at full spin. How long for a long rod to reach the enemy ship?"

"At max speed of 345,000mph in the vacuum, three hours and twenty minutes."

"Fire a long rod at them," he ordered. In three hours he would know if the ship was truly dead in space. If so, a kinetic impact at the speed the rod would generate would be their end.

"The rod will impact in three-hours-thirty-four minutes," Anwar announced.

"Smart move," Elie said. "I want everyone prepared to initiate battle maneuvers in three hours, fifteen minutes.

Three hours, fifteen minutes later, the Systems officer on the battlewagon announced, "Enemy vessel is moving out of the path of the penetrator rod."

"Method?" the Captain demanded.

"Ion drive."

"GC-10 and GC-11, commence laser fire on the enemy," he ordered via comm. "Weapons, all lasers on that ship. Fire at will. I want them covered in enough beams to overpower their shields."

"They are firing EMP pulses at GC-11," Systems reported. "Their shield is down forty percent."

In a much more excited tone, the same officer followed with, "Sir, enemy has fired a particle-based weapon. Targeting GC-10."

"Specifics!" The Captain demanded.

"Plasma."

"Impossible," the commander said. "Not only is it ion-based, plasma is unstable. It would be worthless within a few miles."

"GC-10 has been hit!" the Tactical officer reported the impossible.

Systems told the Captain, "The plasma was encased within a highly magnetized toroid." The officer read the results of the scan. "At GC-10's distance, the toroid reached it in four and one-half seconds. Forward shields were superheated and collapsed. Bulkhead metal melted and the GC-10 has a major breach."

A toroid is coiled material that revolves as it superheats to become plasma. The toroid has a hole in the middle. The weapon is doubly dangerous as the plasma is capable of disintegrating a target and the extreme velocity can cause devastating results from the force generated on impact. Plasma was considered unreliable until decoded Martian files provided a means of magnetizing the toroid to maintain cohesion until impact.

"GC-10, report," the group commander ordered on ship-to-ship.

"Were trying to contain venting," the cruiser's captain responded. "Lost hull integrity. Closing section doors. Don't have a casualty report."

"Can you still fly?"

"Engines were not affected," the reply. "Lost both deck laser cannons. Port and starboard cannons available."

"All ships to non-straight line flight patterns," the Captain ordered. "Continue to move toward the enemy ship, but do not give them an easy target."

He realized attempting to zig-zag a vessel as immense as the battlewagon would not prevent being hit by particle beams moving at the speed of light.

"Tactical, concentrate our forcefield on the hull in direct line with the enemy. When helm turns, you adjust accordingly. Increase power to maximum. I want my shields as thick as possible. Pilot, increase speed by fifty percent. Comms, order the cruisers to match our speed."

"Forty-minutes to recycle the plasma cannon," Genna reported.

"Why longer than normal?" Elie requested.

"The xenon grids that were added," the response. "Slows the recycle rate."

"Targeted cruiser crippled but functioning," Anwar told the bridge. "A lot of frame damage and the two top deck laser cannons are toast. Ship still capable of maneuvering."

"Time to close quarters?" Elie asked.

Casey on Navigation answered, "If we remain on station, at their new elevated speed, five hours."

"Genna, let's test the photon cannon on the battlewagon," the Captain said.

In the simplest terms, a photon is a bundle of electromagnetic energy. It is the basic unit of light and not dangerous. Weaponized it is a beam of ionizing radiation capable of destroying life forms. Photon cannons are the means of taking those characteristics and creating a beam of electromagnetic energy that arrives on target in condensed waves of kinetic force. These force beams are particularly good against force fields generated by electromagnetic energy sources. The photon beam batters the force field, disrupting the flow of energy maintaining shield integrity. Contacting an exposed hull, the waves are strong enough to shatter a hull, releasing deadly radiation inside the ship.

"Firing photon cannon," the First Officer called. Four seconds later she reported, "Minimal effect. Their shielding is extremely dense. The impact rocked them, most likely caused things not tied down to move, but no structural damage. Fifty-minute recycle rate."

"We learned some things," Elie said. "If we use it again, we target a cruiser. I doubt they have generators as strong as the big ship."

While the bridge crews aboard the PT-109 changed, the Captain of the Galvari battlewagon received a stimulant from a medic.

He called his tactical and weapons officers to a conference at his command station.

"They have superior weapons," his weapons expert spoke the obvious. "The reinforcements made following our first encounter strengthened our shield capabilities, but the upgrade required an additional nuclear reactor. The cruisers are not large enough for such an upgrade."

"They have a method of protecting their ion generators," Tactical surmised. "They played dead, but it's obvious the ionic disruptor is inaffective."

"Time until the disruptor energy dissipates?" the Captain asked.

"The radius of influence is already greatly reduced. Total dissipation in three hours," the tactical officer answered.

"They have not used the space-fold drive, but they are fast without it," the Captain said. "Even though we outnumber them three to one and have millions more total tonnage, there isn't a clear advantage. At best we're looking at a stand-off. I intend to change that. Return to your station and prepare the drones for launch in three hours," he told the weapons controller.

To the tactical officer he said, "We have to take advantage of their weakness."

"What weakness would that be?"

"They actually care about others," he answered.

Three hours of no activity, other than the consistent zig-zag flight patterns that brought the Galvari group nearer, was interrupted by a SYNC communication.

Rachelle Paré sat in the command chair. Sean McMannus at comms informed her of the incoming signal.

"This is Captain Paré of the UEC ship *John F. Kennedy*."

"Captain Paré, I am Captain Paulius representing the Galvari Confederation. You are trespassing within Confederation space. You have engaged Confederation ships and caused many deaths. Your crimes have been reported to my superiors and many more Confederation ships have been dispatched. I am ordering you to surrender."

"I'll pass your request on to Captain Casalobos," Rachelle said. Aloud and off mic, she said, "Kennedy, Inform the Captain." To Paulius, she said, "I doubt she will surrender, Captain."

"You have no business here," he countered. "I will give you the option to depart the system."

"Captain Paulius, we have information that you intend to enslave the population of Vista. We cannot allow that," Rachelle said.

"The planet belongs to the Galvari Confederation," Paulius responded. "How we use its assets is our decision. You have no right to interfere."

Elie entered the bridge. She signaled to Rachelle to continue the conversation.

"The people of Vista might disagree," she replied.

"They don't have a say," the Galvari captain countered. "Neither do you."

Ens. Soledad Quevedo, the Argentinian systems officer, called, "Battlewagon is launching drones. Centrifugal cannon is active. The cruisers are shearing away at speed toward our flanks."

"I have command," Elie announced. "Rachelle, meet Mags and prep the fighters. Take a break after that. You have a four-hour window. Folly, add the EM to sonic and crystal force fields," she ordered Fallenitsch, acting pilot.

"Sixty drones at five-hundred-sixty-eight-thousand miles," Soledad reported. "Five hours, forty minutes out. Centrifugal cannon has launched a rod. Centrifuge is reactivated."

"Time to impact?" Elie asked.

"One hour, thirty-eight minutes if aimed at us," Soledad answered. "Target is Vista. Two-hours, fifteen-minutes until the rod reaches the atmosphere. A second projectile has been released. The battlewagon is on a course toward us, surrounded by drones."

"Cruisers?"

"Cruiser One, the damaged one, is at fifty-two relative. Cruiser Two at three-ten relative."

In simple two-dimensional terms, the battlewagon was straight in front, Cruiser One was on their left flank and Two on their right.

"Hans, set a dozen torpedoes to proximity, explosive loads," she ordered Lt.JG Hans Buchholz at the weapons console.

One hour later the shift change returned the team normally on the bridge with Elie.

"Anwar, update on the rods," she requested of her systems operator.

"Six total. Nearest 300,000 miles with approximately 50,000 miles between each one," he answered.

"Lesego?"

"Maintaining a minimum distance of 500,000 miles between us, the cruisers and the battlewagon," the pilot reported.

"Genna, fire a torpedo at the lead projectile. Let's see how the Galvari react," Elie said.

"Door open. Torpedo away," the avatar called. "Thirty-six minutes, nineteen seconds until proximity charge release," she added.

"Cruiser One has fired eight missiles," Anwar announced. Five seconds later he said, "Cruiser Two has fired another eight missiles. Twenty drones have broken away from the battlewagon. Headed our way. Battlewagon and remaining drones are reducing speed."

"There's the response," Elie said. "Overwhelm us and make us decide between the planet or us. How much time before missiles and drones arrive."

"Missiles are two hours out," Systems replied. "Drones are five hours."

"Everyone sit tight. Let's see what the torpedo does to the rod," the Captain said.

The proximity fuse detonated one-tenth of a mile in front of the extremely dense metal projectile. The high explosive charge met the high-speed rod in a flare of eerily silent reds and oranges displayed on the bridge's forward hull.

"Rod was cracked, speed reduced by ninety-percent. Trajectory altered. It will miss the planet by over a million miles," Anwar reported.

"Genna, send another torpedo at the next rod. Thereafter send one in thirty minutes and another thirty minutes later," Elie ordered. "That will eliminate four of the six before we have to relocate."

"Their torpedo altered the rod's course," the junior officer monitoring scans reported to Paulius. "It will miss the planet."

"Any reaction to the missiles launched by GC-10?" he inquired.

"Nothing. They have two hours before the missiles arrive," Systems answered. "The enemy does maintain a minimum distance of 500,000 miles from the battlewagon. They are keeping similar distance to the cruisers. Their pilot is making a lot of adjustments in order to maintain the buffer in three directions."

"The power of our lasers must concern them," he mused aloud. "Any reaction to the drone swarm?"

"No, sir," the reply.

"Pilot, take us to the planet," he ordered. "Weapons, if the enemy ship comes within 500,000 miles fire all lasers on them. Don't ask permission, just do it. I want a full range scan report on the effects if we fire lasers."

Orders delivered, the Galvari captain settled into his seat. "Your move next," he whispered to the image of the PT-109.

Two hours later the Spirit Two fighters launched from the 109.

"Casey?" Elia asked.

"Target zone at relative 51 degrees, up 8 degrees on Y axis. 2.1244728651 seconds," the navigator answered.

"Lesego, space-fold," the Captain ordered.

The 109 returned to normal space behind and above Cruiser One.

"Genna, fire EM pulse. Fire plasma," Elie ordered.

The EMP from the keel rail-gun washed across the rear of the cruiser. With shielding maximized forward, the depleted layer of force field aft was easily removed. The plasma toroid hitting the spaceship at the speed of light disintegrated the rear section of the target. The extreme velocity caused devastating results from the force generated on impact. Hulls and decks crumpled. Exposed electrical conduits sparked. High explosive ammunition, including the remaining missiles, detonated. In the oxygen venting into space the sound was nearly equal to the flume of orange, red, and yellow discharge.

"Complete destruction," Anwar reported. "No survivors, Captain."

"How are the fighters doing?" she asked.

Magpie juked left after launch. Rain soared through the void heading right. Magpie's Spirit crossed the path of the missiles fired by the doomed cruiser. When they altered course to follow she radioed Rain.

"Missile have trackers," she said

"Copy," the reply.

Rain flew toward eight enemy missiles, performed a J-turn and changed her directory by dropping five degrees.

Twenty-thousand miles away, Magpie led the powered projectiles on her tail toward the fifth dense rod hurtling toward Vista. She drove the fighter across the nose of the rod. Four of the missiles glued to her exploded when they came within proximity of the billet of metal. The combined force of the detonations pushed it aside enough to insure a planetary miss.

Rain veered left and up, eight hot rockets of destruction pushed to keep pace with the nimble ship. Utilizing Magpie's example, she passed beneath the speeding rod. Three Galvari missiles exploded with sufficient energy to alter the rod's path. Rain's on-board computer indicated the course change insufficient to make the weapon completely miss the planet.

She performed a loop, pushed the Spirit to its limit, and led the five remaining missiles back toward her target. The velocity of the large projectile had been reduced some by the impact of the triple explosions. By taking advantage of angles available in the dark void of outer space, she intersected it and flew by. Two following missiles reached the rod and detonated. Her computer indicated enough of a wobble was created to make the rod bypass Vista and fly off into open space.

Another J-turn placed Rain head on to the final two missiles. She fired her wing-mounted lasers and slammed down the collective pitch control located at the pilot's left hand. The ship dropped like a runaway elevator.

When the lasers raked the incoming rockets, both exploded. Rain's maneuver took her far from any concussive blow-back. She continued her downward pitch, bringing the fighter around to help Magpie.

While Rain chased down the Galvari projectile, Mags was busy juking around space to give her angles on the missiles tracking her. She detonated two, but the remaining two were on her tail.

"Magpie, hard up on my mark," Rain called.

Rain had pulled in behind the missiles following her wingman. When she called, "Now!" she simultaneously fired her mini laser cannons. Magpie soared up and Rain pitched down and accelerated. Both fighters were well clear when the blasts lit the darkness.

"Much appreciated," Magpie called. "I show the drones two-hours-thirty out."

"They haven't changed directions to track the 109," Rain said. "They must be targeting Vista."

"We're a million and a half miles from the planet," Magpie responded. "Unless they change speeds, it gives us twelve hours to do something about them."

"Roger that," Rain replied.

Captain Paulius watched GC-10's destruction in frustrated silence. The use of space-time to instantly outmaneuver the cruiser was a tactic no Galvari commander had ever imagined, much less faced.

"The two enemy fighters have eliminated all sixteen missiles," Scans reported. "The last two rods have been redirected away from the planet."

Paulius did not respond to the updates.

After several tense minutes in the command center, he said, "Comms, send a report to HQ detailing the loss of GC-10." Accessing the ship-to-ship channel, he contacted the captain of the GC-11. "Rejoin the battlewagon," he ordered.

The Captain's fingers tapped softly on the arms of his chair. The screen before him continued to stream the sight of the Galvari cruiser separating and floating in pieces. Intermittent sparks flashed as electrical systems died. Flashes of color were created as explosives detonated within pockets of oxygen.

He stood, turned, and told his staff, "I'm going to my cabin. Maintain current heading and speed toward Vista. If the enemy ships make any offensive moves, call me.

Otherwise, I do not want to be disturbed until we are within six hours of the planet."

The room watched their commander depart.

The 109 returned to their original position, collected the two fighters, and settled in for an anxious extended intermission.

The battlewagon's captain was back in his chair. Vista was framed on the forward screen. 680,000 miles away. The enemy ship remained 500,000 distant.

He had decided to halt the progress of the forward line of drones. They floated in space 100,000 miles in front of the huge ship. The GC-11 sat on his port flank, 50,000 miles away.

At the current distance, anyone on Vista with a decent telescope would be able to see the battlewagon lit up within the dark expanse. He wondered briefly what the reaction would be among the moderate industrial society.

"Scans, surface cities?" he asked.

"On the surface facing us are three-thousand-seven cities with 250,000 population or higher. Thirty-seven with 500,000 or more," the officer at the scanners' console reported.

"Pilot, move us to 500,000 miles above the upper atmosphere over the largest city," Paulius ordered. "Drone Control, separate the forward swarm into four groups of five. Place a squad 450,000 miles above the next four largest cities. Weapons, if the enemy ship slides in to protect the planet they will probably fall within 500,000 miles. If that happens I want every available laser cannon with line-of-sight to target that ship and fire. Have all other lasers prepared to defend if they space-fold to our stern or flank us."

He sat quietly watching as the video screen displayed the planet grow slightly larger.

"Drone Control, spread the remaining drones around us with their laser cannons facing away," he ordered. On ship-to-ship he radioed the captain of the GC-11. "Place your cruiser on my stern. Prepare for a sudden appearance by the enemy vessel. Target it with your laser cannons and blanket them."

A few minutes later, after considering the tactics displayed by the Earthers, he said, "Weapons, prepare the rail-guns. If they launch their fighters I want EMP rounds fired on them. Follow with missiles. Double the proximity detonation range."

With a strategy for offense and defense in place, he asked, "Time to 500,000 mile mark?"

"One-hour-forty-one-minutes," came the answer.

While Paulius arranged his assets, Rachelle Paré was in command of the 109.

"Kennedy, ETA on the *Renarde* and the *Fairchild*?" she asked aloud.

"*Renarde* is three-hours-fifteen-minutes," the AI answered. "*Fairchild* is eighty-six-hours-fourteen-minutes."

"They're moving," Soledad Quevedo on Systems announced.

"Screen," Rachelle ordered.

The command bridge crew watched as the Galvari Confederation ships and drones redeployed.

"Forward twenty drones are separating into four pods of five. Moving toward the planet at 25,000mph," Soledad reported. "Cruiser is moving to the battlewagon's stern. The remaining forty drones appear to be scattering to form a blanket around the battlewagon. Forward speed of 90,000mph."

"Kennedy, inform Captain Casalobos," Rachelle ordered. "Sean, contact Space Fleet assets and update everyone. It appears the Galvari captain is making his next move."

Elie replaced Rachelle in the Command Chair. Rachelle left to join Mags Moore in the ship's hangar. The 109's commander surveyed her current bridge officers. Other than Folly as pilot, she had limited time with the others.

"Sean, any contact?" she asked Sean McMannus on Comms.

"Nothing from the Galvari," he replied. "The *Renarde* is three-hours-fifteen-minutes from reaching the system. Another six-hours-twenty-minutes to reach our position. The *Fairchild* is three days away."

"Open a channel to the *Renarde*," she ordered. "*Renarde*, this is Casalobos on the 109."

"Hi, Elie, it's Storm," the Fellen replied. "Coop is in engineering with Billy. Do you want me to connect you?"

"No, I just wanted to confirm your ETA."

"We will reenter natural space in four-hours-twenty-two-minutes. Coop told Chaspi to have all three shields up. He's planning on skipping reentry at the rim and using exo-system speed to join you. We're coming straight to Vista," Storm said.

Coop's decision, though dangerous, would get the *Renarde* on site five hours sooner than expected.

"Thanks for the update, Storm," Elie said. "Tell Coop you will be entering at a time we expect to be in a full confrontation. Kennedy will stream conditions non-stop beginning in two hours. I don't want you to leave space-fold and find yourself in a crossfire."

"Gotcha. I'll make sure everybody is aware," Storm replied. "Are you okay until we arrive?"

"I have a good ship and a better crew," Elie answered. "See you in four hours. Casalobos, out."

Elie sat quietly for a few seconds before telling Soledad, "Update the ETA for the *Renarde*. Sean, please inform the crew of the new ETA and expect battle stations in two hours."

"Commence," Paulius commanded.

Eight of the battlewagon's laser cannons moved to target the 109. The same number the cruisers used earlier. Once the last one was in position, they fired. As the beams reached and washed over the enemy vessel's force fields, ten more laser cannon began to reposition. They moved excruciatingly slow in an attempt to go undetected.

The forward pods sent lasers to the surface, the energy beams, in groups of five, slammed into unsuspecting cities, killing hundreds of Vistans. The drones increased their speed.

Behind the forward wave, the remaining drones stayed in close contact with the battlewagon. Twelve arranged along the huge ship's leading edge added their smaller lasers to the eight cannons firing on the 109.

"Shield density dropping," Anwar called. He had replaced Soledad during the shift change an hour earlier.

"Lesego, begin flight pattern Kennedy One. Genna, railgun on the nearest drone squad. EMP followed by rods. It's going to be difficult with five moving targets, but try. Kennedy, I need you to assist Tactical. Set photon cannon to widest spread and fire on the next closest squad. Sweep the plasma cannon across the next group. Rain and Magpie, launch. Engage the two furthermost drone squads. We need to take their attention off the planet. Now, people!" Elie ordered.

Genna was able to destroy two drones. The three she missed broke formation, making it necessary to locate and target them as individuals. The photon spread, directed by the AI, connected with a squad. The beam of electromagnetic energy arrived on target in waves of kinetic force. The force beam was less condensed, but still affective against drone force fields generated by electromagnetic energy sources. The photon beam battered their force fields, disrupted the flow of energy maintaining shield integrity. The photon beam contacted exposed hulls, the waves strong enough to shatter hulls. The release of deadly radiation was unnecessary against autonomic drones, but it did not matter. They were disabled by the crippling force impact.

Within nanoseconds the 109's plasma cannon launched a FTL toroid against a third pod. Kennedy reduced magnetic cohesion to allow the toroid to expand. It would not retain power for long, but the drone squad was near enough that when it reached them all five were disintegrated.

On Elie's HU and at Tactical timers began on the recycle times required by the two weapons.

Rain and Magpie flew as fast as the Spirit 2 fighters could but were unable to engage before more lasers rocked the planet's surface.

Magpie reached impact range first, using her rail-gun to disable a shield before multiple rods penetrated the hull and lay waste to the systems within. While piloting the Spirit 2 to intercept the drones, she had to slip around blasts of EMP beams. Her onboard scan system warned her when the battlewagon's rail-guns cycled to a release point and provided a projected path with only seconds for her to react.

The invisible pulses missed, but made staying on target difficult.

Rain repeated the trusted rod-EMP maneuver, but not before five more rounds of superheated light destroyed structures and caused more Vistan casualties. She finished in time to assist Magpie who was avoiding inbound missiles from the battlewagon while attempting to eliminate the three drones missed by Genna.

Magpie fired a dozen small rods that were passed in space by a FTL EMP burst that caught a drone. The rods shattered the un-crewed ship, but the time needed to remain on target allowed a tracking missiles to get near enough to detonate. The fighter was tossed and lost momentum. As a second rocket closed, Rain used her lasers to slice it into two worthless pieces. Magpie recovered, located a drone seconds after it fired on a city below, and shot it down. Rain watched her six, destroying two more missiles. Working as a team, Magpie destroyed the final drone while Rain lased the last missile. During the confrontation, both pilots exhibited incredible skill by using the three-dimensional aspect of outer space to avoid EMP rounds.

"They are not following a course long enough to target the lasers," Weapons reported. "We have missed on all attempts following the initial one."

On ship-to-ship, Paulus ordered the GC-11 captain to surge forward and take a course 45° relative the enemy ship.

"That will expose your aft," the officer objected.

"Begin firing your forward laser cannons onto the planet," Paulus responded. "That will keep them occupied."

To the Weapons officer he instructed, "Prepare missiles. HE rounds with maximum proximity detonation. Place them between 140° and 200° relative the enemy ship. Launch twenty. Begin when the GC-10 clears us by fifty-thousand miles. I want that ship bracketed. Where are the extra laser cannons?"

"All ten will be in place in thirty-four minutes at the rate of movement you ordered," Weapons answered.

"I did not ask for a general answer," Paulus barked. "Where are they now?"

"Two in place, three in fifteen minutes, two in twenty-two minutes, and three in thirty-four minutes," the quick response.

"You have one priority. Connect your firing sequence to scans. If that ship falls between 60° and 120° and a disc radius of 20,000 miles D of y axis, I want every laser available to fire."

The commander turned his back on the bridge to watch the simulated action occurring between his position and Vista.

"Tactical, time until GC-11 fires on the planet?" he demanded.

"One-hour-twenty-one-minutes."

The Galvari cruiser fired two laser cannons at the planet. Unlike the drones that targeted the largest urban areas, the captain sent random beams toward the orbiting body.

Twenty guided HE missiles were launched toward the 109.

"The missiles are aimed port of our current location," Anwar reported. "Two hours away. Seems like a waste."

"Their heading takes them past us, but the planet's orbit will place it near enough their guidance systems will easily adjust," Casey on Navigation pointed out.

"We'll have to address them soon enough," Elie said. "For the moment that cruiser is the main objective. Genna, photon cannon."

"Firing," the Avatar called. Ten seconds later she reported, "Hit. Their shields held, but the impact knocked them off course."

"Massive energy spike followed by a significant reduction in ship-wide power," Anwar said.

"Plasma," Elie ordered.

"Firing," Genna called. Ten more seconds passed before she said, "Damage to the forward hull. Atmosphere venting."

"The GC-11 is badly damaged," Scans reported.

On ship-to-ship Paulus reached the stricken vessel's commander. "Can you operate?"

"Closing off sections exposed to space," he reported, his tone a combination of tension and urgency. "Nuclear power plant is unharmed but overtaxed. It will be a couple of hours before I can create shields and propulsion."

"Captain," the Scan officer interrupted. "The enemy ship has moved to a position at relative 119°."

Forgetting the problems facing the cruiser, his plan to draw the enemy into a kill zone had worked.

"Weapons, lasers targeting that disc are to fire NOW!" he commanded.

"I have a half-dozen people with concussions," Dr. Singh reported. "One broken wrist."

"Chief Nelson?" Elie asked the next department to report.

"The EM shield generator was overloaded, Captain," the chief engineer responded. "We're working on it, but it may take hours to repair and replace the damaged circuits. One water filtration system failed."

"Genna, tactical systems?"

"Photon cannon housing is unstable," the AI replied. "If we use it the loose connections could tear the hull. All other offensive capabilities available."

"Izzy, Comms?"

"STORM-HATCH collector is damaged. No way to work on it until we can EVA. Streams to Space Fleet off-line. We're no longer in contact with the *Renarde* or Admiral Kebede. I have Rain and Magpie on SYNC. Both report no contact with the Galvari since you ordered us to space-fold to escape the laser attack. Rain said the drones continue to move toward the planet. The battlewagon has ceased movement."

"Anwar, scans?" Elie requested.

"We are 931,410 miles from our original position," he said. "Galvari drones are four hours from Vistan upper atmosphere at their current speed. Twenty missiles launched by the cruiser are ninety-one minutes from impacting the planet's surface. The cruiser suffered catastrophic, but not terminal damage and appears dead in space. The Galvari battlewagon has stopped."

"Kennedy?" Elie asked.

The ship's AI responded, "Performing line maintenance on EM generator for the force field. Water filtration internal system repairs under way. Increased gravitronic output to reduce interior concussive vibrations if we are hit again. Gravity will make human activities twelve-percent more difficult. The biology research lab has a surface deformation in the glass-steel observation portal. I sealed the area in case of further damage."

"Can you boost my personal trans-comm to allow it to reach the fighters?" Elie asked.

"Done," the AI answered.

"Rain, Magpie, it's Elie. You guys alright?"

"Elie, all systems go," Rachelle responded via the universal translator and communication chip imbedded in her neck. "The Galvari are ignoring us. Is the 109 operational?"

"Injured but not crippled," Elie answered. "We have to take out the missiles. With their guidance systems the Galvari can direct them onto dense population sites and cause maximum damage. When we do those drones will react."

"At least the missiles aren't shielded," Rachelle responded. "Mags and I can take out some and avoid the drones."

"The 109 will reengage in ten minutes. Spirit targets the missiles port of center spread. The 109 will cover starboard so you don't get caught in a cross-fire," Elie said.

"And the battlewagon and cruiser?" Mags asked.

"We'll decide when they act," the 109's commander answered. "Stay sharp. Elie, out."

On ship wide Elie announced, "Prepare to return to battle." To her bridge team she said, "We're hurt but not out. Stay alert. Lesego, return us in eight minutes. Be ready to take us back to space-fold at my command."

"Captain, there's a risk of space-time sickness," the pilot reminded her.

Space-time sickness occurs when a ship transfers too often back and forth between space-fold and natural space over a short period of time. It ranges from nausea and extreme discomfort to death.

"I know. We're planning to make our second jump in less than thirty minutes. If we are forced to make a third too quickly, people are going to get sick," Elie said. "Kennedy, warn Dr. Singh. Genna, prep all torpedoes."

Elie checked the display on her command chair's left arm. Forty enemy drones, twenty missiles, a partially disabled cruiser with unknown offensive capability and a Galvari battlewagon two-point-two miles by three miles by one-half mile. A huge vessel with an unknown amount of armament beyond the obvious weapons on its hull. She had the PT-109 and two small fighters.

"Que sera," she whispered.

"The enemy ship has returned," Scans informed Paulus. "It and the two fighters are targeting the missiles with laser fire."

"Drone control, turn the swarm to the enemy ship. Lasers. Drones are to track and provide constant fire on that ship. Weapons, train laser cannon fire on the region surrounding the enemy ship. Send streams of laser beams. Now," he ordered.

On ship-to-ship he ordered the captain of the GC-11 to continue working on repairs.

"Pilot, take us closer. 60,000mph," he commanded. "Time to finish this."

Chapter Twenty-Seven

EMS2

"The 109's communications have ceased," Lt. Perry informed Admiral Patterson. "The *Renarde* is an hour from system entry."

"Continue streaming from the *Renarde*," Patterson ordered. "Time until Admiral Senait arrives?"

"Sixty-four hours and twenty-six minutes," Perry answered.

The Command and Tactical Center (C-Tac) on the thirtieth floor of Space Fleet headquarters north of Toronto was filled with tense personnel. Besides staff monitoring data streaming in from trillions of miles away, tactical analyst reviewed details of the conflict. They hoped to discern possible strategic actions the Galvari might utilize and responses they could suggest to the commanders on sight.

Standing out of the way, but with extreme interest, SF high ranking officers followed events. One non-uniformed person watched and listened.

"Anything you want to add, Dr. Trent?" Admiral Patterson asked her Director of Sciences.

"Not my area of expertise," he replied. "It does appear the 109's weapons and Captain Casalobos' tactics are superior to the Galvari's reliance on bulk and numbers."

"Except for their drones," the Admiral said. "I would sure like to know what's going on right now."

"It is probably the wrong time, but my engineers have reactivated some of the deleted files on the Wraith," he informed her.

"Hallway," she said. "Nothing I can accomplish here until we reestablish communications."

Outside of C-Tac she said, "What have you learned?"

"Not a great deal," he admitted. "The team is forced to digging for files by accessing the avatar's memories. The deeper they try, the more Cassie resists. She appears determined to keep Coop's secrets."

"Has her personality rebooted?"

"A small portion," he answered. "It's significant a hologram-based avatar, disconnected from its artificial intelligence, has enough self-awareness to resist probes."

"Are you suggesting Cassie has developed sentience?" Patterson asked.

"I'm not ready to go there yet," he replied. "But if it becomes a possibility, the continued forced extractions of data could be considered torture."

"The secrets of the Nakki are crucial to our future, Nathan. Cassie is a construct created by nerds in a lab. Even a small amount of information is valuable."

"I understand the value," he replied. "Are you prepared for Coop's reaction if Cassie is injured?"

"The Wraith is your personal property," she reminded him. "You'll be in his crosshairs. I suggest you keep the project dark and be prepared to erase any evidence if necessary."

"Destroy Cassie? What if she is sentient?"

"She's a computer generated avatar," Patterson replied. "We're not God, Nathan. We don't create life. Let me know if you have any breakthroughs."

She left him to return to C-Tac.

Alone in the hallway, he said aloud, "Eliminating her sure feels like playing God."

Chapter Twenty-Eight

Vista System

"Captain, we're using a lot of crystal energy," Nelson warned.

"Understood, Chief," Elie responded.

The two force fields left available powered via laser array and the fusion drive. With dozens of medium strength laser beams connecting from the drones firing on them and the occasional hit by the more powerful cannons on the battlewagon, the 109 was under constant strain. The force vibrations alone made it difficult to respond.

"Eight missiles killed," Anwar called. "Twelve remaining. Six drones taken out. Fifty-four remain. Battlewagon is closing."

"Captain, I have three more crew injured," Dr. Singh reported. "The rest of the crew is nearing exhaustion and under stress."

"Understood, Doctor," she replied. "Rain and Mags, it's Elie. We're under too much enemy fire to bring you in. I have to space-fold out of danger. Go to Vista. Get on the surface and find a hole. I'll contact you as soon as possible."

"Copy that," Rain responded. "Rain, out."

"Mags out," echoed in her head. "Rain, it's Mags. Are we actually bugging out?"

"We have our orders. But she didn't say we couldn't take out a couple more missiles on the way."

"Copy that. Mags, out."

The two fighters began to spiral toward the nearby planet. As they did, the six missiles within their theater took turns falling to well-aimed laser fire.

Aboard the 109 Elie was on the verge of ordering Lesego to space-fold when the trans-comm in her neck spoke to her.

"Elie, it's Coop. Looks like you need a break."

"The *Renarde* just entered natural space," Anwar announced, unable to keep the mix of excitement and relief from his voice.

"Coop, good timing. I'm taking us out of the battle. We need time for damage control. Rain and Magpie are out there. I ordered them to the surface. I plan on putting the 109 on the far side of the planet," she told him.

"Cassandra and Kennedy are communicating," he informed her. "Before you go, Billy has a present for you thanks to Ginae Tabilis."

Aboard the Galvari battlewagon the Scan officer told the Captain, "A ship has emerged on scans. It must have dropped out of space-time."

"What type of ship?" Paulus demanded.

"Unknown. It appears to be opening an exterior hatch," Scan reported.

"Weapons, continue to fire on the first ship. Increase power to lasers. Finish them. Drone control, send the swarm toward the new ship. Fire on it," Paulus ordered.

"The laser cannons are already over heating," Weapons warned. "The radiators cannot maintain the heat transfer if I increase the power."

"Do it!" Paulus yelled, the strain of battle finally breaking the commander's demeanor. The arrival of another ship pushing him over.

"A cube has been dispatched by the new ship," Scans called. "I don't believe my readings, Sir."

"What is it?" Paulus demanded.

"It reads like one of our ionic disruptors."

As the news reached the Galvari captain, the cube, built by Billy and Coop based on schematics provided by the Devee, exploded.

Fifty-four drones shut down, worthless globes of metal drifting in space.

Seconds later the 109 disappeared into space-time.

The Weapons officer did not get an alert in time to stop the firing sequence at increased output in time to abort.

"The forward laser cannons on the battlewagon have super-heated," Sky told Coop. "Catastrophic damage inside the control housings. Twenty-one of thirty are out of action."

"Coop, it's Rain. Orders?"

"Rain, I show two missiles near you. Take them out and you and Magpie go dark. Rest and wait for me or Elie to make contact. Coop, out." He did not wait on a response. He knew Rachelle and Mags would follow orders.

"Sky, lasers on the remaining six missiles. Take them down," he instructed. "Storm, use the QKD and hail the battlewagon."

"Channel is open," she said. "They're receiving but not recognizing us."

"Commanding officer of the Galvari battlewagon, this is Captain Daniel Cooper of the UEC Space Fleet corsair *Renarde*. Your drones are down. Your cruiser is badly damaged. You have Twenty-one laser cannons destroyed and your systems are overtaxed. The Orion Spiral Alliance has declared the planet of Vista as under their protection. A battle group of Space Fleet vessels will arrive in system shortly. You have the opportunity to retreat and leave this system. I suggest you take it."

Coop sat in the pilot's seat, HU display streaming data as scans swept the battlewagon and distant crippled cruiser. Chaspi sat in the co-pilot's chair watching a video representation of the huge ship on her windscreen.

The rest of the crew sat hushed in front of consoles awaiting a response.

"All forward laser cannons are unavailable," the Weapons officer told Paulus. "Nine remain operational."

"Drones unavailable," followed from a console located further away.

"Pilot," Paulus called. "Rotate the ship and bring the stern forward, facing the planet. Weapons, how many missiles do I have?"

"Forty total. Twelve nuclear, twenty high explosive, and eight chemical," the reply.

"Number of largest penetration rods?" he asked.

"Fourteen."

"Comms, channel to the new ship," he demanded, his voice as strong as his body was tense. "Captain Daniel Cooper of the UEC Space Fleet Cruiser *Renarde*. I am Captain Paulius representing the Galvari Confederation. You are trespassing within Confederation space. Surrender or face the consequences."

"Captain Paulus, I admire your tenacity," came the response. "My scans indicated you have more than 30,000 life forms aboard your ship. Do not allow pride to cost those lives, Captain. Retreat. Let the diplomats sort this out."

Paulus replied, "The Galvari do not have diplomats."

Aboard the *Renarde* Coop asked Storm, "Can you hack the internal communications system of the battlewagon?"

"Can't hack a QKD, but access to their internal comms should be simple," the Fellen computer wizard answered. "I doubt it has much of a security system." She concentrated on her console as she used space-normal (SYNC) broadcast bands to probe the battlewagon.

"There it is," she said aloud. "I can give you access until they shut the door," she told Coop. "Maybe a minute."

"Open their ship wide comms and make sure our translators are on," he ordered. He waited on her thumb's up before speaking directly to the people aboard the battlewagon.

"This is Captain Daniel Cooper of Earth. Your ship is compromised. I'm asking you to convince your commander to abort the attack on the planet and withdraw before I am forced to do more damage. I have no desire to see the crew injured or killed, but I will respond to force with greater force. Save your ship. Save your fellow crew members. To the commander I ask that you protect your crew. Withdraw."

As Coop completed his short speech, Storm slashed a finger across her throat indicating their access had been closed.

"You think they will mutiny?" Hiro asked.

"According to the data we received, most of the troops and low ranking crew are draftees from Galvari Confederation planets, but not Galvari. They may not be as dedicated to the cause. Worth a shot," Coop replied.

On the Galvari battlewagon Captain Paulus sat in his command chair. He gave no orders. He watched a hologram of the new Earth ship hover between his ship and the planet. Not on his display, but also hovering in the void, the GC-11 was close to repairing their propulsion and force fields.

He had missiles. He had penetration rods. He had a craft larger than any other in the Confederation.

The Earthers had two relatively small ships and a couple of fighters. They were faster. The weapons they used were more powerful. They disabled his drones with Galvari tech.

Captain Cooper had spoken directly to those aboard his ship, encouraging an uprising.

If he continued to push the enemy, he had no doubt he would lose. The mission to subjugate Vista was a failure, regardless of the outcome of the conflict.

"Comms, ship to ship," he ordered. "GC-11, do you have propulsion?"

"On line now," came the reply.

"Head for the wormhole gate. Return to Galvari," he commanded.

"Yes, sir. And you?"

"We will follow," he replied. "The Confederation needs the data we have collected.

"Comms, contact the UEC ship," he ordered.

When Coop answered, Paulus told him, "I am removing my ship. This is not over, Captain Cooper. Your ships have entered Galvari Confederation space and attacked Confederation ships. You have initiated a war. A response will be made."

"I hope the Galvari response is to open diplomatic channels, Captain," Coop said. "The OSA has to desire to engage in a war. As you have seen, we have QKD capability. Contact my receiver and I will transmit messages to Space Fleet headquarters."

Paulus did not respond to Coop. The huge battlewagon moved away, the injured cruiser with it.

"Sky, place range scans on automatic. Watch them until they exit the system. Set an alarm in case any odd course changes occur," Coop ordered.

"Rain, Magpie, reply," he called.

"Rain here."

"Magpie, copy."

"There are forty drones floating in space. It won't be long before the disruption dissipates and they power up. I'm sending Chaspi to join you in our fighter. Enjoy some target practice."

The two fighter pilots answered. On the *Renarde*, Chaspi rushed from the cockpit and through the command cabin on her way to the dock for Kit.

"She's excited," Cindy said as the girl from Osperantue disappeared through a hatch.

"She deserves the distraction," he said. "And it is good practice."

Chapter Twenty-Nine

Galvari

"I sent Paulus and the two ships to Callustrade 1 the GMSS-8 space station for repairs," Admiral Scendunt told Elder Valens.

"Will you replace Paulus?" Valens asked.

"No reason for that," the Admiral answered. "I've looked over all the data from the conflict with the Earth ships. Our best tactical analysts have combed through the reports. He did well. We are behind the Earthers in weapons and power technology. Not only do they have superior tech, the Captain of the ship designated PT-109 is adept at battle tactics. Twice she has beaten our best battleship. The second time we went in with options determined from the initial encounter over Devisator and two cruisers."

"Your plans?" the Elder asked.

"We are beginning to remove weapons that are useless against the Earthers. The centrifugal cannons have served us well for centuries, but against the speed and firepower of OSA ships, they only take up space. We'll keep drones, but not as many. The space saved by removing large penetration rods and drones will be used by crewed fighters."

"They have the designs for our ion disrupter," Valen said.

"Which limits our drones, but we will use power systems for the fighters from a non-ionic source," Scendunt answered. "Our priority is weapons as capable as theirs. They use photon cannons. Their tactics used for rail-guns were brilliant, delivering EMP pulses and kinetic loads in extremely destructive patterns."

"Photonic cannons are ion based," the Galvari leader said.

"They have a method of shielding them and their fighters from ion disruption. That means they can also operate indo-atmospheric," the military commander told him.

"If we go to war, we lose," Valen surmised.

"Unless you can access the technology we need to equal theirs, we lose," Scendunt agreed.

"If any of our less complacent members use this to secede from the Confederation, nothing will stop the OSA ships from entering our space to assist them. We are looking at the potential for the end of the Galvari Confederation. That is unacceptable, Admiral."

"My fleet and our troops can control wayward planets," Scendunt promised. "I would be lying to say we can defend against the Earthers."

"Then I will get the technology we need," Valens said. "The Galvari Confederation will take the next step in our evolution. Once we can protect our borders, we will expand them."

"Expansion?"

"The OSA, the Trade Worlds, and Earth, Admiral. The Galvari have been content too long. It is time to be true to our nature," Valens said.

Valens' office at the Council of Elders headquarters in the capitol of Galvari was not ornate. The leader of the Confederation preferred functional design. His desk was embedded with the latest electronics, giving him access to information and lines of communication anywhere in the region controlled by Galvari forces.

He sat behind that desk, the city of ancient structures and modern buildings on view through the window behind him. In front of him sat a woman. Unlike the Galvari, with light green pigmented skin, bald skulls, and beak-like nose, she appeared human. Her world was part of the Confederation. It orbited a yellow dwarf star and represented the edge of Galvari influence toward the galaxy's center.

"I gave Admiral Scendunt a mission to plan. What he brought back to me was unacceptable. He's a good officer, and loyal, but has no flare for subterfuge. I require your services, Chessa," he said. "I have an operation that could mean saving the Confederation."

"Who do you want dead?"

The woman seated across from the elder had short brown hair, brown eyes, and was slight of build.

"I do not need an assassin this time. I need a spy," he said. "Our best warships have been bested by a race called humans. Their planet, Earth, is a member of the Trade Alliance Worlds and a newly formed military coalition called the Orion Spiral Alliance. The unique and dangerous concern about humans is they have unlocked the secrets of the Nakki, including space-time flight."

"I've always understood space-time flight, the ability to fold space for travel, a myth," she said.

"It is no longer a myth," he assured her. "Humans have it, as well as extremely advanced weapons. If the Galvari Confederation is to survive, we need those secrets."

"I assume you want me to steal them. Any idea how I'm to accomplish such a task?"

"Your race, the Ize, look like humans. This will help when you encounter Earthers. Before that happens, you need as much intel as possible. On Devisator there is one known as Chimia Wei. She lived on Earth as a Devee spy for decades. I want you to go to Devisator and learn all you can from her," Valens said.

"Why would she talk with me?"

"You have my full backing," he answered. "She is Devee. Whatever she wants in trade, give it to her. But Chessa, do this quickly. Once you have what you need from Wei, you will need to go to Earth. The Confederation does not have unlimited time."

"Have a trader contact Chimia Wei for a meeting," she told Valens. "When it is arranged send a message to my ship, *Daybreak*. I will be on my way to Devisator. I'll expect to hear from you when I exit the wormhole."

When Chessa exited, she was replaced by Valens' fellow Elder, Colythi. The older woman was suppose to be an equal on the Council of Elders, but everyone knew Valens controlled the Council and, therefore, the Galvari Confederation.

"I want you to open diplomatic talks with the OAS," he said.

"We have never talked with our enemy," she protested. "The Galvari act."

"We need time to improve our military assets. Negotiations will provide time. You will limit the harm the OAS could do by keeping them busy avoiding a conflict. For a species with unequaled power, humans refuse to use that power to destroy their rivals. Both times our forces have been bested, they rushed to open diplomatic channels."

"They sound insane," Colythi said. "Why talk when you can rule?"

"We don't have to understand the humans, just keep them distracted while we improve our military."

"Any suggestion where to begin?"

"Give them Vista," he told her. "It's on the edge of our border, has no technological value, and would only be used for crops and labor. Captain Paulus did a great deal of damage with his laser cannons. Let the OAS waste resources on it. Make sure you get something for it. We don't want to appear docile."

"I will put a team together," she promised.

"One more thing, Colythi. Negotiate through the Devee. It is logical since we both deal with the Devee. It will slow communications. Keep in mind, your goal is to give us time."

"I understand."

Chapter Thirty

Vista System

Admiral Senait Kebede arrived in the Vista system. The newly constructed Carrier *Elliott S. Fairchild* dwarfed the 109 and the *Renarde*. With her was the PT-99, *Franklin D. Roosevelt*.

"I'm getting tired of being late to the party," Sindy said.

A meeting had been called aboard the *Fairchild*. In the large and high-tech C-Tac of the flag ship, a gathering of Earth's most famous people.

Besides Kebede, Captain Noa Tal, commanding the new Spirit Fighter Squadron was present. Captain Sam Henderson from the PT-99 joined them at the conference table. Elie Casalobos and Rachelle Paré flew in from the 109. Finally, Coop and Hiro rounded out the assembly. Seven of the ten surviving Space Fleet Rangers in one location at one time.

"I would be more than happy to take a backseat," Elie said. "As is, the 109 will have to return to EMS2 for repairs. My crew needs a break, as well."

"Much earned," Sindy said. "Your action against great er odds will be studied by future officers at the Space Fleet Academy for decades to come."

"Agreed," Sam said. "Do we have a plan for Vista?"

"Tista Korr and I will transfer to the *Fairchild*," Rachelle said. "We'll make contact and determine how best to help their cities recover from the attack."

"You're both welcome to the crew," Sindy said.

"Rys is sending Dwards and assets to assist Petra's crystal mining. We'll stay in orbit as long as needed," Coop said.

"The Battle Group will remain on site for a while," Sindy said. "We can provide personnel and supplies for Vista while covering in case the Galvari return. Meanwhile, the new

Fairchild has an officers' mess to die for. I've invited Tista, Genna, and CC to join us for dinner. Adele (the 99's avatar) will be there also. As time allows, the crew of the Renarde will be brought over, and everyone will be introduced to Noa's Spirit team. For now, let's rejoin in the mess."

After dinner, Hiro returned to the *Renarde*, capable of piloting the Spirit Two fighter the short distance. Coop went to the 109.

Elie rolled off Coop and snuggled against his side.

"Sure you wouldn't like to return to Earth with me?" she asked.

"Nothing I would like more," he said. "But I'm stuck here."

"I guess that means if I don't have weeks for sex, I need to get it all done in one night," she said.

She slid her head across his chest and down his abs, coming to rest on his thigh where she began their next session.

Rachelle and Tista met with Sindy in her office.

"Rachelle, you have already made first contact with Vistans. Use that to find out the best people and best means of making contact with the planet's leaders," Sindy said. "Tista, you were sent out here as the OAS diplomatic representative. This will be your project. Vistans have been introduced to the existence of alien life in the worst way possible. You have to make them understand not all of us are dangerous."

"I'm looking forward to it," the Ventierian said.

"The people we connected with did not know we were aliens," Rachelle said. "I have no idea how they will greet us."

"My understanding is Vista is a steam-industrial society. They have basic radio communications, but no petrol-based engines or other post-industrial inventions. Transportation is steam-driven ships, cars, blimps, and locomotives."

"They also use horse-like animals called cerv. They look similar to large deer or elk on Earth," Rachelle said.

"You'll be stepping back in time," Sindy said. "Wish I were going along."

"If I do my job right, you and others will be visiting Vista soon," Tista said.

"Begin with getting the proper clothing," Sindy said. "Our replicators have the data from the initial visit. You are required to wear METS beneath your outfits. Our mission is peaceful, but you will take no undue chances. If you feel like you are in danger, get out. If you must use lethal force is self-defense, you are authorized. Ready?"

Both women voiced their eagerness to get on with the task at hand.

Chapter Thirty-One
Vista

Rachelle set the LBJ down in a gulley created by a now dried-up creek. Grain stalks like wheat grew lush on either side, further disguising the space craft.

Rachelle and Tista worked their way up the rocky bank. Tista wore an embroidered shirt, slacks, and low-heel knee boots. Rachelle had on a pullover sweater that concealed a combat knife, jeans, and soft leather hiking boots.

"Will I stand out?" Tista asked.

"Your cocoa coloring isn't rare on Vista, but not a lot of non-pink hued Vistans live outside of the cities," Rachelle said. "If you're asking how attractive you are, then yes, you'll stand out."

At the top of the ridge Rachelle pointed north.

"The city of Anders is that way. It was one of the high population areas hit with laser pulses. Scans indicate twenty-percent of the citizenry could have died or sustained major injuries. It is a manufacturing hub. Railways and blimps transport goods. We also determined a military depot is located on the western side of the city."

Next she pointed west.

"The town of Wren is three miles in that direction. It serves the farms and ranches in the region. This is where Tamina Oison came to cull slaves."

"And you stopped them," Tista said.

"The Marines stopped them," Rachelle corrected. "Questions?"

"Did you have to land three miles away?"

The pilot did not reply. She started parting stalks instead.

Sheriff Mark Wine was completing his scan of reports on the devastation caused by beams from outer space. Military and law enforcement were on alert around the planet. Reports by astronomers agreed alien ships orbited above Vista. No one knew if more attacks were coming, but officials needed to be prepared if they did.

When the door to the jail and office opened and closed, he did not look up, saying, "I'll be with you in a moment."

A few seconds later his eyes lifted to find a dark-haired, soft brown skinned young woman watching him. The woman next to her elevated him to his feet.

"Rain," he said.

"Rain is my call sign," Rachelle said. "My name is Rachelle. Rachelle Paré. My friend is Tista Korr. Tista, this is Sheriff Mark Wine."

"Pleased to meet you, Sheriff Wine," Tista said.

"You're not commandoes," Mark said. "You're aliens, same as those who killed and kidnapped my friends. Are you responsible for attacking my world?"

"First, I'll remind you my people freed your friends," Rachelle said.

"Second, Rachelle and a ship from a planet called Earth stopped some very bad people from doing more damage to your world, including plans to land an invasion force," Tista said. "Third, that smells wonderful." She moved to hover over a kettle sitting atop a wood-burning stove.

"Local tea," he said. "Cups on the shelf. Help yourself."

While Tista made happy sounds around sips from her mug, Rachelle took a seat on a barrel-back chair facing Wine.

"We have three ships in orbit," she told him. "There are medical personnel and people ready to help in those areas targeted by the Galvari. We need to speak with the leaders of Vista to offer our assistance. I need you to tell us the best way to do that. We don't want to land ships in urban areas and panic people already traumatized."

"Where are the Galvari?"

"One of their cruisers was destroyed. The other two suffered severe damage and retreated. They have left the system. Our Battle Group will remain on site while diplomats try to get the Galvari Confederation leaders to agree to leave Vista alone."

"Why, Rachelle? Why do your people care about Vista? Where's the profit?"

"Humans can't help themselves," Tista responded to his question as she refilled her cup. She turned to face the Sheriff and took note of his questioning face. "I'm not human. I'm from the planet Ventier. Humans rescued my mother and I from a murderous species called Zenge. Zenge eat their captives, Sheriff Wine. If not for Rachelle's fellow humans, my fate would have been very different.

"Since then I have witnessed Earth defend and rescue entire civilizations from invading forces. I will admit Earth has benefited from new technology, medical advances, and other enhancements provided by the worlds they saved. I also saw them free the residents of a planet called Phisor. Phisor is similar to Vista and had nothing special to offer for humans to intervene, for many to die in battle."

"That all sounds good, but doesn't answer my question," he said.

"Guilt," Rachelle said. "Human history includes the use of slaves for cheap labor. We also feel unworthy for having joined the community of space travelers with advantages discovered and not invented. When we learned of the Galvari's mission to enslave Vista, our leaders felt compelled to intervene."

"One particular leader," Tista added. "It didn't hurt that Rachelle advocated for you. She is one of a small group of important people on Earth."

Wine sat quietly watching his visitors while he contemplated their words.

"We should start with the commander of the military garrison in Anders," he finally said.

Over the course of two weeks several things occurred. The garrison commander required convincing. A trip to the *Fairchild* on the shuttle did that. He arranged meetings with political leaders and transports with people and supplies soon descended on the affected municipalities. The citizens were forced to come to terms with not being the only intelligent life in the galaxy. The trauma mitigated by the realization Space Fleet personal were there to help.

The Galvari Confederation made contact through Ginea Tabilis on Devisator. A truce was accepted and Vista designated a neutral site. In return, the OAS agreed to venture no deeper into Confederation controlled space.

Rachelle and Mark met for lunch in the diner attached to the town of Wren's railroad depot.

"Hard to believe you're an alien," Mark said. "You look and act like a Vistan."

"I could introduce you to a couple of very attractive women from the planet Fell. They have blue skin, golden eyes, and fangs. Or perhaps a resident of Rys. Seven feet tall and covered in shaggy hair," Rachel said. "But it seems your townspeople find me odd enough."

The diner only served a few people a late lunch, but those present obviously knew who Rachelle was. More time was spent in furtive glances and hushed conversations than actually eating.

"Would you like to go somewhere else?"

"No. I'm fine," she answered. "Can't blame them. I remember how I felt when Coop made first contact. We all knew there was life beyond our planet, but to have them arrive was still a shock."

"Coop?"

"Daniel Cooper. His ship is in orbit. He was the first human to make contact with aliens. You'd like him. At his core he's a grunt."

"Grunt?"

"He was a sniper in the military. A grunt is a ground force operator."

"And he went from grunt to space explorer?"

"Long story," she told him. "Our planet has gone through a lot of changes in the last half century."

A young couple entered the diner and walked directly toward Rachelle and Mark.

"Hello, Sheriff Wine," the man said.

"Hello, Van," Mark responded. To Rachelle he said, "This is Van Muller and his wife, Callie. They have a farm north of town. How can I help you, Van?"

"We don't mean to interrupt, but we heard you were here with the lady. We want to thank you. Our daughters were among the people you saved when you were here before."

"We had to tell you how grateful we are," Callie added. "If you ever need anything, please ask. We can never repay you for what you did."

Rachelle, a private person, was moved by the words of these two people.

"It was my team that did most of the work," she said. "I'll make sure each member receives your thanks. Are the girls okay?"

"They always talk about how commandoes saved them from mean aliens," the father said. "When they learned the commandoes were actually good aliens, they were so excited it was all they could talk about."

"We won't bother you any longer," Callie said.

As the two Vistans walked away, Rachelle did something completely out of character.

"Wait," she called. She went to them and hugged each, bringing tears to the mother of the girls.

"You okay?" Mark asked on her return.

Rachelle nodded and gave her food her undivided attention.

The two enjoyed a comfortable silence until Mary Margaret Moore entered the diner.

"There you are," she said, joining them. "A guy sitting in front of your office said you'd be here. Think he said his name was Bard. You're trans-comm is off."

"My what?" he asked.

"Not you. Rachelle. We have these tiny radios implanted beneath the skin in our necks. They also translate languages and translate what we say so you understand us," Mags explained.

"If it's turned off, how have I understood you?" he asked Rachelle.

"I only cut the comm," she answered. "I wanted to have lunch in peace."

"Yeah, I get that," Mags said. "Seems like someone is always busting in and asking questions or giving orders. Is the food here good?"

"Mags, was there something I needed to hear?" Rachelle asked.

"Yep. We're bugging out in forty-eight hours," she said. "Vista is neutral ground and we've done all we can for the injured. Sindy wants us to pick up a model for the ion disruptor that's on the *Renarde* and deliver it to the *Fairchild*."

Mark stood and said, "I'll pay for lunch." He walked toward the counter that doubled as money collector for the diner and ticket purchases for the train.

Mags watched him walk away, turned to her friend, and asked, "Have you tapped him yet?"

"Mags!"

"Come on, Rachelle. I've seen how you look at the Sheriff."

Before Rachelle could respond, Mark returned.

"I have a great idea," Mags said. "Let's take Mark for a trip. LBJ to *Renarde*, then show him the *Fairchild*. You can fly him back. What about it, Sheriff? You up for a little alien abduction?"

Wine, a small town law enforcement officer on a planet where modern transportation depended on steam, handled immersion into the future well.

Meeting Sky and Storm caused him to stammer. It was a toss-up if their blue skin made him lose his breath or how beautiful and built they were. He was more controlled meeting Chaspi. Though her appearance was alien, her infectious personality put him at ease.

Contact with aliens other than humans paled beside the experience of leaving Vista aboard the shuttle and soaring into space. He experienced it from the co-pilot seat as Rachelle handled the yoke. The cockpit's steel-glass canopy provided incredible views.

The trip to the carrier included introductions to Admiral Sindy Senait and a tour of the hanger and Spirit fighters. Noa Tal acted as guide and introduced him to Sky's sister, Stacey.

"Ready for the return flight?" Rachelle asked.

"Honestly, no," he answered. "But I know I have to go. Thank you for showing me everything. You live in an amazing place."

"Funny. I think the same thing about you," she said. "To live where life isn't done at light speed seems perfect."

On the trip home, Mark was treated to the fire and light show created by re-entry.

Rachelle, on Mark's directions, landed the shuttle in the pasture behind his house. She walked with him to the front door. She stayed the night.

Chapter Thirty-Two

Devisator

"I appreciate your meeting with me, Chimia Wei," Chessa said.

"The value offered for my time was worth the deal," Wei responded. "Plus the fact you want my help to hurt the humans."

"I understand you spent many years on Earth," the agent of the Galvari said. "I also heard you attempted to learn the secrets of the Nakki and failed."

"Humans guard those secrets jealousy. I aligned myself with the wrong group. They intended to disrupt the planet's government. I planned on using the confusion to find and steal as many secrets as possible. They failed and I was forced to hide."

"Do you think the secrets can be accessed?"

"If you mean stolen, my answer is *yes*. I should have done things differently and I have had time to decide how. The most important secret is space-time travel. Concentrating on that single goal is the key."

"I agree," Chessa said, massaging the Devee's ego. "How would you go about it?"

"Assuming you can get to Earth, the first step is to hire a local fixer. I will give you the information you need to contact him," Wei said.

"Fixer?"

"A human who fixes problems for a fee. The bigger the challenge, the bigger the cost."

"Of course," the agent said. "Assuming I can reach the planet, won't I be under surveillance?"

"Probably not. Humans are incredibly trusting. If you can pass security on arrival you will, most likely, have access to most of the planet without restraint."

"Amazing. They are that stupid?"

"They consider recognizing individual freedoms as virtuous," Wei replied. "Even for alien visitors."

"How will this fixer help me steal space-time?"

"You need the help of a special human," the former Japanese Princess said. "I believe he is essential to your success. The fixer needs to supply him to you."

"One human being is the key," Chessa said with obvious disbelief.

"I need to tell you a story. It regards a unique group of humans called Space Rangers."

A day later, aboard her ship, *Daybreaker*, Chessa Marquette, assassin and spy, met with the team she assembled to steal Nakki secrets for the Galvari Confederation.

"We're looking at the biggest payday in history," she opened. "I'm not exaggerating to say Elder Valens would give us our own planet for what we are after."

"What are we after?" Kort Durrand asked. He was a former military special operator. After being kicked out of the Confederation services, he offered his skills as a killer for hire.

"Space-time travel," she said.

"Space-fold engines are a myth," Inga Stettz interjected. She was *Daybreaker's* pilot. Originally from the planet Krestor Plā, the woman could fly anything found in the Confederation.

"You are aware the Confederation's biggest and best ships were recently handed their asses?" Chessa asked.

"Rumors," Inga replied.

"The Galvari keep losses very, very secret," her boss said. "In fact, a single ship from a planet called Earth defeated a battlewagon twice. The second time it was accompanied by two cruisers. The Earth ship used space-time travel."

"No shit," Inga exclaimed. "If we had the secret of space-time travel, one planet seems a cheap price."

"How do we get it?" Arcthinical Orvid asked. He was a member of a minority race called Baggers on one of the richest planets within the Confederation. Since he was a child he was known as Clip. He was a master thief.

"I have half a plan," she said. "We won't be able to finish the second part until we're on Earth. It starts with the four of us. I picked you because you have skills needed to succeed and because we all look similar to humans. Inga will have to keep her hair over her tipped ears and Clip needs to not bring attention to his hands."

"What's wrong with my hands?" the thief asked.

"Humans have four fingers," Chessa said. "Baggers only have three."

"Three freakishly long fingers," Inga said.

Clip held his hands out, displaying digits a third longer than normal.

"True," he said. "But I can teach you to love how deep they go, dear Inga."

"Compensation for how little depth his dick can reach," Kort quipped.

"Stay on mission during meetings," Cheesa ordered. "Discuss your body parts on your own time."

"What's the first part of the plan?" Inga asked.

"By the time we enter Earth's system, we need a damn good reason for being there, and a story that will convince the authorities they can trust us on our own on the surface. A Devee traded for information on Earth, humans, and the Trade Alliance Worlds they are allied with. We're going to learn as much as we can and create a cover that's believable," she said. "It will have to be solid. Travel time from the wormhole gate to the planet is three weeks."

"How much time do we have to study the intel and build our story?" Kort asked.

"We will make six channel jumps with an overall time of forty-eight days from now to final gate," she answered. "We'll meet in twenty-four hours to compare notes and discuss ideas. I brought the three of you along because you are the best at what you do and all of you are smart. Prove me right."

Inga interrupted Chessa in the ship's virtual-reality studio (VRS). It was more a small room, but studio sounded cool. The team leader was using the VRS to practice shooting with both hands.

"Kinetic pistols?" Inga asked.

"Always," the answer. "A kinetic weapon is reliable, weighs less, and is more accurate than lasers or rail-guns."

"Limited range," the pilot argued.

"I work up close. I prefer to verify a hit. Did you need me?"

"Quick question. Why only four of us? Seems like a pitiful number to take on an entire planet."

"Stealing the space-time drive isn't a mission where force wins. We need to be quick and trust our teammates. The more people involved, the more opportunities for mistakes. Four of us will also be less likely to raise suspicions."

"Especially if two are female."

"Males have underestimated us before, Inga," Chessa said.

"More than a few are missing body parts because of it," the pilot quipped. "When are you planning on telling us about the humans who are helping us? Do you trust them?"

"When we have a solid plan to get us past security and freedom to travel on the surface, I'll give everyone what you need to know about our human team members. As to trusting them . . . no. Using them to get the prize . . . yes."

"Fair enough. I'll let you get back to target practice."

Inga decided to head for the control center and check systems. There was no reason since any slight abnormality would trigger an alert to her and Chessa. It would give her an excuse to move around.

Kort called to her as she passed the crew lounge and mess, his personal favorite hangout.

"You've known Chessa a while," he said. "What's her story?"

"No one knows a lot about her," Inga answered. "I know she grew up on Callustrade 1."

"Callustrade 1 is a planet-wide Galvari military center," Kort said. "People don't grow up there. Kids don't live there."

"You asked, I answered," Inga retorted and continued on to the control center.

Comfortably seated in the pilot's chair, she thought about projecting the forward external optics onto the VR screen. Since wormhole channels were endless tunnels of grey she could watch the blank screen for the same entertainment value.

Her thoughts turned to *Daybreaker*. She was not a pretty ship, nor ugly. Sleek design, but not deadly like a fighter or flashy like a space yacht. Her hull was dark grey, currently with some red highlights to break the monotone. Rear vents on the left vented gases from the wormhole generator. Matching vents on the right expelled heat from the ionic-propulsion engines. She looked like she could make seventy or eighty-thousand mph. With a disguised fusion generator, two-hundred-thousand mph was possible.

Nothing about *Daybreaker* made you look twice or remember her for long. What was special was how she was designed and constructed to hide whatever Chessa wanted hidden. Like the fusion generator, the ship held a number of secrets. Inga was the pilot for five years and knew there were mysteries known only to Chessa.

Daybreaker had one level dedicated to the crew and comforts like the lounge, VRS, gym, and kitchen. Another was practical, holding engine controls, engineering, computer arrays, and the pilot station she sat in. The third, and final level was storage, engine compartment, gravity control, power generators, environmental, and external access hatches.

Simple, straightforward, and like her current crew, deceptive.

Chapter Thirty-Three

Solar System

"Unknown ship, this is Space Fleet Control on the Mars space station. Identify yourself and state your reason for entering the solar system."

"The hale came over the QKD," Inga told Chessa. "It will be here via SYNC soon. Are we committed?"

Chessa sat beside the pilot in the control room. Kort and Clip stood behind them.

"We are committed," she said. "Wait for the SYNC message and reply the same way. I don't want any potential relationship to the Galvari to raise an alert."

When the time came Inga replied, "This is the *Daybreaker*. We are a civilian carrier, but we are not here to trade. Our planet of origin is Nestor in the Cronus system. We are a non-aligned world. When on a trade mission to Osperantue, we learned about your world. We would like to request permission for two couples to honeymoon on Earth. Over."

"I cannot believe I agreed to this scenario," Kort complained.

After what seemed an extreme amount of time, SFC-Mars responded.

"Welcome and congratulations. Please confirm your purpose is not trade, but honeymoon."

"That's right, Control," Inga said.

"*Daybreaker*, what is your max speed?"

"82,000mph."

"You are aware it will require thirty-two days for you to reach Earth?"

"We are aware," Inga responded. "This was our only opportunity to visit your planet. We are prepared for the trip."

The time required between messages passed. Twice the time needed for SYNC to cover the distance also went by. The four aboard the grey ship worried the story they concocted was too unbelievable.

"*Daybreaker*, this is Commander Henricks. I am the command officer for Space Fleet's shuttle service on the Earth-Moon Space Station, EMS2. We have been developing a system to transport visiting ships between EMS2 and the wormhole gate utilizing space-fold technology. This would reduce your travel time from thirty-two days to thirteen hours. Would you be interested in being our initial customer?"

The four had a hurried discussion about this unexpected development. Chessa made a final decision and Inga responded.

"Commander, could you explain how your system works, whether it is safe, and our cost?"

"*Daybreaker*, we have constructed a barge with space-fold drive. The barge pilot places the dorsal surface beneath your keel and connects your ship with mag-locks. Once you are connected, when the barge enters space-time your ship is covered by the same bubble. We have performed over fifty tests with Space Fleet ships without a single problem. We have not set service fees yet. I would like to offer it to you as a wedding gift."

"Henna slice my heart and bury me in Tarash," Clip said. "I cannot believe this. A wedding gift?"

"I told you the honeymoon story would work," Inga said.

"This isn't just working," Clip said. "This is completely strange. It has to be a trap."

"No," Chessa responded. "Everything we've studied about humans makes me believe their offer is real. Inga, agree."

"Commander, we accept your gracious gift."

"*Daybreaker*, UEC Space Fleet Barge *Savannah,* under the command of Pilot Tastinitch, will arrive your location in fifteen-hours-twelve-minutes. Understand you are required to remain inside your ship at all times. Henricks, out."

"Captain Stettz, the mag-locks have your ship secured to the barge," the pilot of the *Savannah* reported. "Other than engines, you can use all other systems during transport. You will be unable to use communications while in space-fold. My next contact will come after we return to natural space. Tastinitch, out."

"We are going to be escorted to Earth by riding a flying platform with space-fold capability piloted by a Bosine. Unbelievable," Clip said.

"Not as unbelievable as pretending to be married to you," Inga said.

"Speaking of that, when are we consummating our marriage?" he asked.

"Never," she answered.

"No more jokes," Chessa warned. "We have twelve hours to get our stories solid and convince the authorities Kort and I, and you two are married."

"We're in space-fold," Inga announced.

"Truth? I didn't feel anything," Clip said.

"Welcome to EMS2," Tastinitch said. "Mag-locks have retracted. EMS2 Control will take over now and direct you to your docking station. Tastinitch out."

The ensign assigned *Daybreaker* radioed instruction and provided directions for Inga to dock the ship to one of the arms extending from the hub of the massive space station.

A security team was allowed aboard to inspect the alien ship. The two hour sweep of the vessel ended with instructions for the crew to relax until a Space Force representative contacted them.

"If I understand them correctly, Space Fleet handles security in outer space and Space Force is the military force in charge of security between the space station and the planet. A different group enforces the law on the surface," Chessa said.

"Bureaucracy," Kort said. "No matter where you go in the galaxy you have to deal with bureaucrats."

"So we deal," Chessa said. "Be nice. We're honeymooners. Stay relaxed."

Four hours after their ship's inspection they were contacted.

"Captain Stettz, I am Lt. Barbara Wajda of Space Fleet. I need to confirm some information. This won't take long."

Following an hour of back and forth, Lt. Wajda said, "I have everything I need. When you are ready to depart your ship, contact EMS2 Command. You must be escorted to our medical center for a health check. Once you have passed decontamination an escort will be assigned. They will provide you with a map of the station and point out locations with public access. They will also explain protocols for visiting the surface."

The four spies met in the ship's lounge.

"Final chance to back out of this job," Chessa said.

"The major problem, besides the obvious, is our means of escape is tethered to a military space station. We also need their help to return to the wormhole, or take the chance without space-fold and give them time to discover we've stolen their secrets," Kort noted.

"We knew we were going to be at high risk," Chessa replied. "Now that you see how deep we've made it, you can appreciate how crucial it is we keep a low profile. This will not be a grab and run, and we can't fight our way out."

"We locate plans for a space-fold drive, we get to them without alerting the authorities, we make copies and extradite ourselves with no alarms going off. Once we accomplish our goal, we return to our ship, request transport to the wormhole gate, and leave the system before anyone knows anything," Clip said.

"Sounds good to me," Inga said. "What's next?"

"We recon the station," Chessa said. "There's a good chance they have plans here. Let's check out the security. Inga, call for our escort."

They met later.

"This place is huge," Clip said. "And three-quarters of it is off limits."

"Security is impressive," Kort added. "It would take a small army to breach the high security areas."

"The food is good," Inga said. "What? I'm tired of replicated crap made from goo. That place the escort took us to was great."

"It did help us with getting credits we can use here and on the surface," Chessa said. "Wei was right about gemstones. They were the perfect trade item."

"So we head for the surface?" Kort asked.

"The fixer Wei told me about is the best option," Chessa said. "We need to go to a place called Vegas."

Chapter Thirty-Three

Elie was with Pam Patterson and Nathan Trent. They met in Trent's office in the Fleet Engineering section of EMS2.

"Four weeks," Trent said. "Minimum."

"There's a lot of repairs," Pam added. "Plus updates."

"She's taken a lot of abuse," Elie said. "Four weeks isn't asking too much. I'll rotate crews and make sure everyone gets a two-week vacation. Is there a plan for when the 109 is space-ready?"

"Not yet," the Fleet Admiral said. "We're encouraged by the fact the Galvari initiated talks. Tasha Korr and Aya Ishihara are considering going to Devisator to improve communications."

"Speaking of Tasha, what's happening with Tista?" Elie asked.

"She did a professional job on Vista," Pam said. "She and Rachelle are still aboard the *Fairchild*. The Battle Group arrive in system in two days."

"Hard to believe the majority of Space Fleet's ships will be together in the solar system at once," Elie said. "Is the *Renarde* coming?"

"Coop is remaining in orbit over Vista for a few days to make sure the Galvari are honest regarding a truce. I understand Sky, Storm, and Bill Elkman are building a communications array for the government. They will be able to reach us if they are attacked again. Once that's done they are headed back to the planet that showed promise for black crystals."

"Space Fleet engineers are going to be busy," Trent said. "Besides maintenance schedules and up-fits, everyone wants to visit the *Fairchild*. The construction practices of the Aster system ship builders, mixed with our technology, has produced a magnificent space ship."

"The group will visit MSD before coming here," Pam said. "Some of the crew members and Marines have been off world for over a year. Earth is going to see a lot of home comings."

"What about you, Elie? Plans?" Trent asked.

"I'm going to take a week and hike Spain," she answered. "I haven't visited in much too long. Then the Bahamas. Genna and Mags will join me there."

"Good for you," Pam said. "Speaking of vacations, believe it or not we have visitors from a planet called Nestor. They came to Earth on their honeymoon."

"¿Verdad?"

"We brought their ship to port with the new barge project," Pam said. "They're docked in the Traders' Wing. Nice little ship."

"Things are changing," Elie said. "I better return to the 109 and work out shore leave rotations."

"Trent and I have other business," Pam said. "Glad you're home, Elie."

With Elie gone, Pam asked her Director of Sciences, "Where are you with Cassie?"

"Making progress," he said. "It's actually good news the avatar's security protocols are resisting us."

"How could your avatar on your ship, designed and programmed by your nerds, resist you?" she asked.

"The AI and avatar were designed to act as compliments to the captain. Originally that was suppose to be me. I wanted systems that learned how I thought and could make decisions equivalent to what I would do."

"But you gave the Wraith to Coop so he could escape going to prison," she said.

"The AI, now reassigned to the *Renarde*, and the avatar, Cassie, imprinted on him."

"A stubborn, untrusting individual with problems dealing with authority," Pam said.

"You get the picture. The bad news is we have to break through Cassie's reluctance to give up Coop's secrets. The good news is she is blocking us. It means our reboots are restoring the personality traits wiped when the ship returned to Earth. With those traits, her other memories should also return."

"Including the Nakki secrets given to Coop by the pirates who shanghaied him. Stay on it, Nathan. If the secrets pulled from the

Martian hangar have taken us this far, who knows what we might accomplish with the information stored inside Cassie's networks."

Ninety parsecs distant, or two-hundred-ninety light years, Coop sat in the pilot's seat of the *Renarde*. His feet were crossed atop the control console in a relaxed position anyone who knew him would recognize. It was night cycle aboard the ship and he was the only one not in bed.

The screen on the forward hull displayed space looking away from Vista. Besides the wall of stars glowing differently depending on their size and distance, a blue and purple gas cloud streaked across the right side of his vision. Within flashes of light made him think of tropical lightning, hidden within dark clouds.

"Coop?"

"Yes, Cassandra," he responded to the AI.

"I think something is wrong with Cassie."

"You can feel Cassie out here . . . this far?"

"I think so. It's odd."

"What time is it in Indianapolis?"

"Fifteen-hundred CST."

"Call Nathan Trent."

"I'm redirecting to EMS2," she informed him after a few minutes.

"Coop? It's Nathan," came a far-distant voice. "Is there a problem?"

"Just bored," Coop lied to his friend. "Thought I would check on the progress with Cassie."

"Nothing new. I have a crew working on her software and another crew managing the hardware aboard the Wraith. Everyone is trying to be careful. We don't want any further damage done. It takes time."

"Okay. Thanks for the update. We'll talk later."

"He's neither lying nor telling the truth," Cassandra said after the connection ended.

"What is she feeling?"

"Something impossible for an artificial intelligence or related constructs to experience."

"Stop being evasive, Cassandra. What is she feeling?"

"Fear."

At Trent Industries in Indianapolis, inside a hangar converted to an electronic laboratory, the Wraith ship sat in the center of a halo of lights. Inside the ship, seated at the computer and tactical operations console located in the modest cabin, software designer Tyler Porterhouse rubbed his fingers across his brow.

"You are giving me such a headache," he said.

Tyler was the tech who originally added a code to the avatar program that created a sexy, gaming style personality. He did it to entertain himself while completing the multi-layer codes necessary to give the avatar the ability to evolve while remaining coupled to the AI. He intended to erase the protocol before the ship was turned over to its owner. Nathan Trent took possession earlier than expected, and Daniel Cooper flew it to space before he could remotely access the system.

"If I had any clue I was going to have to work this hard, I never would have trashed your personality segments when you showed back up on Earth."

Tyler turned a dial on a heads up (HU) display hovering above the console.

A holographic image of a blonde woman in a military-style tactical outfit appeared in the center of the cabin.

"You look like you could kick ass," he told her. "Now I need to recover those memories from the trash and find any hidden files stored with them. Don't worry, Beautiful. Once I get what the boss needs, I'll delete your whole program so completely, no one will ever recover a single data point."

On the *Renarde,* Coop asked the AI, "Time required to reach Earth?"

"Eighty-eight days, three-hours," the reply.

"Cassandra, I need to talk to someone on Earth. I need you to locate them, initiate contact, and remove any record from the log."

"Is this for Cassie?"

"Yes."

"Who do I locate?"

Chapter Thirty-Four

Las Vegas

"This place is incredible," Clip said.

The four Galvari agents sat at a table in one of the posh lounges at Cesar's Palace. A Space Force shuttle delivered them to a port on the edge of Las Vegas.

"I didn't expect Earth to be so . . . nice," Inga said.

"Stay focused," Chessa said. "We have a job. We're only pretending to be on vacation."

"When are we suppose to meet our contact?" Kort asked.

"His return message said to be here at this time and he would find us," Chessa answered.

"How is he suppose to do that?" Kort asked.

"Because you don't fit in," a handsome man in a perfectly cut suit answered. He joined them without asking permission.

"How so?" Chessa asked.

"Your choice of clothing mainly," he said. "The cute young lady is in an attractive sweater shirt totally inappropriate for the Vegas heat. The tall gentleman with the odd hands is close with the blue suit, t-shirt, and white tennis shoes. Unfortunately it's ten years out of date. The thick chested fellow simply looks like he should be kicking ass, not enjoy his honeymoon. And finally, the tall lady in the stylish double-breasted pants suit. No way in hell you would be married to any of the others."

"That was pretty specific," Chessa said. "Anything else?"

"You're in Las Vegas, in a bar, and none of you have ordered a drink in the half-hour you've been here," he said.

"If we continue our relationship, we'll try to do better," Chessa said.

"Not totally your fault," he responded. "Clothes stores on EMS2 are not known for style. I'm Myron Sweetwell. I understand Wei Zhou Nanke recommended me."

"Chimia Wei called you a 'fixer.' She indicated you could provide help for a fee," Chessa said.

"Fee is determined by the scope of the work required," he said. "Tell me the job, I'll determine the cost."

Chessa outlined the mission.

Sweetwell sat quietly after she finished. After a full minute he told her, "I don't think you have enough to pay for that."

Sweetwell moved the meeting to a room he reserved.

"You want to free Benny Claflin from prison so he can help you break into a secure Space Fleet area and steal plans for a space-fold drive. Of course, you'll also need to find and procure a special crystal if you intend to build your own space-fold drive," he said.

"We can get a crystal," Kort said.

"Not one cut specifically for the laser array," he replied. "They are kept as secure as any other Martian secret."

"Martian secret?" Inga asked.

"Nakki secret," he corrected. "Most humans still call the technology found on Mars as Martian. Only recently have some of us learned about the Nakki."

"We have these," Chessa said. She handed Sweetwell a satchel filled with alien gemstones.

"I recognize most of these," he said.

"There are more on my ship," she told him.

"These will be sufficient," he said, placing the satchel on the floor. "We need to make a plan. Let's start with names and what you bring to the show."

"Chessa," Chessa began, and by doing so signaled the others to comply. "I'm a spy and assassin. I escaped my home world twenty-one years ago. Skills I learned as a child gave me few options for survival in the Galvari Confederation. After five years of successfully completing orders, I was contacted by one of the Galvari Elders. Since that time I have completed sanctioned and non-sanctioned jobs."

"Weapon of choice?" he asked.

"Whatever gets the job done," she answered.

"Okay, big man. What's your story?" Sweetwell asked Kort.

"My name is Kort. Ex-military," Kort responded. "Galvari Special Service. Insertion and elimination of insurgents. Explosives expert. Prefer close quarter weapons."

"You?" he asked Clip.

"Arcthinical, but you can call me Clip. Thief," Clip answered without hesitation. "I can get into any place, take what I want, and get out. Eleven years, no arrests."

"Okay, cutie. Your story."

"I was bought from my family on Krestor Plā and taken to SS-7, the space station over the planet Waterstein. I was a whore until I met Chessa seven years ago. She bought me and since then has taught me to pilot all types of ships and how to kill. I am proficient at both. My name is Inga. Call me cutie again and I'll give you a personal demonstration."

"A demonstration of your skill as a killer or as a whore?" Sweetwell asked. He watched her without making any expression.

Inga stared back, finally smiling and saying, "I like him."

"What about you, Myron Sweetwell?" Chessa asked.

"My parents were both military," he said. "They were stationed in Japan. I practiced to be a ninja. A trained assassin who specializes in edged weapons, but is also proficient with whatever's needed. When I got older I took jobs as private security for the rich and famous. I used the opportunity to meet and make friends with a wide variety of influential people. I met Wei while working for a media mogul who was a member of a group of powerful people intent on destroying Earth's central government."

"How'd that go?" Chessa asked.

"Horribly," he answered. "We were discovered and surrounded by the military. I managed to get Princess Wei to her private shuttle and escape."

"Is our mission possible?" Chessa asked.

"Anything is possible," he replied. "Getting a Space Ranger on your team is a smart move. Did Wei explain who the Space Rangers are?"

"Some," she replied. "Special humans reengineered to be faster and stronger than normal."

"That's an understatement," he said. "They are meta-humans. Six times stronger and twice as fast. They can resist disease and regenerate. They recover quickly from exertion and self-heal if wounded or injured. They also have extended lifespans, though no one knows how long. Just as important, each one brings valuable skills to the show. They were all elite military special operators. Those skills have gotten better and been expanded.

"The captain of the ship that defeated the Galvari battlewagon, twice, Elie Casalobos, is a Space Ranger," he finished.

"And Benny Claflin?"

"Ex-British Special Forces and was head of security for the space station orbiting Mars."

"Why is he in prison?"

"He was a member of the group trying to overthrow the government," Sweetwell answered. "He will be motivated to hurt the UEC and is aware of Space Fleet security protocols."

"Where is he?"

"Maximum security prison in New Mexico, about six-hundred miles from here."

"Can he be freed?"

"If you could put together a team with an assassin, muscle, somebody good with opening locks, an attractive distraction, and a ninja, you might have a chance."

The UEC Detention Center twenty-five miles east of Albuquerque, New Mexico was built after the pandemic. The modern facility held high value targets from around the world. Currently thirty-one criminals were housed in the three story modern building.

Five miles off I-40, the facility was surrounded by open arid flatland. The first floor held administration offices. The second floor was prisoner services like dining hall, gym, library, kitchen and laundry. The third floor contained fifty private cells, secure room for meetings, four conjugal studios, guard station and lounge.

The outdoor areas were surrounded by laser fences.

Myron pulled the multi-purpose transport into a battery recharge and convenience center's long-term parking for haulers and vacationers needing a place for a reprieve from the road. It was on the exit before the off ramp for the road leading to the prison.

The fixer exited the driver's seat and joined the others in the cabin. They occupied bench seats and a small sofa.

"Any final questions?" he asked.

"Seems odd to attempt a jailbreak this time of day," Clip said. "They will be at full force."

"It will be lunchtime," Myron said. "Guards will be less alert and concentrated in the dining room or their own lounge."

"Inga will be on her own," Chessa said.

"She's our insider," he said.

"I'll be fine," she added. "Let's go."

A trailer behind the transport held four motorcycles. Stripped down models with multi-terrain tires and powerful engines. Working together, they had them off in minutes.

"Inga, off you go," Myron said. The female alien from Krestor Plā straddled the machine she only had one day of practice on, turned it toward the road, and roared out of the lot.

"Kort, you're back-up," he said to the big man. "Monitor communications and be ready to get us out. If things go smoothly, you should have it easy. If things go sideways, you have the firepower to cover our escape."

"Chessa and Clip, you have to get to the utility tunnel servicing the prison. Nearest maintenance access is three miles outside the perimeter. You will have all types of locks and security systems to bypass. Practice went well, but you better expect the real thing to have differences. The intel I bought is six-months old."

"I can handle anything we find," Clip assured him.

"We'll be on site on time," Chessa promised. "You?"

"I have the easiest job," he said. "All I have to do is walk in."

Inga parked her motorcycle in a line of similar vehicles in the UEC New Mexico Correction Facility's parking lot. She headed for the first guard station between the lot and the administrative floor. She was under intense observation quickly. Not because she aroused suspicion. The attractive redhead with exotic features wore a salmon colored off the shoulder top, tied in a bow to expose flat abs. It was unbuttoned to show off her cleavage, and threatened to reveal a nice pair of boobs. Blue jeans formed to her hips and legs. She walked like a professional model with attitude.

At the guard station she produced ID.

"Erica Cruz," she said. "Conjugal visit with Alejandro Ramos."

The two guards opened the gate and directed her to the next security checkpoint.

"Who says crime doesn't pay?" one asked the other.

Ten minutes later, Myron parked his cycle and approached the same guards.

"Stephen Reagan," he told them. "I have an appointment to deliver legal paperwork to Benedict Claflin."

After physically checking his briefcase and passing him through scanners, Myron followed in Erica's footsteps.

"Not nearly as nice a scan as the girl's," a guard said.

Three miles away and a quarter mile from a dry gulley where they hid their cycles, Clip bypassed an electronic lock after deactivating a security alert.

He opened the hatch and said, "After you," to Chessa.

Chapter Thirty-Five

Indianapolis

Sandra Campos Valverde sat in a chair in front of a battered metal table being used as a desk. On the other side sat Dr. Manny Hernandez, the top engineer at Trent Industries.

"How can I help the UEC Marshals?" he asked.

"I used my credentials to get to you, Dr. Hernandez. I'm here because Daniel Cooper contacted me and asked a favor," she admitted.

The engineer studied the young woman as if reading a schematic. She was mid to late twenties with curly blonde hair that cascaded across her shoulders. Brown eyes met his, never wavering. She was attractive, but not beautiful. Her gold nose ring, simple as it was, gave her a dangerous appearance. Or maybe that was the vibe she gave off.

"Daniel Cooper is half way across the galaxy," he said.

"Which should tell you how important my visit is," she responded. "It required some effort on his part to reach me."

"Why you?"

"My grandmother was Alessandra Campos. Do you know of her?"

"Yes. She was a Space Ranger. She died helping Coop on a mission."

"My name is Cam. I call Coop 'Uncle Daniel'. He thought contacting you required someone trustworthy. Family."

"What do you need, Señorita Campos?"

"The truth about the avatar, Cassie."

"The Wraith project is kept in a secure facility," he told her. "I am not involved with the program. What do you mean by *truth*?"

"Daniel believes more is being done than an attempt to recover the avatar's evolved personality deleted by one of your software developers. He believes Dr. Trent is trying to restore data he deleted and cleansed. Data given to him regarding the Nakki."

"You want me to find out if Coop's suspicions are warranted. You are asking me to choose between a friend and my employer."

"Yes," she acknowledged.

"Okay," he replied. "There's coffee and tea on the side table. This may take a while."

The engineer opened a holographic display that hovered in the air between them. He stood for easier access to the display of the Trent Industries campus. Cam watched as he tapped a square, turning it into a building that replaced the map. Manny spun the virtual hangar to reveal a door. He tapped it. Nothing happened. He tried again.

"My system should have clearance for everything short of Nathan's office," he said.

"Can you bypass security?"

"I'm an engineer, not a computer expert."

"May I?"

He nodded. Cam stood and slowly turned the building. Returning to the door, she enlarged the view until a security entry pad dominated the hologram. Manny watched with interest as Cam played with the keypad. Next she enlarged the display until the two people seemed to move between gaps in the keyboard and into the circuitry behind the pad. The Deputy Marshal followed one wire to a junction, tapped the spot it interconnected with another wire, and code appeared.

"What is that?" Manny asked.

"Security footage from inside the building feeds through here to data storage," she answered, maintaining her concentration on the code. "I'm trying to find a specific source," she told him as she manipulated the code. Like an archeologist deciphering hieroglyphics, Cam read the code, searching for clues.

After ten minutes of following lines of code to sources, she found the link she wanted. The hologram changed to display the interior of the wraith. A man in short white coat and jeans worked at a console. Standing nearby, a pretty young woman with a blonde ponytail. She wore a tight black t-shirt that accentuated her bosoms and small waist. Matching black panties were her only other clothing.

"Might as well enjoy the company while I'm stuck here," the man said. "At least I can access your appearance logs. Not too much longer and I'll figure out where those fucking Nakki files are hidden."

"Stop replay," Cam said, freezing the virtual display. "Time stamp sets this recording at five days ago. Do you know who we're looking at?"

"The woman is Cassie, the ship's organic holo-avatar. The man is Tyler Porterhouse, one of the company's top software technicians."

"I've never heard of an *organic* holo-avatar," she said.

"Cassie is the one and only," he said. He manipulated the display so only her head and shoulders appeared. "It was something Nathan dreamed up and some of the younger members from different departments were tasked with creating. Together they actualized his concept.

"Basically the engineers constructed a unit that combined the elements of a 3-d printer and an organ transplant printer, then melded it with a hologram projector. The system employed dense ion particles to build a person. Computer engineers married the holo-gram's program to the ship's artificial intelligence operating system. Finally software techs coded the new avatar's personality and conduct profiles. The whole thing was designed to imprint on the ship's captain and learn how to evolve to best serve their needs."

"Serve their needs?"

"It was never meant to include sexual needs," Manny replied. "The purpose was to provide company during extended space travel while equipping the AI with an avatar for real-world contact. As I understand it, Porterhouse added code segments that extended the personality to include characteristics from his gamer obsession . . . sexually charged traits. He intended to erase those segments before signing off on the system, but Nathan took ownership early."

"Dr. Trent gave the Wraith to Uncle Daniel and the avatar imprinted on him," Cam surmised. She stared at Cassie's visage.

"When the ship returned to Earth, Porterhouse deleted the questionable codes remotely. Coop turned the Wraith over to Nathan. The AI was transferred to the *Renarde* and techs were assigned to attempt to recover the avatar's lost personality."

"Then why is he looking for *fucking Nakki files*?"

"I don't know," he admitted.

"I have a more important question."

"What?"

She pointed at the avatar's image and asked, "Why does it look like she's crying?"

Manny ordered food delivered and made more coffee. The two settled in and scanned virtual activity inside the wraith over the past few weeks.

As morning neared, they stopped to talk.

"Nathan is trying to access the Nakki secrets Coop brought back from his trip to the far side of the galaxy. Porterhouse is searching through Cassie's brain looking for the data. Hamed Attalan, a known criminal, is assisting him. They hope that when it was originally stored with the AI, she also had access."

"When Uncle Daniel erased and bleached the AI files, he didn't think about Cassie."

"They could be right."

"Maybe, but the avatar's data source coding is almost as complex as a person's brain," Cam said. "They've recovered a great deal of the personality that was deleted, but haven't located the Nakki memories."

"I'm not a software expert, but it seems to me they should have located them by now, if they exist," Manny said.

"She's fighting," the Brazilian special operator and new UEC Deputy Marshal said. "If you watch, you can tell."

"If she's resisting, they must be there. Porterhouse will keep searching until he can turn them over to Nathan"

"Which presents a problem."

"¿Que?" he asked.

"If they leave her recovered and return the Wraith to Uncle Daniel, she'll tell him what they did."

"So Porterhouse will delete her personality again to cover up, otherwise Coop would go ballistic. What do you plan to do?"
"First, tell him what's happening," she replied. "Second, steal the wraith."

Chapter Thirty-Six

"So you are this month's present from mi amigos," Alejandro Ramos said on entering the conjugal studio.

Inga sauntered across the concrete floor in a sensually permeated walk. On reaching Ramos she reached up and placed her hands on either side of his neck, as if to pull him into a kiss. And she squeezed.

She pinched nerves. Ramos was frozen by the shot of pain followed by neural paralysis. His mouth opened in silent protest. His eyes widened in shock, followed by fear, then rolled up under his lids. Inga let go as the unconscious felon collapsed to the hard floor.

A quick look at the antique watch Myron had given her earlier showed she was ahead of schedule.

Myron Tyler looked at the century old Rolex on his wrist when Benny Claflin was escorted into the private room set up for sanctioned visits.

Two guards entered with the shackled Space Ranger. They released the electrified cuffs binding his wrists and ankles. While one guard stood apart with a laser pistol trained on Claflin, the other had him sit behind a table bolted to the floor. Once seated, his wrists were electronically locked down. He could move them, but more than twelve inches would send a painful shock. More than fifteen inches and the electrical charge would incapacitate him, even if he was enhanced.

When the guards departed, Benny said, "Hello, Sweetwell. Didn't expect to see you. Montack after something?"

"I'm afraid Mr. Montack was arrested in Saudi Arabia," he replied. "I'm here for another employer."

"And what does this person want?"

"We need your services to steal something. In return, I break you out of here, get you off the planet, and you get to travel to a part of the galaxy where the UEC is not welcome. Plus payment that will allow you to live like a king for even your extended life."

"If I say okay, when are you planning this prison break?"

"Now," Myron answered. "I assumed you would consider your freedom valuable."

"And what are we going to steal?"

"A ship and its space-fold drive."

"Myron, mate, get real. Ships with space fold are either in space or docked at Space Fleet facilities. The security will be thicker than jam on biscuits."

"My problem. You just have to fly it. I assume you remember how."

"I'm not certified, but I learned enough while living on MSD," he answered. "I can pilot one."

"Are you in?" Myron asked.

"I'm yours."

Chessa and Clip were forced to stop every quarter mile. He fed the video monitors with digital film of an empty corridor. They would, in turn, send the fake video to the security center in the prison. Next he disarmed motion and pressure sensors. Finally, he disabled the deadly laser grid preventing access or egress through that section of tunnel.

"Let's go," he said, confidently marching toward the section he deactivated.

Chessa trusted the Bagger's expertise, but still allowed him to walk a couple of steps ahead . . . just in case.

She checked the luminescent dial of the antique watch on her left wrist. They were on time.

Inga opened her day-bag and removed the makeup kit security inspected and allowed after two female guards took turns checking her physically for contraband. They had been thorough with her. Not so much with her makeup.

She squeezed red lipstick across the wall directly opposite the exterior panel which opened and closed the door. She pressed a cotton-tipped swab into the thick lipstick smear. Micro circuitry was embedded in the swab's stick. The lipstick was a paste designed to reduce the interference from the wall.

Myron opened his briefcase and placed the papers he removed in front of Benny.

"Read those," he instructed.

Benny read the first few lines. He said, "I have no intention of selling my bloody story."

"Just pretend to read them."

As Benny studied the paperwork, the sham attorney released hidden locks and removed the case's handle. He turned the grip on edge and two rods fell into his open palm. He placed the empty handle on the table top in front of Claflin. He place one rod atop the handle in a cross design, one end angled up and pointed at the shackled prisoner.

"Now what?" Benny asked.

"For the next twelve-minutes-nineteen seconds, you read and I wait," Myron answered.

After Chip assured her all alerts were off, Chessa pushed the panel above her head aside. She jumped, grabbed the edges in her hands, and lifted herself into the maintenance closet. Clip followed.

Quick as a cat, the thief unrolled a personal data sheet. He opened the computer, accessed the detention center's security center, and went to work.

"One minute," Chessa said.

He didn't reply. He did keep his fingers busy.

She said, "Time."

He said, "Done. Security is secure . . . for us."

In the conjugal studio Inga pressed the stem on her watch. The swab activated and the security access panel opened the door. She walked out, turned left and hurried down the empty corridor to the attorney-client rooms. She waved at Myron through the thick window. It required thirty seconds for a second swab to override the recognition protocol and release the lock. She waved again and returned to the studio.

Myron used his second rod to release Benny. While Benny moved to the door, Myron turned the rod around. A hologram of Claflin perusing legal paperwork manifested.

"Sharp," Benny said. "Now what?"

"Go out, turn left, go to the third door on your right. It will have a maintenance room sign on it. Knock," Myron instructed.

"You?"

"I'll see you in a little while. We're on the clock. Go," he ordered.

Benny followed directions. After he knocked, Chessa ushered him inside.

"Clip?" she asked.

"Cameras, scanners, and sensors are back live," he answered. He rolled his tablet, stashed it in a pocket, and said, "Let's go."

The thief dropped down into the tunnel, followed by the escapee, followed by the assassin, who closed the panel behind her.

In the secure meeting room, Myron called for the guard.

"Mr. Claflin has a lot of papers to read and approve," he told the guard. "There's nothing more I can explain. I would appreciate it if you give him thirty minutes to finish."

"No problem," the woman answered. "He can't take the papers to his cell. We'll keep them in a locker in the security closet."

"Thank you. I'll send a courier to collect them."

Myron, briefcase in hand, headed for the exit under the watch of the guard. A quick glance through the window showed Benny Claflin working his way through the documents.

As he reached the first security gate, Inga was explaining to another guard . . .

"Señor Ramos is sleeping," she said. "There is another hour available. Let him rest."

"You mean recover, don't you?" the guard quipped. "Don't know how much you charge, chiquita, but you're obviously worth it."

"Gracias. Too bad you cannot afford me," she responded.

The guard escorted her to the first gate toward the final exit.

In the parking lot, Myron started his bike, but waited to exit until he saw Inga exit the front door.

By the time Myron reached the Interstate, in the gully, Benny climbed on the cycle behind Clip. They took off across the flatlands, followed by Chessa.

When the trio arrived at the convenience center, Myron and Inga already had their rides on the trailer and secured. The last two bikes were quickly loaded and strapped down.

Kort took the wheel while the others settled inside the cabin.

"Where we headed?" Benny asked.

Myron removed his suit coat and sat.

"First, I have people waiting to switch vehicles. The motorcycles we're hauling are a tad obvious," he said. "After that, Indianapolis."

Chapter Thirty-Seven
Vista System / Earth

"Okay, Cam. If you and Manny can figure out a way to get to the Wraith and get it outside, you will need a pilot," Coop told the hologram image.

In Manny Hernandez's private office, using his personal STORM-HATCH communicator (He did, after all, create the system with Storm and Sparks.), Cam contacted Coop.

"The fleet is in system," she said. "Any suggestions."

"It will have to be someone willing to buck authority and willing to risk their career. Do you know where the 109 is located?"

"Dry dock on EMS2," she answered. "It was on the news. Crew is being shuttled to the surface on leave."

"Find Lt. Mary Margaret Moore," he said. "Explain what's happening. I'm sure she'll help."

"Should you contact her first?" she asked.

"I'm too far to use my trans-comm, even with Cassandra's boost. I don't want to bring attention to her. When the Wraith goes missing, Admiral Patterson will suspect I'm involved and check my contacts," he explained.

"What about this one?"

"You're on Manny's private S-H. He can erase his log. I'll have Cassandra remove this one from our records," he replied.

"If, big if, I can actually steal the ship and Lt. Moore agrees to pilot it, where does she take it?"

"Fell," he said without hesitation. "The AS clan will bring her back via wormhole. If she takes a two-week leave, there will be enough time for the return trip. By then the theft will be known and I will have a private conversation with Elie. She'll figure out an excuse to pick Mags up at the system rim."

"A lot of potential fails," Cam said.

"We have no choice, Cam. Cassie's life is at risk," he countered.

Manny interrupted. "Coop, why not simply talk to Nathan?"

"Because I don't know what his reaction would be," he answered. "He could increase security, or worse, shut her down. Believe me, Manny. I plan on talking with him once Cassie is safe."

"We'll handle things," Cam promised. "I really wish you were here."

"I trust both of you. And I will be there as soon as I can."

Cam and Manny knew that meant three months, but said nothing.

They ended the communication. There was a skeleton of a plan and a chance of success. Coop knew he was placing good people in peril. Cam could be kicked out of the Marshals; Mags would be facing a potential court-martial if she agreed to help; Manny would be fired, and all of them could go to prison. He had no intention of allowing them to pay such high prices for helping him.

"Cassandra?"

"Yes, Coop."

"Contact Clyde."

"Now what?" Manny asked.

"We need the most important piece before we make a plan," Cam answered. "Contact Lt. Moore."

Chessa moved into the passenger seat next to Myron, who was driving. They had transferred to a luxury RV with hover/thrusters available for impassable sections of the highway. The high-end home on wheels also had air-ride suspension to overcome the potholes and cracks, providing a somewhat comfortable ride.

"I apologize for the poor condition of our roads and bridges," Myron said. "Infrastructure went to hell when extreme liberals were elected to run the old USofA's government. By the time people rose up and returned sanity to the system, only vehicles with off-road capability or hover engines could use the highways between metropolitan areas. Then the Pandemic hit. Must seem strange for aliens to see this, considering our capacity for space travel."

"I've visited many worlds," she responded. "I don't make judgements. Civilizations operate differently. Now that we have Claflin, what's next?"

"We're going to steal the only ship with space-fold drive not surrounded by Space Fleet Marines. And this time it won't be a smart, well-timed operation. We have to get it out, get Claflin in it, and everybody escape without being identified."

"Do you have a first step?"

"I do. Contact an arms dealer."

"I have to admit we were surprised to hear from you," Arty said.

"Things change," Coop replied. He was alone in his cabin. The connection with the Nakki vessel nicknamed Clyde by Veresk D'Sey and Arty, the verbal guide who performed as the go-between with the illusory Nakki, completed through a means unknown to him.

"I need a quick ride to my solar system," he said. "When I finish business I have there, I will accept the invitation to meet face-to-face with the Nakki."

"It will require two days for Clyde to reach your current location. Another day to transport you to Earth," Arty responded.

"Fine. How do I contact you when my work is done? I won't have Cassandra."

"With your permission I will add myself to the private contact list on your translator-communicator chip."

"Granted."

"As you do for your friends, say 'Arty' followed by your nickname and we will be connected."

"I will need a power source to boost the signal," Coop pointed out.

"I will hear you, Captain. Call when you are ready. I will see you in forty-seven hours, eleven minutes."

"Hello, Dr. Hernandez. We haven't talked since we recovered the *Star Gazer* and delivered it to Earth. Congratulations on the STORM-HATCH project. You made everyone's life bunches better with FTL communication," Mags said.

"Thank you, Lieutenant. Sparks came up with the concept. I simply built a workable array," he responded.

"Mags, please."

"And I'm Manny to my friends. I have someone for you to meet, Mags. This is Sandra Campos Valverde."

Before her image fully appeared on Mags' holo-comm receiver, the fighter pilot said, "You're Cam. Coop and Elie have told me about you."

"Good. It will make this simpler . . . Mags. Uncle Daniel contacted me to investigate a personal matter. After I did and reported, he told me to connect with you," Cam said.

"Sounds like spook and spy business," Mags rejoined. "How do I fit in?"

"We need a pilot who can fly a Wraith class ship."

"Since I know of only one Wraith, and I understand it is locked away at Trent Industries, what's the deal?"

"Mags, Nathan Trent has his software people attempting to force secrets out of the avatar, Cassie," Manny told her. "Secrets Coop does not want to share."

"I met Cassie when we went after the Prophet," she said. "Is she in danger?"

Cam was surprised Daniel, Manny, and now, Mags Moore, acted as if the avatar was alive. Not only alive, but important to them. Operating in outer space and operating on Earth led to the development of differing points of view. Still, she had been moved by the sadness she perceived in the hologram's eyes.

"She is," Manny confirmed. "We intend to steal the Wraith and free Cassie. Coop suggested you might be willing to fly it to Fell."

"I'm in," she said.

"Mags, there could be serious consequences," Cam interrupted. "We're breaking a lot of laws. Uncle Daniel said you could face court-martial."

"Yeah, I get it. Sounds like fun compared to the crap I've been wading in the last couple of months," she replied. "I'll tell Elie I want two weeks surface leave. Where do we meet?"

"There's a shuttle port at the Indianapolis Speedway," Manny answered. "Let us know when and we'll pick you up."

"Will do. Mags out."

Off line, Mags said aloud, "Kennedy?"

"Yes, Mags," the AI responded.

"Did you hear that?"

"I did."

"Then you understand it has to be erased and deleted from the comms' log?"

"I do. It's done, and thank you for risking your career for one of my kind," the AI said.

"By *my kind* you mean a friend. You're welcome."

At Trent Industries, Manny said, "There's your first piece. Ready to make a plan?"

"I have a feeling we're all going to end up locked away and forgotten. Let's try really hard to figure out a way to do this and not let that happen," Cam said.

Chapter Thirty-Eight
Vista System / Earth

On Earth two different teams with different agendas were making plans to accomplish the same goal . . . theft of the Wraith ship on the Trent Industries campus.

Above Vista a huge silver hued ship shaped like a kidney bean arrived. On board the *Renarde*, Coop called everyone to the lounge.

"I'm going to apologize for waiting to the last minute, but I wasn't entirely sure this was going to happen. Cassie, Cassandra's AI is in trouble. I'm hitching a ride on Clyde to Earth. Cindy will be in charge while I'm gone. I'll take Kit," he said, intentionally keeping his announcement terse.

"I don't think so," Cindy said. "I'm sure I speak for everyone. If there's a friend in trouble, we all go. There is more than enough room in Clyde's hangar."

The others voiced agreement, overlapping each other in their desire to be heard.

"Listen up!" he demanded. "What I'm doing is not only illegal, but is breaking several Space Fleet regulations. I can't let you throw your careers away."

"Storm and I can always return to Fell," Sky said.

"We would join them," Hiro replied for himself and Cindy.

"I've always wanted to be an outlaw," Billy said. "I have money to live a dozen lifetimes on and the Fairchild name to protect me. I'll protect Chaspi."

"I have always wanted to be a pilot. A real pilot. You have helped me achieve that dream. I would hate myself if I did not help you now," Chaspi said.

"Listen to us, Coop," Cindy said. "We can keep the *Renarde* hidden in Clyde. If we do need to leave, this ship has the most advanced detection avoidance tech available. We'd be on site to help, and no one ever has to know."

"How would you explain not being over Vista?" he asked.

"Damn, Coop. We're sixty-trillion miles from Earth," Hiro said. "We can tell them we're giving children tours of the system and they would never know."

Coop looked over his resolute crew.

"Cassandra. Contact Clyde and inform him there is a change of plans. Tell him to prep for *Renarde's* arrival."

Cam, Manny, and Mags met in Manny's office.

"We have an advantage by already being inside the perimeter security," Cam said. "Getting to the building holding the Wraith won't be difficult. There is security, but only two lightly armed guards. They expect the first line of guards to handle anyone attempting to enter the campus without authority. I can take them out without raising an alarm."

"Without killing anyone," Manny emphasized.

"Non-lethal force," she assured him. "People who will try to stop us are not the enemy."

"You sure you can get into the hangar?" Mags asked.

"I checked the building out when Manny pretended to give me a tour of Trent Industries. The lock-out system is simplistic. They are not taking an attempt to break in as realistic," Cam answered.

"What can I do?" Manny asked.

"We have communications. You can stay in your office and watch video feeds of the campus," she said. "If you see any reaction moving toward us, give me an alert."

"That's all? Stay in my office."

"Oversight is key to our escape, Manny. Without you, Mags and I are blind," Cam said. "You're also our cover. Right now, we came in to visit. That puts us on the visitor log. If we did steal the Wraith, it would not take long to put together the ship being gone and us not here. Because of your position, security doesn't search your vehicle. After we leave, we'll sneak back in by hiding in your ride."

"We snatch the Wraith, evade the entire fleet, space-fold to the system rim, and reengage for Fell," Mags said. "Other than being blasted by my friends, what could go wrong?"

"No *we*, Mags. Once the hangar door is open, you're on your own," Cam said. "I can't go to Fell and disappear for the time it will take to return by wormhole. I'll leave the same way I got in, with Manny."

"It all seems simple," Manny said.

"The best plans are," she said. "The problems come when you begin, then nothing is simple."

"The problems will begin when the mission begins," Myron said.

The RV was parked in the lot of an abandoned strip mall in northern Indianapolis, two miles west of Trent Industries. The team members each had a personal tablet with satellite view of the engineering giant's expansive campus.

"We go in the morning," he said. "When the day security replaces the night crew, the number of guards is reduced by half, with a lot less firepower. Inga drives the kitchen supply truck we commandeer through the security check at the delivery gate. The rest of us will hide in the back behind the food and goods for the campus kitchen. In all the years Trent Industries have operated in Indianapolis, no one has attempted to break in. Lots of cyber attacks and surveillance, but no physical attacks. My source says security is lazy and over confident."

"So getting in is a snap," Kort said. "How about getting out with alarms going off?"

"Benny will hop the fence in the Wraith and drop us off before heading for space," Myron answered.

"You're planning on shock and confusion to give me time to reach a place I can use space-fold," Benny said. "Not much of a strategy, Myron."

"It's all we have," the fixer responded.

"You have the reference points for the nav computer. It's a multi-gate location with a trade center space station. It's a place where sketchy deals are often done," Chessa said. "We should be able to get their in ten days, as long as Space Fleet escorts us to the system rim. If we're not there in two weeks, use the second set of coordinates to reach a Galvari secret outpost. They will contact Elder Valens and take care of you."

"No worries. I can handle myself. There better be a reward waiting," Benny said.

"You'll get your pay," Cassie assured him. "We all will."

"Which leaves the big hole in the plan between getting in and getting out," Kort said.

"That's where you come in, Kort," Myron said. "Once we're inside the perimeter, finesse is over. My armorer source came through with heavy duty weapons. You and Inga are going to attack the computer development lab three buildings south of our object. While you pull security to that location, Clip gets the rest of us into the hangar. Chessa and I cover while he disconnects any locks on the hangar doors and Benny flight checks the Wraith. When they are ready to go, you and Inga will have five minutes to disengage with security and join us. Clip opens the doors, Benny exits and hops the perimeter. We return to the RV and he flies off with the ship."

"Sounds too simple," Inga said.

"Believe me, when all hell breaks out, and it will, it won't seem too simple then," Myron promised.

The next day Manny Hernandez arrived for work. The guard at the main gate waved him through, not wasting time to inspect his personal ride or have him run it through scanners. After parking in his space behind the primary engineering R&D building, he waited until the area was clear to usher Cam and Mags from their hiding place and through the employee entrance. Both wore calf-length white lab coats with fake id badges.

To avoid people, they used the stairwell instead of the lift to go to Manny's third floor office.

"Step one was a success," Cam said. "Let's hope the rest of the day goes as well."

"This is exciting," Mags said. "I feel like a spy."

"I've felt like throwing up since I got out of bed," Manny said. "Which was a waste of time. I was awake all night."

Cam opened her long white coat and pulled a hand-held weapon from a thigh holster and checked it before returning it. She noticed Manny's anxious stare.

"Don't worry. It's a stun gun. Fires small darts with contact charges that knock the target out. Non-lethal like I promised."

"And the knife in your left boot?"

"It can be lethal," she admitted. "I've never gone to work without it. I promise to leave it sheathed unless I'm forced to pull it."

"I have my METS on beneath my clothes, so I'm set to go," Mags interjected, taking Manny's attention away from Cam. "When do we . . . what the hell was that?"

A blast sounded. An explosion large enough to make the safety glass in the windows shimmer, and small items on desktops and shelves bounce. A second, equally powerful peal followed.

Manny rushed to his computer.

"The exo-surface vehicle research center is being attacked," he said. "What would anyone want from there?"

"Nothing," Cam said. "It's a diversion. Someone else is after the Wraith."

She ran for the door, Mags on her heals.

Most employees working on the campus sheltered in place. A handful ran from the area where smoke rose into the air. Heads ducked and paces accelerated as another blast sounded.

Armed security guards passed them, paying the two women running away from the explosions a second look.

Cam reached the hangar ahead of Mags. She had the stun gun in hand, silently cursing her pledge to Manny and wishing she had something with more impact.

"The door is open," she told Mags on arrival. She handed the unarmed pilot the weapon. "It has nine rounds," she said. "Try for skin. If your target is big, hit them twice."

"What about you?"

The Brazilian pulled her combat knife.

"Oh, yeah. You and Coop are related."

Cam removed the lab coat, dropping the white bull's-eye on the ground before slipping through the door. Mags copied her and followed.

A woman lay sprawled on the concrete floor a few feet inside. Cam checked her out.

"She's alive," she whispered. "ID badge says she's a software engineer. Probably working on Cassie with Porterhouse. The hangar is well lit. Stay behind equipment and in shadows. The Wraith is pointed toward the hangar's double doors. If we get the chance, you up for flying it out of here?"

"Affirmative," the terse reply.

"Stay low," Cam said as she crouched and moved around a cargo sled.

The booted foot would have caught her flush across her face if not for the predatory reflexes honed over years of dangerous work. Her left arm blocked the blow, but the force managed to rock her backward. Mags' body kept Cam on her feet when she unexpectedly cushioned the smaller woman's fall.

Cam regained her balance and slashed at her attacker with the knife.

Chessa reacted as quickly, pulling away from the deadly arc. She was not expecting the human to block and recover from her kick so quickly. Nor the blade. She reached for the kinetic pistol procured from the arms dealer. As it cleared the holster belted at her waist, the blonde female reacted with her own kick, catching Chessa's hand and sending the pistol through the air.

Cam threw a right cross at the taller woman, expecting and having it blocked. She followed with an upper-cut; one using the tip of the knife and not knuckles leading.

Protecting her jaw from deadly metal, Chessa swung her right forearm across the path of the blade. The tip was deflected, but the edge sliced sleeve and skin, leaving a bloody incision.

Before Cam could press her advantage, a shot rang out. Behind her Mags dropped to her knees, clutching a hand against her abdomen. She had been aiming the stun gun at the hooded and masked assailant when Clip, working on the panel controlling the hangar doors, fired his pistol.

Chessa, cradling her arm, moved toward the wraith. Clip stepped into the open to cover her. Myron, hearing the shot fired, appeared at the ship's rear cargo ramp.

Cam dropped down next to Mags, expecting the worse.

"I'm okay," she said weakly. "Wind knocked out of me. The METS stopped the projectile. Watch your back!" she croaked.

Life-saving reflexes acted once more. The ex-assassin picked up the stun gun from the floor where the pilot dropped it. She spun, using her knee as a pivot, and lifted the weapon. Three disks were rapid fired, leaving the rectangular shaped barrel at high velocity. All three hit Clip. Even though covered from head to toe to disguise his appearance, the trio of darts delivered shocks at the same time, easily penetrating cloth. The darts sent the spasming thief down. He lay unconscious.

Cam helped Mags behind the cargo sled. She turned to defend their position. Across the wide expanse of the building's interior, a side door was violently forced open and two more people entered. A large one and a smaller one, both wearing hoods and masks. They carried large weapons with circular drums. Cam recognized the personal cannons. The drums held high-explosive rounds capable of blowing up armored transports. They explained the blasts heard earlier. If they used those weapons on them, they were dead. Mags suit would not protect her this time.

She risked looking around the sled's rear. One person was carrying the person she stunned toward the Wraith. The smaller cannon-toter had set her weapon down and used strips of cloth from the damaged sleeve to wrap the knife wound. The big one stood sentinel, his weapon trained in her direction.

As she tried to decide her next move, and Mags recovered from the body blow, another man came down the ramp. He was not masked and carried a limp form in a white coat. He easily tossed the body aside before addressing the group.

The man carrying the stunned shooter disappeared up the ramp, following the bald, black man who appeared in charge. The woman she fought hesitated, the followed. The two with the mini-cannons walked away from the ship in her direction. She was about to boost Mags and make a desperate escape when they stopped. They turned to face the hangar doors.

Benny walked down the ramp, Porterhouse slung over his shoulder. The engineer went down and out with one well-place tap. Not before he pronounced the Wraith as intact and flight ready.

"What the bloody hell is happening out here?" he demanded as he roughly deposited his unconscious load on the ground.

"Visitors," Chessa said. "Talented ones," she added as Inga tied the cloth to stop her blood flow.

Myron arrived with the limp Clip cradled in his arms. "He's out. He didn't unlock the doors before going down."

Benny told Kort and Inga, "When the engine fires, blow those doors off their tracks. I'll leave the ramp down until you board, then we go."

He went up the ramp. Myron followed with Clip. Chessa hesitated, but could think of no other options. She left Kort and Inga, who, weapons in hand, moved away from the ship for a clear path to the doors.

Kort considered firing a round into the cargo sled, but decided the two hiding behind it no longer represented a danger. When the indo-atmosphere engine came on, he and Inga fired two rounds each at the large doors. Wood, steel, and other metals violently blew outward, leaving a gaping hole obscured by smoke.

They hurried to the Wraith's rear entrance, rushing up the ramp. Seconds later the ramp ascended, the ship hovered as its tripod landing gear rose into the belly. The Wraith eased forward, cleared the opening, and disappeared.

Cam covered Mags just before the hangar doors were destroyed. They both stood and watched the ship lift, leave the hangar, and fly away.

They hurried through the door they had entered, retrieved the white lab coats, and made their way through the confusion to Manny's office.

After recounting their experience, Cam asked the engineer to contact Coop.

On Clyde Arty told Coop, "You have a call, Captain. Would you like me to route it here?"

"Yes. This is Cooper."

"Uncle Daniel, it's Cam. Someone took the Wraith before we could. Most of them wore masks, but one didn't. It was Benny Claflin."

"I thought he was in prison."

"He was broken out a week ago. Probably by the same team that helped him steal the Wraith," she said.

"Are you, Mags, and Manny okay?"

"We're fine. There's no telling where Claflin went."

"He'll head for the rim and then out of the system," Coop said. "I'll handle it from here, Cam. Stay safe. Coop, out."

"Now what?" Hiro asked.

Coop turned to face Arty.

"Can you track the Wraith?"

"I can," the hologram answered.

"You pulled me out of space-time twice. Can you do it again?" Coop asked.

"Clyde's tether is capable of it."

"My work isn't done until I get the ship and Cassie back. Will you help me?"

"Of course," Arty answered.

Chapter Thirty-Nine

Myron finished bandaging Chessa'a wound.

"I'm only assuming antibiotics will prevent infection," he told her. "I'm not fluent in alien metabolism. I would suggest you get the cut closed."

"I have bio-paste on the *Daybreaker*. I will be fine until then," she replied.

"I can't believe we pulled it off," Clip said.

"*We*?" Kort rejoined. "You were out cold for most of the action."

"We did do it," Inga said. "We'll be heroes when we get back."

"You actually believe Claflin will deliver the Wraith and the space-fold drive to you?" Myron asked.

"Of course," Clip said. "It's worth a fortune to him."

"A fortune he can trade for anywhere in the galaxy," Myron responded. "Which is a distinct possibility. Just as possible, Space Fleet will catch him."

"How? He has space-fold," Inga said.

"In my experience, Space Fleet and the other Space Rangers are extremely good at screwing up attempts to cause Earth problems," he said.

"It won't go well for us if we have to return to Galvari without the secret to space-fold," Clip said. "Especially if the Elders find out you were on the ship and turned it over to a criminal."

"*You*?" Kort asked.

"I was unconscious, remember?" Clip said.

"We deal with whatever happens," Chessa said. "Right now we have to get back to the *Daybreaker*. We'll go to the trade center and see what happens. Either he shows up or he doesn't."

"I may have something that could help," Myron said. "While we were aboard the Wraith I found a flexible tablet." He pulled a thin plastic-alloy sheet from a pocket on his tactical pants. "I believe this belonged to the technician working aboard the ship when we boarded it. I only had a quick glance, but I bet there may be some valuable information here. I doubt there is a space-fold drive diagram, but other secrets of benefit."

He handed the flex-tablet to Chessa.

"Free?" she asked.

"The satchel of gems will more than cover my costs and provide me a comfortable life," he answered. "Besides, this was the most fun I've had in a long time. You're welcome to the RV for as long as you need. I suggest you drive to Chicago and use the station there to shuttle up to EMS2. Directions will be in the nav computer. Drop the RV wherever you wish. It can't be linked to me."

"Thank you, Myron Sweetwell," Chessa said. "It's been interesting."

Cam and Mags exited Manny's vehicle in a parking garage in the downtown business district.

"Do you honestly think Coop will find the Wraith?" Manny asked.

The looks returned by the two women were answer enough.

"Okay. You're right. I don't know why I asked. What will you two do now?"

"We're going shopping," Mags said. "I have two weeks and it will not be wasted. After that and a night being pampered at one of Indianapolis' nicest hotels and spa. Tomorrow we are going to the speedway and drive vintage race cars. Next week, the Bahamas."

"Cam?" Manny asked.

"I'm with her," she answered, linking arms with Mags.

"The Wraith is in the hangar," Arty announced.

The entire crew departed the lounge for Clyde's massive hangar. The small Wraith ship sat beside the *Renarde*. Coop used the hatch behind the cockpit to enter. He found Benny Claflin passed out in the pilot's seat. He pulled him out of the seat, laid him on the cabin floor, and used electronic cuffs he brought with him on his wrists. With Claflin secure, he opened the rear cargo hatch.

Hiro and Billy volunteered to carry the wayward Space Ranger away. The others left with them, leaving Coop alone in the ship.

"Cassie?" he called.

The hologram of the young woman appeared. After a moment it solidified.

"I thought you would never show up," she said, placing both arms around him in a hug. This was followed by a deep kiss.

"Arty?" Coop asked aloud.

"Yes, Captain," the bodiless voice answered.

"Is Cassie able to exit the Wraith and move around inside Clyde like before?"

"Indeed she can."

Coop and Cassie joined the others in the lounge. She was introduced to everyone but Hiro. The two met when Coop and Hiro used the Wraith to get to the Prophet in the Aster system.

"The oddest thing was being separated from Cassandra," she told Storm later. "It's comforting to be near enough to communicate again."

"Are you sure about the plan?" Cindy asked.

"The truth is our best option," Coop answered. "We caught a ride on a Nakki super ship because Cassandra felt something wrong with Cassie. We arrived in time to prevent Benny Claflin from escaping with a space-fold drive that wasn't under proper security. I placed you in charge with orders to take Benny to EMS2. To repay the Nakki, I remained on board with the Wraith. I'm going to meet with the Nakki and will return or get in touch when I can."

"We should go with you," Storm said.

"All of us," Chaspi added.

"No," he replied. "I trust all of you, but this is my responsibility. The *Renarde* has work to do and a capable crew. This could be the way to completely restore Cassie."

"Doesn't fly," Hiro said. "Coop, each of us joined this crew because you are the captain. If you abandon the ship, there is no *Renarde*."

"Hiro's right," Billy interjected. "Chaspi and I left the Marshals to join you. Hiro, Cindy, and Sky left their homes on Fell. Storm left the 109. We all want to help Cassie."

"I don't want to be the reason you leave your friends," Cassie added.

"If I may, Captain," Arty interrupted. "I can refit the *Renarde* to support Cassie as an organic holo-avatar. It would also reestablish the AI-Avatar connection."

"Sounds like you're surrounded and outnumbered," Cindy said. "Time to surrender, Coop."

Coop surveyed the people in the lounge, including two holograms.

"Arty, connect me with Admiral Patterson. She could be on EMS2 or somewhere on the surface," Coop told the Nakki construct.

"She is in her office at Space Fleet headquarters on Earth," Arty replied. "Speak when you are ready."

"Pam, it's Coop."

"Hello, Coop. Is something happening on Vista?" she asked.

"I'm not in the Vista system," he told her. "I'm aboard a Nakki ship in our system."

"No one has reported an unidentified alien ship," she said. "We're on high alert. An unknown vessel would have been seen."

"The ship is cloaked, Pam," he explained. "I assume you called a Level One alert because of the theft of the Wraith from Trent Industries."

"What do you know about that?"

"I have the Wraith and Benny Claflin. I haven't had a chance to talk with him, but I believe he planned on trading the space-fold array for his freedom."

"How do you *have* him?" she asked.

"He's tied up. I'm going to toss him in the Wraith and drop them off near EMS2 where they can be picked up. Pam, the crew of the *Renarde* is joining me for a trip to visit the Nakki. Cassie is going, too. I know what you and Nathan have been doing, Pam. I plan on meeting with the Nakki, repairing Cassie, and returning to talk with you and Nathan. Any problem with that?"

After a long hesitation, Admiral Patterson said, "No."

"Pam, you need to keep a closer watch on your secrets," he said. "I doubt this will be the last time someone tries to steal them. Cooper, out."

"Now that was badass," Billy said.

Chapter Forty

Galvari / Nibiru

"You've been gone a long time," Valens said.

"Earth is a long way," Chessa answered.

"My contact on Devisator tells me a ship with space-fold drive was nearly stolen."

"Your contact is mistaken. The ship was stolen. Unfortunately the pilot recommended by Chimia Wei failed to escape," the woman from Callustrade 1 said.

"It was an expensive gamble," the Elder said.

"One that paid off." She handed him the flexible tablet. "It does not contain the Nakki secrets we hoped for, but there are many of Earth's technological programs."

"Very good, Chessa," he said. "With these we can upgrade our own systems and outline methods to counter theirs. When we decide to meet them in battle again, we will have the advantage."

Alnilam, Alnitak, and Mintaka are the stars which form the constellation humans call Orion's Belt. The Nakki home world orbits Alnilam, seven-hundred-thirty-six lightyears from Earth.

"We've been here a week," Hiro said. "It's beautiful, but it's getting tedious. Are we ever going to meet a Nakki?"

"Eventually," Coop answered. "Arty keeps telling me to practice patience."

The two friends sat side-by-side on a banister. Behind them, a marble faced edifice rose two stories. Below, seated around a stone table, Storm, Sky, and Cassie were talking and laughing.

"How can she exist outside?" Hiro asked.

"People keep asking me and I keep answering *I don't know*. It has become my go to answer."

Across the courtyard, a wide berth of stairs rose up into a wide portico. A building stood there, reminiscent of an expansive Italian villa. A woman with long, curly auburn hair watched them.

She wore a black outfit with off the shoulder body hugging top and harem-style pants that moved in the soft breeze.

"Do we wait or go?" Hiro asked.

"I vote go," Coop answered, tired of waiting.

The two Space Rangers walked down to the patio. They directed the attention of the women to the building behind and above them. The three joined Coop and Hiro to ascend the marble staircase.

They reached the portico and stood before the woman. This near it was obvious she was as lovely and stately as her surroundings.

"A late welcome to Nibiru," she said. "I am Ki. I appreciate your patience. My fellow Nakki and I have been discussing your arrival. We were expecting Daniel Cooper, not his friends as well."

"Is it a problem?" Daniel asked.

"Not at all," she assured him. "Just an adjustment. I have asked KSS-delta-one-nine-one-six to invite the rest of your party to join us."

"Who?" Storm asked.

"Arty," Coop answered.

"Please, come with me," Ki said.

They followed her through the front doors of the building, entering a huge foyer. The ceiling soared thirty feet overhead. A painting depicting planets orbiting a blue-white star covered the canopy. Twin stairwells rose up before them, curving before coming together again on the floor above. Statues reminiscent of those depicting Greek and Roman mythological figures found in museums on Earth were placed in niches carved into the orbicular walls. Granite tables topped with urns of colorful exotic flowers were strategically placed to please the eye.

Ki continued walking across the polished tiles, passing beneath the stairwells and through a case opening. She entered a room with a polished wood table and eight chairs facing a raised dais with eight high-back chairs.

Tapestries of muted colors hung from the ceiling around the square room. One wall held a carved frieze of men and women amid strange animals.

The Nakki woman directed them to the long table. Once they were seated, she stepped onto the raised platform and sat in one of the center-most chairs.

An uncomfortable silence followed during the time required for the rest of the *Renarde's* crew to arrive and take seats. Coop simply shook his head at whispered queries.

A door opened between two tapestries and people who appeared as human as Ki entered the chamber. They took seats facing the crew.

Ki stood and said, "Allow me to introduce everyone. On your far left is Enell."

A grey-haired male whose hair swirled wildly around his head gave a simple seated bow.

"Next is Kint."

The middle-aged man appraised them with deep, dark eyes. He had a beard six inches long, perfectly cut in a thick rectangle.

"Beside Kint is Nina."

Nina was a young, attractive woman. She wore her blonde tresses long, spilling over the shoulders of a simple blue ankle-length frock. She smiled in greeting.

"Next is Aun."

The black man seated in the chair had a presence of power. Taller than the others, he was also the most relaxed.

Ki looked to her left, introducing the male Nakki in the chair beside her open one.

"This is Nan."

He was light skinned with arresting blue eyes.

"Then Tu."

Tu was older, but obviously muscular. His solid bulk dwarfed the chair he occupied.

"Finally, Inanna, Tu's sister."

If Ki was beautiful, Inanna was drop dead gorgeous. Raven locks, black eyes, and lush lips. The body-hugging dress with deep v top revealed a body rivaling Sky and Storm.

Ki took her seat.

"We are the Judges," Aun said. "It is our responsibility to watch over the galaxy. When a situation arises that threatens the continued existence of a planet, a species, or a race we vote as to whether action should be taken. If it is decided intervention may be required, we dispatch an agent.

"Our agents are independent actors. They investigate the situation. A final decision to actively intercede or not is their decision. If they choose to become involved, they have access to Nakki technology to support their enterprise."

"Why do you care if one group is attempting to eliminate another?" Coop asked.

"The Nakki seeded and cultivated a great number of the civilizations in the galaxy," Inanna answered. "We have watched elements mix with deposits of organic paste evolve into life. Life, the most basic form, survived and became a life form. In some cases, Nakki biologists intervened to improve the strain. We are invested in the success of civilizations. The destruction of a species is contrary to our goals."

"The ones in danger do not have to be descendants of the seeding," Tu interjected. "There are more planets with life derived independently of Nakki involvement than those seeded. Our concern is genocide of any type. Short of eradication, we watch for the destruction of civilizations in other ways. Natural disasters, self-destruction, and falling under the control of a more powerful society are examples."

"To better answer your question, let me make it simple," Ki interrupted. "The galaxy if filled with children. We are the adults."

"D'Sey offered me the chance to be one of your agents," Coop said. "I haven't changed my mind."

"The people of Osperantue have been capable of traveling between star systems for 5,000 years," Enell said. Chaspi perked up. "They have invested their time and energy into improving the lives of the residents of Osperantue. Their growth as star travelers led them to becoming tourist guides.

"The residents of Fell have become technological wizards," he said, garnering the attention of Sky and Storm. "To their credit, they used technology to bring peace to their planet. They also used it to enrich those with the most inventive minds."

"It is what all of the worlds in the Trade Alliance does," Storm responded defensively. "It is how we improve our civilizations."

"It is," Enell agreed. "Which is what makes humans even more remarkable."

"We have not asked you here to offer you a place as an agent, Daniel Cooper," Ki said. "Of thousands of worlds, two have stepped up to use their technological superiority to defend planets and their inhabitants from attacks by civilizations devoid of civility. Hela, on the far side of the great black hole, and Earth. It is our hope your two worlds continue to evolve in the direction of benefactors. The galaxy needs more adults."

"I don't understand," Billy said. "I still don't get why we are here."

"Our other responsibility is to watch for danger," Aun said.

"Daniel Cooper has been a driving force within your world's expeditionary ventures," Nan, the pale Judge, said. "It is crucial that he continues to shepherd the powers leading the planet in the right direction. Humans are bringing other worlds together. Together they are acting to protect weaker species from predators. Your alliance stands in the way of expansionist societies who will attempt to destroy you in order to continue their path of dominance and destruction. Facing such enemies will be your short term future. Having to accomplish it while developing your own foundation will tax your resolve."

"And our long term future?" Coop asked.

"The Nakki will need allies," Aun said. "There is a species intent on taking the Milky Way as theirs."

"The Basfor Flyn of the Sagittarius Dwarf Galaxy," Coop said.

"Exactly," Aun said. "They attempted to destroy our work once. We believe they are preparing to do so again. The experience and growth humans and Helacene will struggle with will prepare you to stand with the Nakki to face them."

"Why does a race as advanced as the Nakki need allies?" Cindy Shaw asked.

"Our numbers are diminished," Nina replied. She was the final Judge to address the visitors. "The unfortunate truth is our civilization has passed our tipping point. We are creatures of near immortality. With that gift comes a terrible price. We cannot reproduce. In their attempt to escape the tedium that accompanies an extended lifespan, many Nakki have left Nibiru in search of adventure. We are a scattered, unconnected people."

"It is why we refer to our seeds around the galaxy as our children," Ki said.

"So this is nothing more than a rah-rah moment," Cindy said. "You pat Coop on the head and send him back to continue acting as humanities' lead sled dog."

"I understood none of that," Aun admitted.

"She's calling this meeting a waste of time," Coop said.

"This meeting is to provide you with context," Aun said. "The reason for your visit it to provide access to Nakki technology. You will be free to mix with the population. There are a number of facilities where you will have access to the innovations created over the centuries. But there are two caveats."

"Here it comes," Cindy whispered. "The price we pay."

"Your evolution can be enhanced, as it was when you discovered and unlocked the secrets left on Mars, but too much of our advancements will inhibit your natural growth. Select three designs or devices to take back and share, but only three."

"Out of all of the inventions created over more than 500,000 years," Coop exclaimed. "Selecting three will be impossible."

"It's three or none," Aun countered.

"The other caveat?" he asked.

"Before you return to Earth you travel to the other side of the galaxy and assist Veresk D'Sey."

"I was told he could handle his own battle," Coop responded.

"The Kashōn have proven to be more resolute in their decision to destroy the Helacene Alliance. Our other agents are engaged in equally difficult situations. D'Sey will not ask for help, but he needs it."

"Why don't you help him?" Chaspi asked.

"We do not directly interfere with disputes between civilizations," Nanna replied.

"Sending us is interfering," Chaspi countered.

"Don't bother, Chaspi," Coop told the young pilot. "The convoluted answer is as confusing as an impossible puzzle. The Nakki have their own way of defining interference. It's like they have decided to provide advanced tech to help us face our enemy, but limit the help to three pieces. We will need to work to succeed."

"You have as much time as you wish, Daniel Cooper," Ki said. "The perimeter blocks have been removed. You have access to the city. Everyone knows who the eight of you are. Any questions will be answered. The hologram you named Arty will remain with you as well. I am your contact if you need anything special. Arty will contact me for you."

"You're assuming I agree to your conditions," Coop said.

The eight Judges all gave him questioning looks. Ki asked it.

"Do you?"

"I have my own caveat," he said. "I'm not committing myself, my crew, or my ship to a protracted engagement against the Kashōn. We have our own battles to wage on this side of the galaxy. We assist D'Sey until the tide changes for the Helacene, or one-hundred days . . . Earth length days."

The Judges sat watching the visitors without comment.

Ki finally spoke.

"Agreed."

Epilogue

Seated on benches on the star-drenched patio, the seven crew members and Cassie held their own meeting.

"Did you know they were telepathic?" Hiro asked.

Coop shook his head and said, "I know little more about the Nakki than you."

"You have Nakki secrets stashed away," Cindy said. "Isn't that why all the fuss over restoring Cassie and recovering the files you deleted?"

"Most of the information is what you just learned," he answered. "The most important secret was the reason some people survived the regeneration process that created Space Rangers and others did not. If the solution was discovered, how long do you think it would take for influential people to force the government to reactivate the program?"

"What's the plan?" Cindy asked.

"I don't want to be here more than a week," Coop said. "To reduce our search to a reasonable level, each one of us will take on a category, find where the data is located, pick our favorite innovation, and present it to the group. By vote we select our three choices and get to Hela as soon as possible.

"Storm, communications. Sky, computer enhancements. Billy, propulsion. Hiro, ship and surface defensive measures. Cindy, ship and surface offense. Chaspi, navigation and piloting improvements. Cassie, artificial intelligence. I will look into personal combat gear. If you stumble on anything out of context but valuable, bring it to the table."

"I have a headache," Storm said. "The Nakki have been more than helpful, but I have scanned so much data on communication system my eyes hurt."

"We all sympathize," Coop said. "Question is, did you find one of our three treasures."

"No," she answered. "We have FTL communication already. They have a system using black hole energy to increase distance and speed, but we aren't going to be operating over the vast distances to make it worthwhile. I did pick up some ideas to improve STORM-HATCH, but I can implement them without needing designs."

"I have an interesting discovery," Sky said. "All of the Nakki operational computers use artificial intelligence. They imbue the systems with sentience from conception instead of waiting to see if they develop self-awareness over time. They don't use avatars. The AI's are created without potential for ego, id, or super-ego and operate on a single level of consciousness. We could use their methods to empower machines, reduce the number of personnel, and without fear of meltdowns."

"The AI would be intelligent, self-aware, but void of any unique personality traits," Cassie said. "I don't see that as an improvement."

"It's still a possibility," Coop said. "Billy?"

"I looked at trans-dimensional drive, but the power required would mean space-station sized ships," he said.

"Like Clyde," Coop said.

"Yep. I found something better. A design improvement able to increase space-fold interstellar speed from one parsec, or three-point-two trillion miles per twenty-four hours to one lightyear per day, or six-trillion miles."

"You're talking twice as fast!" Chaspi exclaimed.

"We will put it up for vote, but it sounds promising," Coop said.

"Hiro?"

"I was shown schematics on an active denial system that is an improvement over the crowd-control ADS used on Earth. Millimeter-wave beams can be fired at another ship. They can penetrate most forcefields. The radiation enters a ship and those on board absorb it into their skin. It results in intense pain within five seconds. To escape the pain, the ship has to move away. It will allow us to avoid lethal options as our only option when faced with a confrontation."

"Interesting. An affective defensive weapon," Coop said. "Cindy?"

"More bust than anything," she said. "The weapons on file are nothing we don't know about. There was data on reducing size and increasing output, but our scientists are already working on those improvements. Our best bet is locating black crystals. They give us more flexibility than anything else I found."

"Amazing that in all these centuries the Nakki haven't made any major innovations in offensive capability. As far as black crystals, Arty already provided potential planets to search," Coop said. "Chaspi, anything better?"

"The Nakki use a variety of propulsion systems, but the only exotic one is trans-dimensional, so navigating is unique," she replied. "Since it is not an option, the system doesn't matter. They use a transfer case that allows them to transmit their thoughts directly to the piloting controls. Because we're not telepathic, I'm not sure if it can be adapted for our brainwaves.

"I did look over the tether ray used to pull us out of space-time. First, they have a scanner capable of penetrating space-time and wormholes. We could track vessels using either. The tether requires too much power for it to be viable on Fleet ships. You need a Clyde-size generator. However, the technology used has been adapted into a much smaller version used to snare and hold animals or as a non-lethal weapon. It's designed like a lance; six-feet long with a four-inch circumference."

"The tracker and the snare both sound like they have potential," Coop said. "Good work. Cassie?"

"Sky told you how the Nakki imbue AI's with single mind sentience. I found out how holo-images used for communication can exist outside of a structure with imaging hardware."

She placed a disc on the stone table. It was the size of a hockey puck.

"It's a portable rebounder," she told them. "The Nakki have them placed wherever they may want to use a holo-gram. When they travel, they drop them on the surface of the planet and have instant access."

"I assume these are what allow you to maintain your structure when outside, like now," he surmised. "If we can get some, or the plans for building them, you would be able to expand your environment."

"Actually, I discovered I only require one," she responded. "If I carry a rebounder, I can travel where there are no imaging hardware systems. The range is limited to three miles from my origination."

"Cassie, that's great," Chaspi said. "It's like you would be free."

"Up to three miles," the avatar corrected her. "Essentially, I have unrestricted mobility and a solid body within that zone. That's if we vote for it."

"Nothing we could take from here is as important as this," Chaspi said. She looked around for an endorsement and was rewarded with universal agreement. "Good. I would hate to hurt somebody."

"What did you find, Coop?" Hiro asked.

From a bag, he placed his personal laser pistol on the table.

"This is our Gen-2 laser gun," he said. "We reduced the size and weight from the original design when we were able to use a black crystal instead of batteries for power. Those changes improved accuracy. By hinging the forward compartment housing the mirrors and light emitter, we could fold it beneath the barrel and allow us to use a modified holster to carry the weapon. When we lost access to the crystals, production stopped. Unfortunately, normal crystals, in the size formatted for the array, weren't strong enough to produce a beam."

From the same bag he produced another pistol. This one the size and appearance of a traditional explosion-based weapon like the old Army M1911 .45.

"The Nakki fabricated a miniaturized light and mirror array that utilizes a white crystal and is contained in the grip. The trigger is a button, and the beam has two settings. Lethal option delivers a full-strength laser beam. They incorporated a non-lethal setting. It reduces the strength and can cause discomfort up to full stun, depending on how long you maintain contact."

"Wicked cool," Billy said, lifting the pistol. "It's half the weight of a Gen-2 and nothing compared to the original."

He handed the weapon to Cindy Shaw.

She handled it, pretended to aim and fire, and looked over the design.

"Me like," she said, placing it back on the table.

"We have agreed on the rebounder. We need to choose two other items. We'll select between the technology to create advanced artificial intelligence, increasing space-fold drive from three-point-two trillion miles per twenty-four hours to six trillion, an active denial system to drive enemy ships away with killing anyone, a tether snare within a lance, the ability to track ships in space-fold or wormholes, and a third generation laser pistol."

The first group vote unanimously agreed on increasing the miles covered per day with space-fold.

ADS, tracking ships, and the improved laser pistol made the cut for more discussion and the final piece of tech.

"ADS will give us the capability of turning away an entire ship without any deaths," Hiro argued.

"If Benny Claflin had escaped, the ability to track the Wraith would mean following and recovering it. We would also know what ships are using wormholes and where they are located. This could be invaluable in a war," Chaspi said.

"The improvements on a personal weapon increases a soldier's chances of survival," Coop said. "You have heard the arguments. It's time to decide."

Coop and Ki met in a garden.

"We will take the hologram rebounder schematics and a couple of discs, the plans for improving the array for space-fold drive, and the ship-to-ship active denial system," he informed her.

"Everything will be delivered to your ship," she replied. "When will you leave."

"Immediately after I make a stop in the Aster system."

The End

July 20, 2020

APPENDIX

Characters You Should Know

Daniel Cooper. "Coop"

A former Can-Am Army Ranger and sniper. Survived the Space Ranger's Project and joined the Navy Air Service. Uses the enhancements from the biological reengineering experiment to become the Navy's best test pilot. He is tapped to test fly the new space-fold equipped ships and eventually named the Captain for Space Fleet's first deep space exploration and military-capable vessel, the SFPT-109, *John F. Kennedy*. Current assignment: the Corsair Class *Renarde*.

Kennedy

The SFPT-109's Artificial Intelligence (AI) operating system.

To prevent confusion the ship is referred to as the 109, or the *John F. Kennedy* while the AI is simply Kennedy.

Genna

Genetic Engineered Neuro-Network Avatar. Connected to Kennedy while an embryo, she was created to keep the AI sane by providing "real world" contact for a sentient-potential program stuck in a two-dimensional existence. Genna eventually becomes the 109's First Officer.

Elena Casalobos. "Elie"

Former Spanish Legionnaire and Space Ranger. Long time love of Daniel Cooper. She also followed the path from Can-Am Naval pilot, to space ship test pilot, to Space Fleet fighter pilot. She replaced Coop as Captain of the 109 after an assassination attempt put him out of action.

Nathan Trent

Space Fleet's Director of Science and CEO of Trent Industries. With the help of his wife, Mara Galetti, a linguist, he broke the Martian code and recreated the advanced technology found on Mars for use by Space Fleet.

Pamela Patterson

Space Fleet's first Commanding Admiral.

ASkīlamentrae. "Sky"

A communications and computer expert from the planet Fell. Aboard the refugee alien ship when Coop made first contact. She joined him as his co-pilot in the fight against the Zenge armada and became his lover. She eventually returned to Fell, but returned to join the crew of the *Renarde*.

AStermalanlan. "Storm"

Fellen communications genius and Sky's cousin. She became Coop's Comm-Tac during the Zenge conflict and joined him and Sky as a threesome. Storm remained when Sky returned home. She helped create the FTL communication system used by Space Fleet to provide real-time connections across trillions of miles of space. Elie Casalobos recruited her to the 109. Coop recruited her to the *Renarde*.

Titus A. Barnwell, Jr. "Tab"

Former US Marine Intelligence officer. Space Ranger. Appointed the UEC's first Marshal for law enforcement. He leads the fight against the Camarilla Dissolvere.

Senait "Sindy" Kebede. SF Admiral.

Anton Gregory. SF General. Currently in the Astor System.

Rachelle Paré. SF Fighter Pilot. Currently assigned to the 109.

Noa Tal. SF Squadron Commander. Currently in the Aster System.

Samuel Harrington. Captain of SFPT-99, the Franklin D. Roosevelt.

Hiroshi "Hiro" Kimura. Planetologist. Member of *Renarde.*

Benedict "Benny" Claflin. Under arrest as a member of the Camarilla Dissolvere.

Alessandra "Ali" Campos. KIA on the Space Rangers' first operation.

Rolf Berkel. KIA during the Space Rangers' first operation.

Reoccurring Characters

Guy Arcand: Chairman of the Board of Governors of the UEC. Earth's leader.

Mary Margaret "Mags" Moore: Fighter Pilot on the 109.

Cam: Brazilian member of Barnwell's Marshals and granddaughter of a Space Ranger. Sandra Campos Valverde.

Chaspi: Bosine from Osperantue. Space Fleet Academy graduate. Deputy Marshall. Currently pilot aboard *Renarde*.

William "Billy" Elkman: Engineering graduate of Space Fleet Academy and assigned to *Renarde*. Grandson of Elliott Fairchild, the man who discovered the Martian hangar. Was a Deputy Marshal.

Cassie: Three-dimensional hologram avatar on the Wraith-class ship, Cassandra.
    Nathan Trent gifted the ship to Daniel Cooper.

Tasha and Tista Korr: Mother, daughter Judges from Ventier hired by UEC to assist Earth co-exist with other planets.

Aya Ishihara: Director of Exo-Legal Affairs.

Dr. Manny Hernandez: Head engineer for Trent Industries and co-inventor of the STORM-HATCH FTL communicators with Storm and Sparks.

Trade Alliance Worlds

A loose alliance of planets who utilize wormholes to facilitate trade between their civilizations.

Aster System: Aster Farum 1. Aster Farum 2. Aster Farum 3.

Fell: Home to the AS clan: Sky, Storm, Sparks, and Stacy.

Rys: Home of the Lisza Kaugh and Dwards. Discovered power crystals.
   Colony Planets: Seguerra. Fathom Oren. Neuvarusry.

Osperantue: Earth's first contact.

Stamalah 3: Known for charting wormhole channels.

Ventier: Interstellar Switzerland. Supply judges to mediate trade disputes.

Parria: Professional cargo haulers.

Devisator: A planet of women. Matchless traders.

From the files of Trade Alliance Worlds there are fifty-six known sentient species encompassing one-hundred-forty-two races. Twenty-four have wormhole travel.

There are another one-hundred-twelve known systems with planets capable of sustaining life, but no sentient beings.

[1] Earth Moon Space Station in fixed orbit above the Earth.

[2] HU: Heads Up. Information displayed on the interior of the plexi-shield.

[3] The FTL tachyon-based communications system. Solid-state Tachyon Operations & Retrieval Monitor / Hernandez-ASparquilla Tachyon Communications Housing.

[4] CONNEXIONS. Book #4 in the Space Fleet Sagas.

[5] CONTACT AND CONFLICT. Book One is the Space Fleet Sagas.

[6] Leader of the all-female Devee civilization from the planet Devisator

[7] First Published in Space Fleet Sagas. A Collection of Adventures. ©2017.

[8] Multi-Environmental Tactical Suit

[9] Light is basically moving energy. A laser produces intense energy that can travel over long distances. That is why a laser can become a weapon while the light from an incandescent bulb cannot.

To do this, a laser has to produce light in a nonconventional way. "Laser" stands for *light amplification by stimulated emission of radiation*. In other words, a laser produces light by stimulating the release of photons, or light particles. A laser needs four basic parts to do this:

Lasing medium: a source of atoms that get excited and emit light of a specific wavelength. The medium can be a gas, liquid, solid or semiconductors. Spaceships use gallium nitride, indium gallium arsenide and gallium arsenide semiconductors pumped with electrical currents in the form of quantum wells. This method creates the strongest beam. Handheld weapons use gas because its lighter.

Energy source: primes or pumps the atoms in the lasing medium to an excited state. The smaller lasers use batteries. They require replacement or recharging.

Mirrors: a full mirror and a half-silvered mirror. The mirrors allow the emitted light to bounce back and forth within the lasing medium cavity and ultimately to escape to the outside.

Lens: some type of lens to focus the beam.

The lasing process revolves around storing and releasing energy. An energy source injects energy into the lasing medium. The energy excites electrons, which move up to higher energy levels. When the electrons relax, they emit photons. The photons move back and forth between the mirrors, exciting other electrons as they go. This produces powerful, focused light.